Friday's Footprint

TWELVE STORIES AND A NOVELLA

Nadine Gordimer's Africa – the continent where she was born and still lives – is a large world. In this new book, her fifth, she records again her intensely perceptive observation of the nuances of human relationship. Each of these stories deals with critical moments in the lives of men and women when character is tested and inner strength, or its lack, tilts the scale. They take place in the crepuscular abodes of today's foreign residents in Cairo, in road camps, crocodile-haunted rivers, the humming business district of Johannesburg. But the inner world of her characters is broader still. It is the universal world of aspiration, achievement, and despair.

In the novella, "An Image of Success," she records through the eyes of a young lawyer the chance moment when a girl's love of wildflowers proved the turning point in the career of a business magnate. The unwrinkled perfection of Nadine Gordimer's style enables her to endow this and the other stories in the book with a reality that can come only from the testimony of the five senses and the thinking mind transmuted into words. As the *London Observer* said of an earlier collection, "Her attitude toward language is that of a woman towards the man she loves and as a result she winds it round her little finger."

(Continued on back flap)

With each new book her stature as one of the finest of modern writers is reaffirmed. It is with pride that we present the novella and twelve stories that comprise *Friday's Footprint.*

FRIDAY'S FOOTPRINT

and Other Stories

ALSO BY NADINE GORDIMER

Novels

A World of Strangers

The Lying Days

Short Stories

Six Feet of the Country

The Soft Voice of the Serpent
and Other Stories

FRIDAY'S FOOTPRINT

and Other Stories

ALSO BY NADINE GORDIMER

Novels

A World of Strangers

The Lying Days

Short Stories

Six Feet of the Country

The Soft Voice of the Serpent and Other Stories

Friday's Footprint

AND OTHER STORIES

By Nadine Gordimer

THE VIKING PRESS

NEW YORK · 1960

Published in 1960 by The Viking Press, Inc.
625 Madison Avenue, New York 22, N.Y.

Published in Canada by
The Macmillan Company of Canada Limited

"Friday's Footprint" (with the title "A View of the River"), "Little Willie," "The Bridegroom," and "Our Bovary" first appeared in *The New Yorker*; "Check Yes or No," "The Gentle Art," and "The Path of the Moon's Dark Fortnight" (with the title "The Path of the Moon") in *Mademoiselle*; "A Style of Her Own" (with the title "The Lady's Past") and "An Image of Success" in *Cosmopolitan*; "The Last Kiss" in *The London Magazine*; and "A Thing of the Past" in *Encounter*. Copyright © 1957, 1958, 1959, 1960 by Nadine Gordimer. The lines quoted on page 133 are from the translation of the *Bhagavad Gita* by Swami Prabhavananda and Christopher Isherwood, published by Harper and Brothers.

Library of Congress catalog card number: 60-5857

Printed in the U.S.A. by American Book-Stratford Press, Inc.

For Mrs. Toni Cassirer
with love and admiration

Contents

FRIDAY'S FOOTPRINT

and Other Stories

Friday's Footprint

The hotel stood a hundred yards up from the bank of the river. On the lintel above the screen door at the entrance, small gilt letters read: J. P. CUNNINGHAM, LICENSED TO SELL MALT, WINE AND SPIRITUOUS LIQUORS; the initials had been painted in over others that had been painted out. Sitting in the office off the veranda, at the old, high, pigeonhole desk stuffed with papers, with the cardboard files stacked round her in record of twenty years, she turned her head now and then to the water. She did not see it, the sheeny, gnat-hazy surface of the tropical river; she rested her eyes a moment. And then she turned back to her invoices and accounts, or wrote out, in her large, strong hand, the lunch and dinner menus: Potage of Green Peas, Crumbed Chop and Sauter Potatoes—the language, to her an actual language, of hotel cooking, that was in fact the garbled remnant influence of the immigrant chef from Europe who had once stuck it out in the primitive kitchen for three months, on his way south to the scope and plush of a Johannesburg restaurant.

She spent most of the day in the office, all year. The only difference was that in winter she was comfortable, it was even cool enough for her to need to wear a cardigan, and in summer she had to sit with her legs spread under her skirt while the steady trickle of sweat crept down the inner sides of her thighs and collected behind her knees. When people came through the squealing screen door onto the hotel veranda, and hung about in the unmistakable way of new arrivals (this only happened in winter, of course; nobody came to that part of Central Africa in the summer, unless they were obliged to) she would sense rather than hear them, and she would make them wait a few minutes. Then she would get up from the desk slowly, grinding back her chair, pulling her dress down with one hand, and appear. She had never learned the obsequious yet superior manner of a hotelkeeper's wife—the truth was that she was shy, and, being a heavy forty-year-old woman, she expressed this in lame brusqueness. Once the new guests had signed the register, she was quite likely to go back to her bookkeeping without having shown them to their rooms or called a boy to carry their luggage. If they ventured to disturb her again in her office, she would say, astonished, "Hasn't someone fixed you up? My husband, or the housekeeper? Oh Lord—" And she would go through the dingy company of the grass chairs in the lounge, and through the Ping-pong room that smelled strongly of red floor polish and cockroach repellent, to find help.

But usually people didn't mind their offhand reception. By the time they arrived at the river village they had traveled two days from the last village over desert and dried-out salt pans; they had slept out under the crushing silence of a night sky that ignored them and held no human sound other than their own small rustlings. They were inclined to emerge from their jeeps feeling unreal. The sight of Mrs. Cunningham, in her flowered print dress, with a brooch on her big bosom, and her big, bright-skinned face looking clerically dazed beneath her thick permanent, was the known world, to them; Friday's footprint in the sand. And when she appeared in the bar, in the evening, they found out that she was quite nice, after all. She wore a ribbon in her large head of light curly hair, then, and like many fat women, she looked suddenly not young, but babyish. She did not drink—occasionally she would giggle experimentally over a glass of sweet sherry—and would sit reading a week-old Johannesburg paper that someone had brought up with him in his car.

A man served the drinks with light, spry movements that made everything he did seem like sleight of hand. "Is that really Mrs. Cunningham's *husband?*" newcomers would ask, when they had struck up acquaintance with the three permanent guests—the veterinary officer, the meteorological officer, and the postmaster. The man behind the bar, who talked out of the curl of his upper lip, was small and slender and looked years younger than she did, although of course he was not—he was thirty-nine and only a year her junior. Outdoors, and in the daylight, his slenderness was the leanness of cured meat, his boy film-star face, with the satyr-shaped head of upstanding curly hair, the black, frown-framed eyes and forward-jutting mouth, was a monkey face, lined, watchful, always old.

Looking at him in the light of the bar, one of the permanent guests would explain, behind his glass, "Her second husband, of course. Arthur Cunningham's dead. But this one's some sort of relative of her first husband, he's a Cunningham, too."

Rita Cunningham did not always see nothing when she turned to look at the water. Sometimes (what times? she struggled to get herself to name—oh, times; when she had slept badly, or when—things—were not right) she saw the boat coming across the flooded river. She looked at the wide, shimmering, sluggish water where the water-lilies floated shining in the sun and she began to see, always at the same point, approaching the middle of the river from the other bank, the boat moving slowly under its heavy load. It was their biggest boat; it was carrying eight sewing machines and a black-japanned iron double bedstead as well as the usual stores, and Arthur and three store boys were sitting on top of the cargo. As the boat reached the middle of the river, it turned over, men and cargo toppled, and the iron bed came down heavily on top of their flailing arms, their arms stuck through the bars as the bed sank, taking them down beneath it. That was all. There was a dazzle of sun on the water, where they had been; the water lilies were thickest there.

She had not been there when it happened. She had been in Johannesburg on that yearly holiday that they all looked forward to so much. She had been sitting in the best seats on the stand at the Wanderers' Ground, the third day running, watching the international cricket test between South Africa and the visiting New Zealand team. Three of her children were with her—the little boy had the autographs of all the men in both teams; and Johnny was there. Johnny Cunningham, her husband's stepbrother, who had worked with them at the hotel and the stores for the last few years, and who, as he did every year since he had begun to work for them, had driven her down to Johannesburg, so that she could have a longer holiday than the time her husband, Arthur, could spare away from his work. The arrangement was always that Arthur came down to Johannesburg after his wife had been there for two weeks, and then Johnny Cunningham drove himself back to the hotel alone, to take care of things there.

Ever since she was a girl, she had loved cricket. At home,

up in the territory, she'd have the radio going in the hotel office while she worked, if there was a cricket commentary on, just as some people might like a little background music. She was happy, that day, high up in the stand in the shade. The grass was green, the figures of the players plaster-white. The sweet, short sound of the ball brought good-natured murmurs, roars of approval, dwindling growls of disappointment following it, from the crowd. There was the atmosphere of ease of people who are well enough off to take a day's holiday from the office and spend it drinking beer, idly watching a game, and getting a red, warm look, so that they appear more like a bed of easy-growing flowers than a crowd of human faces. Every now and then, a voice over the loudspeaker would announce some request or other—would the owner of car TJ 986339 please report to the ticket office at once; a lady's fob watch had been lost, and would anyone . . . et cetera; an urgent telegram, I repeat, an urgent telegram awaits Mr. So-and-so. . . . The voice was addicted to the phrase "I repeat," and there were mock groans here and there, among the crowd, every time the voice began to speak—she herself had exchanged a little shrug of amusement with someone in the row ahead who had turned in exasperation at the umpteenth "I repeat" that day. And then, at exactly quarter past three in the afternoon, her own name was spoken by the voice. "Will Mrs. Rita Cunningham, of Olongwe, I repeat, Olongwe, please report to the main entrance immediately. This is an urgent message for Mrs. Rita Cunningham. Will Mrs. Cunningham please report . . ."

She turned to Johnny at once, surprised, pulling a face. "I wouldn't know," he said, giving a short, bored laugh. (He preferred a good fast rugby game any time, but Arthur, wanting to give him a treat, had said to his wife, "Get a cricket ticket for Johnny too, take Johnny along one of the days.") She said, smiling and confused, bridling, "Somebody's making a silly ass of me, calling me out like this." "Awright," he said, slapping down his box of cigarettes and getting up with the quickness of impatience, "I'll go." She hesitated a moment; she had suddenly thought of her fourth child, the naughty one, Margie, who had been left playing at the house of the Johannesburg relatives with whom the Cunninghams were staying. "Oh, I'd better go. I suppose it must be Margie; I wonder what she's gone and done to herself now, the little devil."

Johnny sat down again. "Please yourself." And she got up and made her way up the stand. As soon as she got to the entrance she saw her sister Ruth's car drawn up right at the gates where no one was allowed to park, and before she had seen her sister and her brother-in-law standing there, turned toward her, a throb of dread beat up once, in her throat.

"What happened? Did she run in the street—" she cried, rushing up to them. The man and the woman stared at her as if they were afraid of her. "Not Margie," said the man. "It's not Margie. Come into the car."

And in the car, outside the cricket ground, still within sound of the plock of the ball and the voice of the crowd rising to it, they told her that a telegram had come saying that Arthur had been drowned that morning, bringing a boatload of goods over the flooded river.

She did not cry until she got all the way back to the hotel on the bank of the river. She left the children behind, with her sister (the two elder girls went to boarding school in Johannesburg, anyway), and Johnny Cunningham drove her home. Once, in the middle of a silence as vast as the waste of sand they were grinding through, she said, "Who would ever have dreamt it would happen to him. The things he'd done in his time, and never come to any harm." "Don't tell me," Johnny agreed, his pipe between his teeth.

In Johannesburg they had all said to one another, "It'll hit her when she gets back." But although she had believed the fact of her husband's death when she was away from the village, in the unreality of the city—once she saw and smelled the village again, once she stepped into the hotel, it all seemed nonsense. Nothing was changed. It was all there, wasn't it? The wildebeest skins pegged out to tan, the old horns half buried in the sand, the plaster Johnny Walker on the counter in the bar; the river.

Two days later one of the store boys came over to the hotel with some checks for her to sign, and, standing in the office doorway with his old hat in his hand, said to her in a hoarse low voice, as if he wanted no one, not even the dead, to overhear, "He was a good man. Missus, he was a very good man. Oh, missus." She cried. While she wrote her name on the checks and silently handed them back to the elderly black man, it came: strong pity for Arthur, who had been alive, as she was, and was now dead. When she was alone again she sat on at the desk staring at the spikes of invoices and the rubber stamps and the scratched and ink-stained wood, and she wept in pity for the pain of that strong, weathered man, filling his lungs with water with every breath under the weight of the iron bedstead. She wept at the cruel fact of death; perhaps that was not quite what her relatives in Johannesburg had meant when they had said that it would hit her when she got home—but she wept, anyway.

Slowly, in short bursts of confidence that stopped abruptly or tailed off in embarrassment, people began to talk to her about the drowning. This one spared her this detail, another told her it and spared her something else; so it was that she had put together, out of what she had been told, that silent, unreal, orderly picture, scarcely supplemented at all by imagination, since she had very little, that she sometimes saw rise on the river and sink out of sight again.

The facts were simple and horrible. Arthur Cunningham

had been doing what he had done dozens of times before; what everyone in the village had done time and again, whenever the river was flooded and the bridge was down. The bridge was either down or under water almost every year, at the height of the rainy season, and when this happened the only way to reach the village was by boat. That December day there was a pack of stuff to get across the river—all the food for the hotel and the store goods, which had come up North by truck. Arthur Cunningham was the sort of man who got things done himself; that was the only way to get them done. He went back and forth with the boys four times, that morning, and they were making some headway. "Come on, let's see if we c'n git things going," he kept chivvying at the white assistants who were in charge of unloading the trucks, and were sweating with haste and the nervous exhaustion of working under his eye. "I dunno, honestly, I've got my boat, I've got my team of boys, and what's happening? I'm waiting for you blokes. Don't tickle that stuff, there, man! For Christ's sake, get cracking. Get it on, get it on!"

The Africans took his manner—snarling, smiling, insulting in its assumption (true) that he could do everything his workers did, but in half the time and twice as well—better than the white men. They laughed and grumbled back at him, and groaned under his swearing and his taunts. When the boat was fully loaded for the fifth trip, he noticed the black-japanned double bed, in its component parts, but not assembled, propped against a crate. "What about that thing?" he yelled. "Don't keep leaving that behind for the next lot, you bloody fools. Get it on, get it on. That's a new bed for the Chief's new wife, that's an important order." And he roared with laughter. He went up to a pimply little twenty-two-year-old clerk, whose thin hair, tangled with the rims of his glasses, expressed wild timidity. "You shouldn't be too young to know how important a nice comfortable big bed is? You expect the old Chief to wait till tomorrow? How'd'jou feel, if you were waiting for that beautiful bed for a beautiful new woman—" And while the young man peered at him, startled, Arthur Cunningham roared with laughter again.

"Mr. Cunningham, the boat's full," another white assistant called.

"Never mind, full! Put it on, man. I'm sick of seeing that bed lying here. Put it on!"

"I don't know how you'll get it over, it makes the whole load top-heavy."

Arthur Cunningham walked up to his clerk. He was a man of middle height, with a chest and a belly, big, hard, and resonant, like the body of a drum, and his thick hands and sandy-haired chest, that always showed in the open neck of his shirt, were blotched and wrinkled with resistance to and in tough protection against the sun. His face was red and he had even false teeth in a lipless mouth that was practical-looking rather than mean or unkind.

"Come on, Harris," he said, as if he were taking charge of a child. "Come on now, and no damn nonsense. Take hold here." And he sent the man, tottering under the weight of the foot of the bed while he himself carried the head, down to the boat.

Rita had married him when she was twenty-three, and he was sixteen or seventeen years older than she was. He had looked almost exactly the same when she married him as he did the last time ever that she saw him, when he stood in the road with his hands on the sides of his belly and watched the car leave for Johannesburg. She was a virgin, she had never been in love, when she married him; he had met her on one of his trips down South, taken a fancy to her, and that was that. He always did whatever he liked and got whatever he wanted. Since she had never been made love to by a young man, she accepted his command of her in bed as the sum of love; his tastes in lovemaking, like everything else about him, were formed before she knew him, and he was as set in this way as he was in others. She never knew him, of course, because she had nothing of the deep need to possess his thoughts and plumb his feelings that comes of love.

He was as generous as his tongue was rough, which meant that his tongue took the edge off his generosity at least as often as his generosity took the sting out of his tongue. He had hunted and fished and traded all over Africa, and he had great contempt for travelers' tales. When safari parties stayed at his hotel, he criticized their weapons (What sort of contraption to you call that? I've shot round about fifty lion in my lifetime, without any telescopic sights, I can tell you), their camping equipment (I don't know what all this fuss is about water filters and what-not. I've drunk water that was so filthy I've had to lean over and draw it into my mouth through a bit of rag, and been none the worse for it), and their general helplessness. But he also found experienced native guides for these people, and lent them the things they had forgotten to buy down South. He was conscious of having made a number of enemies, thinly scattered in that sparsely populated territory, and was also conscious of his good standing, of the fact that everybody knew him, and of his ownership of the hotel, the two stores, and whatever power there was in the village.

His stepmother had been an enemy of his, in that far-off childhood that he had overcome long ago, but he had had no grudge against his young stepbrother, her son, who must have had his troubles, too, adopted into a house full of Cunninghams. Johnny'd been rolling around the world for ten years or so—America, Mexico, Australia—when he turned up in the territory one day, stony-broke and nowhere in particular to go. Arthur wasn't hard on him, though he chaffed him a bit, of course, and after the boy'd been loafing around the river and hotel for a month, Arthur suggested that he might give a hand in one of the stores. Johnny took the hint in good part—"Got to stop being a bum sometime, I suppose," he said, and turned out to be a surprisingly good worker. Soon he was helping at the hotel, too—where, of course, he was living, anyway. And soon he was one of the family, doing whatever there was to be done.

Yet he kept himself to himself. "I've got a feeling he'll just walk out, when he feels like it, same as he came," Rita said to Arthur, with some resentment. She had a strong sense of loyalty and was always watchful of any attempt to take advantage of her husband, who had in such careless abundance so many things that other men wanted. "Oh for Pete's sake, Rita, he's a bit of a natural sourpuss, that's all. He lives his life and we live ours. There's nothing wrong with the way he works, and nothing else about old Johnny interests me."

The thing was, in a community the size of the village, and in the close life of the little hotel, that life of Johnny Cunningham's was lived, if in inner isolation, outwardly under their noses. He ate at table with them, usually speaking only when he was spoken to. When, along with the Cunningham couple, he got drawn into a party of hotel guests, he sat drinking with great ease but seldom bothered to contribute anything to the talk, and would leave the company with an abrupt, sardonic-sounding "Excuse me" whenever he pleased. The only times he came "out of his shell," as Rita used to put it to her husband, were on dance nights. He had arrived in the territory during the jive era, but his real triumphs on the floor came with the advent of rock-'n'-roll. He learned it from a film, originally —the lounge of the hotel was the local cinema, too, on Thursday nights—and he must have supplemented his self-teaching on the yearly holidays in Johannesburg. Anyway, he was expert, and on dance nights he would take up from her grass chair one of the five or six lumpy girls from the village, at whom he never looked, at any other time, let alone spoke to, and would transform her within the spell of his own rhythm. Sometimes he did this with women among the hotel guests, too; "Look at old Johnny, giving it stick," Arthur Cunningham would say, grinning, in the scornfully admiring tone of someone praising a performance that he wouldn't stoop to, himself. There was something about Johnny, his mouth slightly open, the glimpse of saliva gleaming on his teeth, his head thrown back and his eyes narrowed while his body snaked on stooping legs and nimble feet, that couldn't be ignored. "Well, he seems to be happy that way," Rita would say with a laugh, embarrassed for the man.

Sometimes Johnny slept with one of these women guests (there was no bed that withheld its secrets from the old German housekeeper, who, in turn, insisted on relating all she knew to Rita Cunningham). It was tacitly accepted that there was some sort of connection between the rock-'n'-roll performance and the assignation; who would ever notice Johnny at any other time? But in between these infrequent one- or two-night affairs, he took no interest in women, and it seemed clear that marriage was something that never entered his head. Arthur paid him quite well, but he seemed neither to save nor to have any money. He bet (by radio, using the meteorological officer's broadcasting set) on all the big races in Cape Town, Durban, and Johannesburg, and he had bought three cars, all equally unsuitable for road conditions up in the territory, and tinkered them to death in Arthur's workshop.

When he came back to the hotel with Rita Cunningham after Arthur was drowned, he went on with his work as usual. But after a week, all the great bulk of work, all the decisions that had been Arthur's, could not be ignored any longer by considerate employees hoping to spare the widow. She said to Johnny at lunch, in her schoolgirlish way, "Can you come to the office afterwards? I mean, there're some things we must fix up—" When she came into the office he was already there, standing about like a workman, staring at the calendar on the wall. "Who's going to see that the store orders don't overlap, now?" she said. "We've got to make that somebody's job. And somebody'll have to take over the costing of perishable goods, too, not old Johnson, Arthur always said he didn't have a clue about it."

Johnny scratched his ear and said, "D'jou want me to do it?"

They looked at each other for a moment, thinking it over. There was no sign on his face either of eagerness or reluctance.

"Well, if you could, Johnny, I think that's best. . . ." And after a pause, she turned to something else. "Who can we make responsible for the bar—the ordering and everything? D'you think we should try and get a man?"

He shrugged. "If you like. You could advertise in Jo'burg, or praps in Rhodesia. You won't get anybody decent to come up here."

"I know." The distress of responsibility suddenly came upon her.

"You could try," he said again.

"We'll get some old soak, I suppose, who can't keep a job anywhere else."

"Sure," he said with his sour smile.

"You don't think," she said, "I mean just for now—Couldn't we manage it between us? I mean you could serve, and perhaps the Allgood boy from the garage could come at weekends to give a hand, and then you and I could do the ordering?"

"Sure," he said, rocking from his heels to his toes and back again, and looking out of the window, "I can do it, if you want to try."

She still could not believe that the wheels of these practical needs were carrying her along, and with her, the hotel and the two stores. "Oh yes," she said, distracted, "I think it'll be okay, just for the time being, until I can . . ." She did not finish what she was saying because she did not know what it was for which the arrangement was to be a makeshift.

She took it for granted that she meant to sell the hotel and the two stores. Two of the children were at school in the South, already; the other two would have to follow when they had outgrown the village school, in a year or two. What was the point in her staying on, there, in a remote village, alone, two thousand miles from her children or her relatives?

She talked, and she believed she acted, for the first six months after Arthur was drowned, as if the sale of the hotel and stores was imminent and inevitable. She even wrote to an agent in Johannesburg, and an old lawyer friend in Rhodesia, asking their advice about what sort of price she could expect to get for her property and her businesses—Arthur had left everything to her.

Johnny had taken over most of Arthur's work. She, in her turn, had taken over some of Johnny's. Johnny drove back to Johannesburg to fetch the two younger children home, and the hotel and the stores went on as usual. One evening when she was doing some work in the office after dinner, and giving half her attention to the talk of hotel matters with him, she added the usual proviso—"It would do in the meantime."

Johnny was hissing a tune through his teeth while he looked up the price of a certain brand of gin in a file of liquor wholesalers' invoices—he was sure he remembered Arthur had a cheaper way of buying it than he himself knew—and he stopped whistling but went on looking and said, "What'll you do with yourself in Johannesburg, anyway, Rita? You'll have money and you won't need a job."

She put down her pen and turned round, clutching at the straw of any comment on her position that would help her feel less adrift. "Wha'd'you mean?"

"I suppose you'll buy a house somewhere near your sister and live there looking after the two little kids."

"Oh, I don't know," she parried, but faltering, "I suppose I'd buy a house . . ."

"Well, what else could you do with yourself?"

He had made it all absolutely clear to her. It came over her with innocent dismay—she had not visualized it, thought about it, for herself: the house in a Johannesburg suburb, the two children at school in the mornings, the two children in bed after seven each night, her sister saying, you must come down to us just whenever you like.

She got up slowly and turned, leaning her rump against the ridge of the desk behind her, frowning, unable to speak.

"You've got something, here," he said.

"But I always wanted to go. The summer—it's so hot. We always said, one day, when the children—" All her appeals to herself failed. She said, "But a woman—it's silly—how can I carry on?"

He watched her with interest, but would not save her with an interruption. He smoked and held his half-smoked cigarette between thumb and first finger, turned inward toward his palm. He laughed. "You are carrying on," he said. He made a pantomime gesture of magnificence, raising his eyebrows, waggling his head slowly and pulling down the corners of his mouth. "All going strong. The whole caboodle. What you got to worry about?"

She found herself laughing, the way children laugh when they are teased out of tears.

In the next few weeks, a curious kind of pale happiness came over her. It was the happiness of relief from indecision, the happiness of confidence. She did not have to wonder if she could manage—she had been managing all the time! The confidence brought out something that had been in her all her life, dormant; she was capable, even a good businesswoman. She began to take a firm hand with the children, with the hotel servants, with the assistants at the stores. She even wrote a letter to the liquor wholesaler, demanding, on a certain brand of gin, the same special discount that her late husband had squeezed out of him.

When the lawyer friend from Rhodesia, who was in charge of Arthur's estate, came up to consult with her, she discussed with him the possibility of offering Johnny—not a partnership, no—but some sort of share, perhaps a fourth share in the hotel and the stores. "The only thing is, will he stay?" she said. "Why shouldn't he stay?" said the lawyer, indicating the sound opportunity that was going to be offered to the man. "Oh, I don't know," she said. "I always used to say to Arthur, I had the feeling he was the sort of man who would walk off, one day, same as he came." In view of the steady work he had done—"Oh I must be fair," Rita hastened to agree with the lawyer. "He *has* worked terribly hard, he's been wonderful, since it happened"—the lawyer saw no cause for concern on this point; in any case the contract, when he drew it up, would be a watertight one and would protect her interests against any such contingency.

The lawyer went home to Rhodesia to draw up the contract that was never needed. In three months, she was married to Johnny. By the time the summer rainy season came round, and he was the one who was bringing the supplies across the river in the boat, this year, he was her husband and Arthur's initials were painted out and his were painted in, in their place, over the door.

To the meteorological officer, the veterinary officer, and the postmaster—those permanent residents of the hotel who had known them both for years—and the people of the village, the marriage seemed quite sensible, really; a matter of convenience—though, of course, also rather funny—there were a number of jokes about it current in the village for a time. To her—well, it was not until after the marriage was an accomplished fact that she began to try to understand what it was, and what had brought it about.

At the end of that first winter after Arthur's death, Johnny had had an affair with one of the women in a safari party that was on its way home to the South. Rita knew about it, because, as usual, the housekeeper had told her. But on the day the party left (Rita knew which woman it was, a woman not young, but with a well-dieted and massaged slimness) Johnny came into the office after the two jeeps had left and plonked himself down in the old cane chair near the door. Rita turned her head at the creak of the cane, to ask him if he knew whether the cook had decided, for the lunch menu, on a substitute for the chops that had gone off, and his eyes, that had been closed in one of those moments of sleep that fall like a shutter on lively, enervated wakefulness, flew open. He yawned and grinned, and his one eye twitched, as if it winked at her, of itself. "Boy, that's that," he said.

It was the first time, in the seven years he had been at the hotel, that he had ever, even obliquely, made any sort of comment on the existence of his private life or the state of his feelings. She blushed, like a wave of illness. He must have seen the red coming up over the skin of her neck and her ears and her face. But, stonily, he didn't mind her embarrassment or feel any of his own. And so, suddenly, there was intimacy; it existed betwen them as if it had always been there, taken for granted. They were alone together. They had an existence together apart from the hotel and the stores, and the making of decisions about practical matters. He wouldn't have commented to her on his affair with a woman while Arthur was alive and she herself was a married woman. But now, well—it was in his careless face—she was simply a grown-up person, like any other, and she knew that babies weren't found under gooseberry bushes.

After that, whenever he came into the office, they were alone together. She felt him when she sat at her desk with her back to him; her arms tingled into gooseflesh and she seemed to feel a mocking eye (not his, she knew he was not looking at her) on a point exactly in the middle of the back of her neck. She did not know whether she had looked at him or not, before, but now she was aware of the effort of not looking at him, while he ate at table with her, or served in the bar, or simply ran, very lithe, across the sandy road.

And she began—it was an uncomfortable, shameful thing to her, something like the feeling she had had when she was adolescent—to be conscious of her big breasts. She would fold her arms across them when she stood talking to him. She hated them jutting from her underarm nearly to her waist, filling her dress, and, underneath, the hidden nipples that were brown as an old bitch's teats since the children were born. She wanted to hide her legs, too—so thick and strong, the solid-fleshed, mottled calves with their bristly blond hairs, and the heavy bone of the ankles marked with bruises where, bare-legged, she constantly bumped them against her desk.

She said to him one morning, after a dance night at the hotel—it simply came out of her mouth—"That Mrs. Burns seems to have taken a fancy to you."

He gave a long, curly-mouthed yawn. He was looking into space, absent; and then he came to himself, briskly; and he smiled slowly, right at her. "Uh, that. Does she?"

She began to feel terribly nervous. "I mean I—I—thought she had her eye on you. The way she was laughing when she danced with you." She laughed, jeering a little.

"She's a silly cow, all right," he said. And as he went out of the bar, where they were checking the empties together, he put his hand experimentally on her neck, and tweaked her earlobe. It was an ambiguous caress; she did not know whether he was amused by her or if—he meant it, as she put it to herself.

He did not sleep with her until they were married; but, of course, they were married soon. He moved into the big bedroom with her, then, but he kept on his old, dingy rondavel outside the main building, for his clothes and his fishing tackle and the odds and ends of motor-car accessories he kept lying about, and he usually took his siesta in there, in the summer. She lay on her bed alone in the afternoon dark behind the curtains that glowed red with the light and heat that beat upon them from outside, and she looked at his empty bed. She would stare at that place where he lay, where he actually slept, there in the room with her, not a foot away, every night. She had for him a hundred small feelings more tender than any she had ever known, and yet included in them was what she had felt at other rare moments in her life: when she had seen a bird, winged by a shot, fall out of flight formation over the river; when she had first seen one of her own children, ugly, and crying at being born. Sometimes, at the beginning, she would go over in her mind the times when he had made love to her; even at her desk, with the big ledgers open in front of her, and the sound of one of the boys rubbing the veranda floor outside, her mind would let fall the figures she was collating and the dreamy recapitulation of a night would move in. He did not make love to her very often, of course—not after the first few weeks. (He would always pinch her, or feel her arm, when he thought of it, though.) Weeks went by and it was only on dance nights, when usually she went to their room long before him, that he would come in, moving lightly, breathing whisky in the dark, and come over to her as if by appointment. Often she heard him sigh as he came in. He always went through the business of lovemaking in silence; but to her, in whom a thousand piercing cries were deafening without a sound, it was accepted as part of the extraordinary clamor of her own silence.

As the months went by, he made love to her less and less often, and she waited for him. In tremendous shyness and secrecy, she was always waiting for him. And, oddly, when he did come to her again, next day she would feel ashamed. She began to go over and over things that had happened in the past; it was as if the ability to re-create in her mind a night's lovemaking had given her a power of imagination she had never had before, and she would examine in re-creation, detail by detail, scenes and conversations that were long over. She began always to have the sense of searching for something; searching slowly and carefully. That day at the cricket. A hundred times, she brought up for examination the way she had turned to look at Johnny, when the voice called her name; the way he had laughed, and said, "Please yourself." The silence between them in the car, driving back to the territory. The dance nights, long before that, when she had sat beside Arthur and watched Johnny dance. The times she had spoken distrustfully of him to Arthur. It began to seem to her that there was something of conspiracy about all these scenes. Guilt came slowly through them, a stain from deep down. She was beset by the impossibility of knowing—and then again she believed without a doubt—and then, once more, she absolved herself—was there *always* something between her and Johnny? Was it there, waiting, a gleaming eye in the dark, long before Arthur was drowned? All she could do was go over and over every shred of evidence of the past, again and again, reading now yes into it, now no.

She began to think about Arthur's drowning; she felt, crazily, that she and Johnny *knew* Arthur was drowning. They sat in the Wanderers' stand while they knew Arthur was drowning. While there, over there, right in front of the hotel, where she was looking, through the office window (not having to get up from the desk, simply turning her head), the boat with the eight sewing machines and the black-japanned double bed was coming over the water. . . . The boat was turning over. . . . The arms of the men (who was it who had taken care not to spare her that detail?) came through the iron bed-head, it took the men down with it—Arthur with his mouth suddenly stopped forever with water.

She did not say one word to Johnny about all this. She would not have known how to put it into words, even to herself. It had no existence outside the terrifying freedom of her own mind, that she had stumbled down into by mistake, and that dwarfed the real world about her. Yet she changed, outwardly, protectively, to hide what only she knew was there—the shameful joy of loving. It was then that she started to talk about Johnny as "he" and "him," never referring to him by name, and to speak of him in the humorous, half-critical, half-nagging way of the wife who takes her husband for granted, no illusions and no nonsense about it. "Have you seen my spouse around?" she would ask, or "Where's that husband of mine?"

On dance nights, in the winter, he still astonished guests by his sudden emergence from taciturnity into rock-'n'-roll. The housekeeper no longer told any tales of his brief ventures into the beds where other men's women slept, and so, of course, Rita presumed there weren't any. For herself, she learned to live with her guilt of loving, like some vague, chronic disorder. It was no good wrestling with it; she had come to understand that—for some reason she didn't understand—the fact, the plain fact that she had never committed the slightest disloyalty to Arthur all through their marriage, provided no cure of truth. She and Johnny never quarreled, and if the hotel and the businesses didn't expand (Arthur was the one for making plans and money) at least they went on just as before. The summer heat, the winter cool, came and went again and again in the reassuring monotony that passes for security.

The torture of imagination died away in her almost entirely. She lost the power to create the past. Only the boat remained, sometimes rising up from her mind on the river through the commonplace of the day in the office, just as once her nights with Johnny had come between her and immediate reality.

One morning in the fourth winter of their marriage, they were sitting at table together in the hotel dining room, eating the leisurely and specially plentiful breakfast of a Sunday. The dining room was small and friendly; you could carry on a conversation from one table to the next. The meteorologist and the postmaster sat together at their table, a small one near the window, distinguished by the special sauce bottles and the bottles of vitamin pills and packet of crispbread that mark the table of the regular from that of the migrant guest in a hotel. The veterinary officer had gone off for a weekend's shooting. There were two tables of migrants in the room; one had the heads of three gloomy lion-hunters bent together in low discussion over their coffee, the other held a jolly party who had come all the way from Cape Town, and the leaders of which were a couple who had been in the territory and stayed at the hotel twice or three times before. They had received a bundle of newspapers by post from the South the day before, and they were making them do in place of Sunday papers. Johnny was fond of the magazine sections of newspapers; he liked the memoirs of famous sportsmen or ex-spies that were always to be found in them, and he liked to do the crossword. He had borrowed the magazine section of a Johannesburg paper from one of the party, and had done the crossword while he ate his bacon and fried liver and eggs. Now, while he drank a second or third cup of coffee, he found a psychological quiz, and got out his pencil again.

"He's like a kid doing his homework," said Rita, sitting lazily in her chair, with her heavy legs apart and her shoulders rounded, smoking over her coffee. She spoke over her shoulder, to the people who had loaned the paper, and smiled and jerked her head in the direction of her husband.

"Isn't he busy this morning," one of the women agreed.

"Hardly been able to eat a thing, he's been so hard at it," said the man who had been at the hotel before. And, except for the lion-hunters, the whole dining room laughed.

"Just-a-minute," Johnny said, lifting a finger but not looking up from his quiz. "Just-a-minute—I got a set of questions to answer here. You're in this too, Rita. You got to answer, too, in this one."

"Not me. You know I've got no brains. You don't get me doing one of those things on a Sunday morning."

"Doesn't need brains," he said, biting off the end of his sentence like a piece of thread. " 'How good a husband are you?'—there you are—"

"As if he needs a quiz to tell him that," she said, at the Cape Town party, who at once began to laugh at the skepto-comical twist to her face. "I'll answer that one, my boy." And again they all laughed.

"Here's yours," he said, feeling for his coffee cup behind the folded paper. " 'How good a wife are you?'—"

"Ah, that's easy," she said, pretending to show off, "I'll answer that one, too."

"You go ahead," he said, with a look to the others, chin back, mouth pursed down. "Here you are. 'Do you buy your husband's toilet accessories, or does he choose his own?' "

"Come again?" she said. "What they mean, toilet accessories?"

"His soap, and his razor and things," called a man from the other table. "Violet hair-oil to put on his hair!"

Johnny ran a hand through his upstanding curls and shrank down in his seat.

Even the postmaster, who was rather shy, twitched a smile.

"No, but seriously," said Rita, through the laughter, "how can I choose a razor for a man? I ask you!"

"All they want to know is, do you or don't you," said Johnny. "Come on, now."

"Well, if it's a razor, of course I don't," Rita said, appealing to the room.

"Right! You don't. 'No.' " Johnny wrote.

"Hey—wait a minute, what about the soap? I do buy the soap. I buy the soap for every man in this hotel! Don't I get any credit for the soap—"

There were cries from the Cape Town table—"Yes, that's not fair, Johnny, if she buys the soap." "She buys the soap for the whole bang shoot of us."

Johnny put down the paper. "Well, who's she supposed to be a good wife *to,* anyway!"

All ten questions for the wife were gone through in this manner, with interruptions, suggestions, and laughter from the dining room in general. And then Johnny called for quiet while he answered his ten. He was urged to read them out, but he said no, he could tick off his yesses and nos straight off; if he didn't they'd all be sitting at breakfast until lunchtime. When he had done, he counted up his wife's score and his own, and turned to another page to see the verdict.

"Come on, let's have it," called the man from the Cape Town table. "The suspense is horrible."

Johnny was already skimming through the column. "You really want to hear it?" he said. "Well, I'm warning you—"

"Oh, get on with it," Rita said, with the possessive, irritated, yet placid air of a wife, scratching a drop of dried egg-yolk off the print bosom of her dress.

"Well, here goes," he said, in the tone of someone entering into the fun of the thing. " 'There is clearly something gravely wrong with your marriage. You should see a doctor or better still, a psychiatrist' "—he paused for effect, and the laugh—" 'and seek help, as soon as possible.' "

The man from Cape Town laughed till the tears ran into the creases at the corners of his eyes. Everyone else laughed and talked at once. "If that isn't the limit!" "This psychology stuff!" "Have you ever—!" "Is there anything they *don't* think of in the papers these days!"

"There it is, my dear," said Johnny, folding the paper in mock solemnity, and pulling a funereal, yet careless face.

She laughed with him. She laughed looking down at her shaking body where the great cleft that ran between her breasts showed at the neck of her dress. She laughed and she heard, she alone heard, the catches and trips in her throat like the mad cries of some creature buried alive. The blood of a blush burned her whole body with agonizing slowness. When the laughter had died down she got up and not looking at Johnny —for she knew how he looked, she knew that unembarrassed gaze—she said something appropriate and even funny, and with great skill went easily, comfortably sloppily, out of the dining room. She felt Johnny following behind her, as usual, but she did not fall back to have him keep up with her, and, as usual after breakfast, she heard him turn off, whistling, from the passage into the bar, where there was the aftermath of Saturday night to clear up.

She got to the office. At last she got to the office and sat down in her chair at the roll-top desk. The terrible blush of blood did not abate; it was as if something had burst inside her and was seeping up in a stain through all the layers of muscle and flesh and skin. She felt again, as she had before, a horrible awareness of her big breasts, her clumsy legs. She clenched her hand over the sharp point of a spike that held invoices and felt it press pain into her palm. Tears were burning hot on her face and her hands, the rolling lava of shame from that same source as the blush. And at last, Arthur! she called in a clenched, whimpering whisper, Arthur! grinding his name between her teeth, and she turned desperately to the water, to the middle of the river where the lilies were. She tried with all her being to conjure up once again out of the water *something*; the ghost of comfort, of support. But that boat, silent and unbidden, that she had so often seen before, would not come again.

The Last Kiss

When people become characters, they cease to be regarded as human; they are something to be pointed out, like the orange tree that President Kruger planted, the statue in the park, or the filling station that once was the first church hall. Mr. Van As was a character, formed, as many characters are, by neglect. He was an Afrikaner who had started up as a cartage contractor before gold was discovered, when the town was a coal-mining village between black hills of coaldust on the high veld of the Transvaal. His donkey-drawn wagons moved the swaying household goods of the Cornish miners from the station to their cottages. Then there was gold; the shafts went down, the houses and shops went up. Mr. Van As bought a team of dray horses and four wagons, and he moved machinery and equipment for the gold mines as well as smart new furniture for the influx of miners and tradespeople. He bought a large corrugated iron shed and converted it into a storage place; he had an office, and an expensive trap for his personal use. His wagons, with VAN AS FOR CARTAGE painted across them in two-foot letters, were seen all over the village. He was an elder in the church. He built himself a house with white cake-frill railings to the veranda, an ornamental turret, and an onion dome of corrugated iron—the first time that indispensable material, the very stuff of which the Witwatersrand was built, night-cold all winter, blazing noon-hot all summer, was made the soul as well as the substance of local architecture. Inside, neither plush nor ball fringe was spared, and there were mirrors in mahogany frames to multiply the heads of his wife and daughters.

As he became self-conscious, of money and fine possessions, so the village, now a little town, became self-conscious too; civic pride required a mayor and a gold chain for him to wear, and councilors for him to consult with. Van As was mayor, and wore the gold chain for three years running, and the first stone building in the town, a bank, still standing, has one of its stones inscribed: "15th July, 1912. This foundation stone was laid by His Worship the Mayor, Councillor G. G. Van As."

Years later, a photograph of him as he appeared at this time, in mayoral robes and chain, and with the tusklike mustache that was the one thing he never lost, was discovered in the unsalable rubbish cluttering a corner of one of the local auctioneers' salesrooms, and was reproduced in the local paper; it looked about as credible as a picture of a manifestation of ectoplasm.

The town outgrew Van As. As he got older, it got younger, more vigorous and brash, became more and more of a show-off. He was all right for Masonic gatherings and Dutch Reformed church bazaars and the Sons of England ball, but would he have done to open swimming galas, judge beauty queens, or welcome a visiting Hollywood film actress making an appearance in person? His English was not very good; his Afrikaans, though that was his mother tongue, was not much better. It had not been necessary to talk much at the beginning of the town; it had been enough to be solid and prosperous and wear the gold chain well. If he had lasted on into the rise of Afrikaner nationalism and the Nationalist government of South Africa, he certainly would not have done to welcome a minister of state on an official visit to celebrate the milling of the billionth ton of gold ore: one of those Nationalist ministers with their stern public faces, their apocalyptic manner, and the urbanity that coats politicians invisibly as the oil on a duck's back.

But he did not last even into the era of the motor van. By the twenties, there were two other cartage contractors in the town, each with a motor removal van, a lumbering, tin-hooded thing that kept furniture clean and dry in all weathers, and that had to be cranked up like a giant clockwork toy being wound. Van As's wife died in 1922, with the birth of their fourth or fifth daughter, and perhaps that was one of the reasons why he hesitated too long about exchanging his horse-drawn wagons for the new vans, and lost his lead in the cartage business. It was an unsettled year, anyway, on the Witwatersrand, with strikes and their attendant disruption of business life; liquor shops were closed for months and there was some glorious rioting in Johannesburg, when the streets ran with looted whisky and imported chocolates. People said—when they thought back on it—that it was with his wife's death that Van As began to go down; but then people like to pend the insidious slither of misfortune from some ill omen—it is part of the craving for order, for a fate to take their lives out of their hands. Mrs. Van As turned her face to the wall, and luck turned away with her; it makes a starting point.

Van As continued to live in his grand house, with his eldest daughter, a girl of about eighteen, as housekeeper and mother to the rest. The weather vane had not fallen down yet and the good plush furnishings were still in fine condition. But the valuable cartage contracts for new gold mines opening up went to the men with the modern motor transport, and Van As for Cartage lost some of his old contracts, too, when they came up for renewal. He had begun to let go, it seemed, and there was no closing his hand on anything, after that. He had lent money; it was not paid back, and the securities proved worthless. It was many years since he had been mayor, almost as many since he had been dropped from the city council. He speculated on the wrong things and sold the cartage business. He was declared bankrupt.

It was perhaps the mark of his failure, his inability to adapt, that he and his immediate surroundings remained the same. He did not leave the ornate and dating house (it had been in his wife's name and was bequeathed to his daughters); he continued to wear the great tusky mustache that had once become the dignity of a city father. Nothing fades so quickly as what is unchanged. By the thirties, when the youngest child was ten years old, and the eldest had provided grandchildren, the house was a landmark of positive antiquity for a town that young. The rusty weather vane screeched drunkenly on windy days, the white railings had never been repainted, and, looking in through the living-room window from the street, you could see the motheaten plush, and the places where little balls were missing from the fringe on the pelmet. The Van Ases could not afford to change anything. The eldest daughter's husband got phthisis working underground on the mines, and had only his disability pension to get along on, so her family, too, came back to live under the old roof with the onion dome. Old Van As—already it seemed he had never been known as anything else—had a job in a produce store, the sort of job a bright youth may start with when he leaves school; if a middle-aged man has a job like that, people take it to mean that he is fit for nothing else.

It was about this time that a cinema went up on a vacant plot near the house (the old residential areas were being taken in by the expanding business center of the town, and it was no longer fashionable to live within walking distance of the post office) and Van As took to dropping in there two or three nights a week. Did he develop a passion for seeing films? Nobody ever asked him. Not even his children. He went down the road to the cinema as some old men go to the pub, and are out of the way. The children were all busy trying to find space and importance for the growing paraphernalia of their interests; one had boy-friends, another played the piano and wanted to practice to enter a talent contest, a third collected butterflies and was trying for a scholarship.

Van As couldn't manage anything for them, so they had to manage for themselves.

He was no longer an elder of the church, of course; and church-going had been so much a part of the social position that he had lost, that he didn't go to church any more, as if his presence would have embarrassed himself and God, just as the current mayor (a dentist who had made money on the stock market, had a house with a cocktail bar, and had instituted a publicity campaign for the town, with luminous signs that said: YOU ARE NOW ENTERING INDUSTRIAL NOORDDORP—WELCOME AND PROSPERITY) and his councilors would have been embarrassed if Van As had walked into the council chamber. In the forties, he lost his job at the produce store and for a while he was to be seen wandering about the town, looking long and steadily into shop windows, as if deliberating some important purchase. It was then that he began to be known as poor old Van As. But his enforced idleness did not last. The war was well under way by then, and the next thing was old Van As in uniform: he got a job in the recruiting office in

Johannesburg. It was a mild sort of joke in the town. Some of the older city fathers who had continued to do well for themselves and who chose to regard his decline as a kind of eccentricity, poked him in the chest of his private's ill-fitting uniform and bellowed (it was well known that he seemed to have got rather deaf), "Well, we've nothing to worry about now, eh, Van As? Hitler's had his chips, now, with you around." And old Van As would wheeze and laugh, mumbling something unintelligible under his straggling mustache.

Week after week, he sat in his same seat in the cinema. It was one of the cheap seats, two rows from the front, and often he had the whole row to himself, because to sit there was to be grotesquely *vis-à-vis* the huge faces on the screen. All through the winter he was sunk to the ears—pale, sagging ears, tufted with albino bristles—in his army greatcoat. If he had brought along several thicknesses of newspaper, and spread himself out on them on the floor, it would not have seemed too incongruous; he camped in the ugly little cinema, with its red lights in brackets, like animal eyes, on the wall, and its wooden floorboards gritty with peanut shells, with the air of the homeless in a park.

Winter and summer, his presence was always known by his cough. At least two or three times in the course of a program it would break out: the fully orchestrated cough of chronic bronchitis, beginning with a stifled wheeze, like silent laughter, rising to a counterpoint of gulping, roaring, retching, and then dying, through more wheezing, to silence. Old Van As's cough.

He coughed on the train, too, the early train that took him to his job at the recruiting office in Johannesburg every day. The morning air made him cough even more. Old Van As's here; ladies, going into Johannesburg to do the important shopping they couldn't trust to the local shops, and, in those days of petrol rationing, unable to travel in their cars, avoided the coach from which they heard that cough coming. It was unpleasant, coughing and spluttering in a railway carriage. Anyway, it was embarrassing to find oneself shut up with poor old Van As, sitting there calmly in that ridiculous uniform, poor old thing, at his time of life. What could one say to him? And one couldn't ignore him; after all, he wasn't just a tramp. No one had really spoken to him for *years*—it was so awkward. And the Van As girls were nice girls, actually; especially Essie (she had got her scholarship and was a nursery-school teacher)—thoroughly sensible and sweet with the children.

The high-school boys and girls who clambered onto the train every morning on their way to school in the next Witwatersrand town (Noorddorp's high school couldn't accommodate them all, before the new high schools were built) didn't notice old Van As or his cough. They filled his carriage and a number of others, willy-nilly, yelling and fooling, great, well-grown South African children whose legs and bodies defeated the purpose of school uniform so thoroughly that, on them, it was not modest and drab but robustly provocative, in the best vaudeville tradition. The girls' short serge gym frocks showed inches of thigh above black stockings straining to cover strong, curved legs and bulging calves; heavy breasts jutted under the tightly buttoned shirts. The enormous hairy legs of boys in football shorts that barely contained their muscular buttocks, stretched across the aisles; at fourteen or fifteen they weighed a hundred and seventy pounds and had the terrifying belly laugh that comes with newly broken voices and new beards breaking erratically through adolescent pimples. They wrote four-letter words on the carriage doors. They stuck gum on the seats and pummeled and flirted, and were as unmindful of old Van As as they were of everyone else outside the violent and raucous orbit of their time of life.

The war ended and they left school and others grew up

into their places and their ways, and old Van As was discharged from the army, but continued to travel to Johannesburg every day, to another job. Nobody knew exactly what it was; some old man's small occupation. He was out of uniform, of course, but still, when it was cold, he wore his army greatcoat over his stained suit. And he still coughed.

Very rarely, the children would make some halfhearted attempt to bait the old man; it was really hardly worth the trouble, since he seemed to travel between invisible blinkers, simply sitting till he got there, sometimes dozing, scarcely even looking out of the window. Once someone had offered him a stone wrapped up in a sweet paper; but he had put up his hand, coughing by way of response, and shaken his head in innocent thanks and refusal. Months went by during which the boys and girls merely battered past him with their school cases and heavy feet, and he was forgotten. Then one of the boys got hold of one of those fake dog's messes, made out of rubber, and when it had been tried in all the likely places and on all the likely people, and seemed to have exhausted its potentialities of diversion, a girl who wanted to impress the boy snatched it up and planted it in the old man's corner seat. Sure enough, he boarded the train at his usual place, the coach two from the end, and sure enough he sat on the thing, but he never noticed it and there it stayed, while the girl sat with her hand over her mouth, her brass-bold eyes watching him for a move. Her friends pressed in on either side of her, and the huddle shook with jeering laughter. For a while, the old man seemed to look at them rather than through them; his wrinkled eyelids flickered once or twice like a film clearing from the narrow apertures of his eyes. He might have been some harmless, slow-reacting creature in a zoo, dimly hearing the sound of pieces of thrown orange peel bouncing off its hide.

Just before the train reached the station at which the children got off, the girl demanded, "You sitting on something of mine." It did not occur to the old man that she could be addressing him. "You sitting on something of mine," she said again, impatiently. He cupped his ear in surprise. "I say there's something of mine you sitting on."

He shuffled fussily to his feet, looking all round him. The girl snatched the object, prancing, insolent, while her friends clutched each other in joy. But the old man had not even seen what it was supposed to be, and he sank down heavily to his place again.

The next morning, the misfired joke was forgotten; the same girls were giggling and whispering over a *True Romances* paperback. They were unaware of him, but the old man sat looking at them.

A day or two later, by one of those simple chances that might so easily never have happened, the old man missed the train, and took a later one. The girl who had played the joke (she looked exactly like the others, she might have been any one of them) missed the train, too, and caught the later one. That train was almost empty, since it was too late for workers or schoolchildren. By habit, the old man got into the second coach from the end; perhaps also out of habit, so did the girl. She flung down opposite him, panting and cross because she would be inexcusably late for school. She brought with her a smell of dusty serge, ink, and the verdigris odor of her greasy yellow hair, which was curled every night but washed infrequently. She gave him the uninterested, ignoring look with which she regarded old people and little children, and became absorbed in a new *True Romances* she had bought herself. The sun shone directly in her eyes, and, without taking her attention from the magazine, she got up and bounced down on the other side of the compartment, on the seat beside him.

Ever since she had come into the empty compartment he had been looking at her, mildly, from his own distance, as if he both saw her and didn't see her. He sighed as she sat down beside him.

It was the old man with the cough, she told, the old man with the cough who was always on the seven-thirty. "*Ô my God,* man, the old pig, what a nerve, eh?" (These giant children spoke the coarse, slangy hybrid of English and Afrikaans that had grown up out of their situation as the progeny of half-educated parents in a bilingual country.) Her friends yelled with laughter until she lost her temper. Her teacher refused to listen to yet another wild tale. But the girl's father, who never knew where she was, what she was doing, or when she came home at night, roused to the promptings of some primitive tribal honor (he liked a fight, anyway) and swore, *vragtig,* he'd like to get his hands round his neck; he'd put the police on the man.

So one day in 1951, when Van As was nearly seventy, he was arrested for kissing a schoolgirl in a train. One of the great robust schoolgirls with the spread thighs and the heavy breasts, female but not yet woman: the female of all erotic fantasy, from adolescence to senility, conjured up by glands, mindless, nameless, almost faceless.

Old Van As! That poor old thing, deaf as a post, with no teeth and the smelly old mustache. Ugh! People giggled with revulsion, grinned with disgust. Why, no woman had looked at him, surely he hadn't had anything to do with one for twenty, thirty years. Since his wife died. He'd never married again, or anything like that—of course not, old Van As! No one would dream of thinking of a woman in connection with him. What on earth got into him? The old devil, eh? Who would have thought it? Well, the old devil . . . You know, the one who coughs so that you can't hear the picture . . .

that's him . . . harmless-looking old bird in an army great-coat.

In the Johannesburg papers there was an inch of space saying that an elderly ex-soldier was alleged to have attempted criminal assault on a fourteen-year-old schoolgirl. The photograph of Van As in his mayoral robes and chain was taken out of the auctioneer's junk room and reproduced in the local paper, with the caption: FORMER MAYOR KISSES SCHOOLGIRL. "G. G. Van As, once mayor of Noorddorp and city councillor for six years, appeared in the Magistrates' Court this week on the charge of kissing a fourteen-year-old schoolgirl, Anna Cornelia Jooste, 17 Dantry Road, Mooiklip."

FOND OF HER DOLLS, SAYS MOTHER was one of the subheadings to the story. All at once, it seemed that a dirty, lecherous old man had frightened a tender little girl. His daughters (especially Essie, who was so well known) could hardly hold up their heads. What a disgrace to them, what a nuisance to them he was, everyone said. Someone even whispered that it was a pity he'd lived on so long; his wife was dead nearly thirty years and he had no friends—not much good to himself or anyone.

His daughter Essie got a lawyer to defend him and he got off, of course: momentary loss of memory—some such plea. The salacious indignation of the town took a little longer to let him off. It was not so much what he had done—that was scarcely to be talked about; while the first kiss was something to make your eyes prick in the cinema, it was assumed that the last must be ridiculous and obscene—but that, for one crazy moment, he had stepped out of character, out of old Van As, the tusky mustache, the comic soldier, the cough in the cinema, and signaled.

It was as if the town's only statue, a shabby thing of an obscure general on a horse, standing in a dusty park and scrawled over by urchins, were to have been observed, bleeding.

The Night the Favorite Came Home

Duncan Miller and Freda Grant arrived at Roodekraal Mine the night the favorite came home. Freda was a South African herself, and Duncan had lived in the country on and off for many years, but when they walked into the house on the mine property where they were to be guests for the night, it was as if they had walked into some foreign village on the birthday of a local saint of whom they had never heard.

"Don't mind the racket, eh," said their host, Alfred Ardendyck, coming across the lawn in a stream of bright light from the front door, to greet them. "Vera backed the winner today, and the whole house's been celebrating since three o'clock. She promised the kids half-a-crown each and they just tearing around instead of going to bed. Please to meet you, Mrs. Miller. Well, Dunkie, you old bastard—how's it, eh? Come inside, Mrs. Miller." And he took Freda's overnight case from her and shepherded the couple up the steps and into the house.

Freda felt foolish rather than guilty at being called "Mrs. Miller"; Duncan had thought it simpler not to explain to a chap like Ardendyck that he and Freda, though they had lived and worked together for years, were not actually married, and never pretended to be. Ardendyck had been in the same hut with Duncan as a prisoner-of-war in Germany for three years of the war. Duncan had suddenly met him again, after thirteen years, one morning in a Johannesburg street, and in the course of the long talk in a bar that had followed, Duncan had promised that when one of their field trips took Freda and him up Alfred's way, in the Northern Transvaal, they would stop over at the Roodekraal Mine and spend the night at Alfred's house.

"This business of chaps one knew in the war," Duncan had said to her, "it's like one's first girl. Afterwards you develop the faculty of natural selection, you seek out your own kind or the kind you aspire to be. But the first one's simply a girl. A prototype, one of those basic outline drawings that represent the female population in a comparative graph. In a prison camp, the chap who sleeps and lives next to you is simply a man, the prototype friend. Alfred was a good sort. I don't know what he's like at home, of course. I can only think of him in the simplest human terms—he used to play cards with the guards and swap the cigarettes he won off them, with me, for my chocolate. I didn't know what he thought about." And Duncan smiled at Freda, his glasses moving with a gleam; he was a small, lean, ugly man, with the smile of a shy girl. Only she, of all the people he had ever known, knew what *he* thought about; of that she was aware. No one else. Certainly not the little girl he had once been married to, when he was a student.

They entered the Ardendyck house past three gaping boys

in short pajamas that bared big pink legs and large feet. "Garn you three, buzz off." Their father gave them the verbal equivalent of an affectionate cuff, and, grumbling, they retreated just far enough up the passage to let the guests go by into the living room. Sobbing and shouting came from the radio, there was a hissing crescendo, as if a dragon were shut away somewhere, coming from the kitchen, a one-eyed spaniel lay, belly up, before the fire, and two guests, a gray-haired woman with pearl earrings weighing down her ears, and a skinny man with the open collar of his shirt showing his Adam's apple, turned in the composed expectancy of greeting. "This's Bill Hamilton, and over here's his wife, Cora, another one of these girls who cleaned up on the race this afternoon." There was an air of placid triumph about Mrs. Hamilton; she took, as if they were only her due, the polite exclamations of surprise and congratulation that Freda and Duncan immediately offered.

Freda was carrying a flowered drawstring plastic bag that held toilet bottles that couldn't be trusted not to leak in a suitcase, and, of course, her books. She was being urged toward Mr. Hamilton's swing chair, beside the fire, and at the same time was being asked by Alfred Ardendyck, "What'll you have? What you gonna have, eh, Mrs. Miller?" She realized that she was not going to be shown to the room were she and Duncan were to sleep, and hastily sat down and stowed away her belongings beside her chair, like someone who has brought a musical instrument along to a party and is alert enough to discover at once that it is not to be a musical evening after all. She prided herself, in a quiet, solitary way, on the way in which she adapted herself to her company; she could sit at a tribal beer drink (the work that she and Duncan did—research into the relation between malnutrition and African tribal life, on the one hand, and detribalized urban life on the other—

sometimes brought them invitations of this kind) or among the black ties and crackling shirt-fronts at the formal dinner of some dull learned society, with equal naturalness. It was her form of humility; her way of showing that she knew and believed that her own particular way of life was not to be valued above other people's.

"What race meeting was this?" she said, taking her whisky and water from Alfred, with a smile, and then turning conversationally to the gray-haired woman. The burst of laughter, the yell from Alfred Ardendyck, over at a cabinet whose front was let down like a drawbridge to bear a full load of whisky and brandy and gin bottles, orange squash and Coca-Cola and fancy glasses—this outburst made her memory wince to attention; her laughter came only a split second after theirs, as if her question really had been a joke. Who else in that room could have believed it to be anything else? There wasn't a child above the age of five, in South Africa, who didn't know about the Durban July Handicap. The first Saturday in July, when it was run, came round as regularly as Christmas, and was publicized nearly as much. The newspapers spoke of "the classic of the South African turf" and the posters announced, seasonally, S.A. IN GRIP OF JULY FEVER. She had seen the posters herself, of course, that morning, before they left Johannesburg, on every street corner. But her mind must have traveled over them harmlessly, like a magnet over a surface on which there is no particle with which it has affinity.

At this point a small boy, younger than the three who had hung about the front door, ran into the room and threw a half-eaten piece of toast into the fire. The bigger ones followed and stopped short, eyeing him from outside the orbit of grownups in which he had taken sanctuary. At the same time, a heavy woman came in forcefully, fresh from some sort of bustle, her legs—muscular and heavy-boned and shapely as a wrestler's—

and great strong feet bearing crushingly down on black sandals with very high heels.

She was grinning as if she couldn't help it; the grin retained its personal, private, and gleeful nature through the pleasantries of introduction. "I've just been getting the kids' supper down their necks," she said to Freda, standing with her hands on her hips, as if looking round for the next thing that had to be done; dazed and exhilarated. "They're nearly as bad as I am; and I don't know if I'm coming or going." She giggled suddenly. Then she said, with grandeur, "I won eighty-five pounds today!"—and giggled again. "So you must excuse me."

"It must be a wonderful feeling," said Freda. "I mean it's a different sort of money. Not like money you've worked for; it's like magic."

"Go out now, Basil, man, go on out, all of you," said Mrs. Ardendyck, tossing her head at her sons. They broke into a stir of grumbling exclamations, grunting, moaning, shrilling. "Awh-h-h-h!" "Mommy!" And they settled down again, perhaps a foot nearer the door, in attitudes of exaggerated protest, one hanging his arm thuggishly round the neck of his brother, another unplaiting the cord of his pajama trousers. Mrs. Ardendyck sat down on the sofa, beside the radio-gramophone. She looked as if she would get up again at once; but instead, she yelled, "Alfred, you so-and-so, you've gone and pinched my drink." Powerful as an ostrich's, her leg tipped against a little three-legged table, rocking the empty glass and full ashtray that stood on it.

"Don't be a clot, Vera, here's your drink on the mantelpiece, where you left it."

She crossed her legs, leaned back in her chair, and took the glass from him, eyeing it imperiously before she drank from it.

"Trouble with you women, you getting too big for your boots, after today," said Bill Hamilton.

Mrs. Ardendyck ran her freckled, square-fingered hands through closely curly, brilliantined, bright hair. "You'n my old man are so darned jealous you could spit blood. You are! You are!"

"But the money's all in the family, isn't it?" said Duncan. "The husband can't lose if the wife wins, can he?"

Alfred gave a snorting laugh. "That's what you think."

"You should've seen him this afternoon," said Mrs. Ardendyck, a woman confident of the attention of her audience. "Boy, you should have seen him. I was shouting Full House—it was just when they came round the second bend and until then the radio hadn't even mentioned that horse's name, he was right out of the running, he didn't get away at all, you know, and then suddenly he came up like that. There I was yelling Full House for all I was worth, and *he's* saying all the time, Shut up, shut up, let's hear the race. Then Bojangles is mentioned for the first time. He nearly puts his hand over my mouth—"

"Ataboy!" said Bill Hamilton, while Alfred swaggered with laughter.

"Honest to God," said Mrs. Ardendyck, "I'm telling you. He tries to do this"—she put her hand over her mouth; her shrewd hazel eyes signaled a furious pantomime of indignation. "It's Bojangles, he yells—and I'm pulling his hand away all the time—it's Bojangles, lemme listen! And there we are struggling, and he's shouting Bojangles and I'm shouting Full House, and we never heard a thing over the radio. Not a thing! I'm telling you! Next thing is, the race's over and they waiting for the photo-finish. But I wasn't worried, you know."

"She fancied Full House right from the beginning," Alfred explained to Duncan. "She said to me, the end of February it must have been, I want you to put something for me on Full House. And I thought she was crazy, man, I wanted to talk her out of it—" He began to replenish everyone's drinks. The noise of frying rose higher, and the smell of fat came into the warmth of the room and made the spaniel restless. The radio changed tempo and the eldest boy said, "Oh boy!" and began to jump about, pumping the arms of his brother. Mrs. Ardendyck had settled down to discuss her success with Duncan and Freda. "I had three separate bets on him, you know. I got him twenty-to-one, twelve-to-one, and seven-to-one. I would have got him ten-to-one the last time, but Alfred, the clot, put off going to town to lay my money for me that day, and by the time he got round to it, the odds were down."

"Vera just can't go wrong," said Mrs. Hamilton feebly. "She fancies something, you can be sure your money's safe. Five of us were in with her." She stayed Alfred's hand as he was about to put a brandy on the arm of her chair. "No *thanks*. I'm still feeling what I had this afternoon."

"Oh come on, Cora," said Mrs. Ardendyck. "For Pete's sake. You only live once and you can only win the July once a year. Snap out of it, man."

"Here's how." Alfred rounded up the room. "To Bojangles and me, good losers—"

A peevish catcall from Mrs. Hamilton and a yell from Mrs. Ardendyck drowned his toast.

A large African woman had been looking coyly round the door, disappearing, and coming back again, for the past ten minutes. "Hey," Alfred grunted at her at last, as if he were questioning the inexplicable movements of an animal who could not understand words, but knew very well certain tones of voice. Mrs. Ardendyck had slipped into the technical jargon of punters, with the expert's careless assumption that the layman cannot possibly be ignorant of whatever subject the expert's happens to be, and Freda was listening to her with the absolute attention of incomprehension. "Emma wants you in the kitchen," Alfred called to his wife, and she got up, her balance in question a moment on her high heels. "I was going to turn out a smart dinner tonight, but once Full House was in I wasn't going to spend the afternoon in the kitchen. Not me. You don't blame me. All us girls in the syndicate had made a pact, we were going to meet at the club if we won. So there we were, on the phone to each other, and down to the club. It was a real party, Cora?"

Mrs. Hamilton looked put out because she did not feel as she felt she ought to feel. "I drank two brandies much too quickly. I don't like drinking in the afternoon at all."

"Look at me," said Mrs. Ardendyck, "on top of the world. You know what I do when I've had one too many? Two Alka-Seltzers and a tablespoon of glucose." She slapped her middle. "Don't feel a thing."

"Emma *wants* you."

She tousled Alfred's hair, making him spill some of his drink. "Hell, no, Vera— You're tight, you know." She crossed her goose-fleshed, quaking red arms in short sleeves and jeered at him; for a moment, the irritations, dissatisfactions, and reproaches that twined and intertwined, making the strong and pliant stuff of everyday, showed through the swimming bright surface of celebration. Yesterday, before the race was won, and tomorrow, the day after the day the race was won, appeared briefly. Then Mrs. Ardendyck did a few dance steps in time to the samba that was coming from the radio, and stopped short, indicating, with a jerk of her head and a grimace, the servant in the kitchen. "You should have seen that one in there when the result was announced. I was doing a war-dance, man, and she ran in in a real state. Missus, are you sick, she said, Missus, are you sick. I reckon she thought I was potty or something. Okay, Emma, I'm coming," she yelled, and went up the passage arguing with her sons, who followed her.

In a few minutes, Duncan and Freda and the Ardendycks

went into the next room for dinner. The children had gone to bed and the Hamiltons, it appeared, had eaten before they came. "Well, you know where the bottle is, Bill," said Alfred with an expansive gesture, as those who were to dine filed out.

The food was the sort of food Freda and Duncan never cooked for themselves and that turned out to be much nicer than they remembered. There was a strong vegetable broth and liver and onions and a steamed pudding. Duncan kept taking off his glasses and resting them on the table a minute or two, while he looked at the world without them; something he always did when he had had a few drinks and was feeling at ease. Freda refused a whisky with her dinner because she had had two stiff ones already and she knew that if she had any more she would not feel equal to getting up at five o'clock next morning, as she and Duncan must do, if they were to keep to the schedule of their journey and their work.

Before the soup was drunk, there was a tattoo on the front door and Mrs. Ardendyck said, triumphantly, "The Mackenzies, I'll bet. She was in the syndicate with me, too. Going to get herself a new bedroom carpet. You'll see, the whole lot'll be over at our place before the night's out."

A little woman with a round, excited face tied like a pudding in a silk scarf that was printed with pictures of Edinburgh Castle and the legend "God Save The Queen," walked in carrying a covered dish. "Ah brought you a few wee as-paaragus rolls, Vera. Ah've no ideer what they'll be like. Ah'm that worked up. I couldna even remember how many spoons of flour was needed." All through the meal people kept arriving; Mrs. Ardendyck kept up a two-way conversation, through the open door into the living room, where her guests were gathered, and with her table companions. "Don't forget I want a helping of the sweets!" one of the men called, from the living room. "We haven't reached the sweets stage yet, keep your hair on!" she shouted back. Alfred was telling Duncan about his job on the mine. Once Freda asked Mrs. Ardendyck whether she had decided what to do with her winnings, and, ample and commanding at the head of the table, smiling at what she heard with that part of her attention that belonged to the room next door, she said, "One thing, I'm definitely buying myself a bottle of some perfume I've seen. Grace Kelly's perfume. Ten pounds a bottle."

Alfred turned at this. "Like hell you are. You must be out of your mind, Vera."

She ignored him and said to Freda with the disdainful air of a spoiled, petulant beauty, "It's the only one I like, out of the lot. Too wonderful."

The moment the last mouthful of pudding was eaten, Mrs. Ardendyck scraped back her chair; "C'mon dear." She touched Freda on the shoulder—and with the touch noticed Freda, for a moment, the space of a rift in her elation, for perhaps the first time since Freda had come into the house, seeing, in that moment, shrewdly and bluntly, right through Freda's polite friendliness and attention. She continued rather gingerly, "Let's go in to the others, Mrs. Miller. Come on, folks."

The living room was full. Canvas chairs had been brought in from the stoep, and people were sitting on the little tables that were meant to hold glasses.

"Well, you girls certainly livened up the old club this afternoon."

"How's it, Vera?"

"I'll say. Why didn' you come over and have a spot with us, Henry? We all called out to you but you weren't having any."

"Next time we won't ask him, that's all."

"Dreamt about anything for next week's double, Vera?"

"I'm sure to tell you."

Duncan stood about with a group of men who leaned their weight against whatever support of wall or furniture offered, but Bill Hamilton had kept Freda's chair for her, and no one would hear of her giving it up. She protested quite strenuously, but giving it up, finding room for herself wherever she could, was a privilege of intimacy she was not to be accorded. The chair had got pushed closer to the fire and she sat wedged in, one cheek hectically flushed and the other turned to a man named Iggulden (she and Duncan had been introduced to everyone, as they came into the room). Iggulden drank his beer and said, "I hear you people travel all over the show," and they began to talk about the weather and the roads in various parts of the country, which was what travel meant, to him. Freda responded to him with ease and respect, for she knew that he was the kind of man who, though he might not share your enchantment with a historic ruin, or your interest in a tribal dance, would not get petulant if you lost your way, and if the lorry stuck, would certainly be able to climb out and fix it. The man called across to his wife, a woman who sat bolt upright on a kitchen chair in the draft from the door, and had not ventured to take off her coat or embroidered woolen gloves, "Sybil, here's someone who's been just about everywhere in the country." But the woman seemed to reject the imputation of her interest as if it were something quite outlandish. She screwed up her face with wifely impatience. "What?"

She looked at Freda; a smile, expressionless and laconic, came and ended abruptly as if the current had failed.

Freda's companion could not help having toward her the attitude of a man to an offering which has not been well received; he lost confidence in their conversation, and it died. For a little while Freda was on the periphery of a three-sided male conversation of which she was a shadowy fourth, but the men began to draw closer and closer round the point of the story one of them was telling, and when she laughed at the innocuously coarse climax, they became aware of her with such surprise and discomfiture that she felt she had been eavesdropping, and sat back in her chair.

Voices competed all round her like barkers on a fairground.

". . . Grace Kelly's perfume. It was specially made for her by one of these blokes in France."

"Man, no. I think I'll have a beer."

". . . but I wouldn't dare tell Alec's mother. She's always trying to get us to sign the pledge and she won't even take a bazaar raffle ticket."

"There's no more ginger ale. What'll you have with your brandy, Les—Coke?"

"D'you know what time I was in town this morning? Quarter past eight. They were just taking the dust-sheets off in Bassett's . . . the girls in the showroom always have a yap with me. Those black coats are lovely, I know, but I think it's too late in the season. Then I spent about an hour at the perfume counter. Here—and here—and here— Man, I just had it all over, I tell you. . . . Yes, ten quid a bottle; it's the only one I'd have."

One couple had brought a small boy and he had wakened the Ardendyck children; they burst in dodging and tumbling among the grownups, and stayed, in the face of threats, until their presence was forgotten, when they would leap up on impulse and rush to some other part of the house, carrying off a dish of peanuts or a bottle of Coca-Cola. Someone had turned up the radio, in the unconscious desire to provide the excitement of the opposition of one kind of blare against another. Duncan, kept by Alfred Ardendyck at his side, had the bewildered yet pleased look of the class swot who has suddenly been taken up by the gang.

Beneath the protection of the room's uproar, Freda was returned to her own private existence; she looked out, at noise and knickknacks and people—a room so full and at the same time so bare. There were no pictures, unless you counted those of embroidered wool, there were no books or papers. Her gaze went quietly over the curtains with their design of red and yellow cactus, the carpet with its beige and maroon scrolls, the mantelshelf with its population of china figurines, glass animals, and miniature liquor bottles. There was no line, no object, no color that spoke to her silently as she had so often found inanimate things do, even in the most unexpected and alien places. The title of a book she had read, a cup like one she had drunk out of in another place, a photograph, cut out of a newspaper and pinned on the wall, of something she had laughed at or admired—these were the things that leaped seas, made plain foreign tongues, and gave into the stranger's hand the connecting thread of his own identity.

She got up and made her way across the room, murmuring good night at dazed, loosely animated faces wherever they happened to turn to her momentarily. "Mrs. Miller!" Alfred sang out. "Come an' have a drink. This old Dunkie's been pulling a fast one. You better keep him in his place. Come on, have a whisky—" But he was so caught up among shouts of laughter, glasses thrust at him, the fragments of anecdotes and arguments whipping his burly center like a top, that he did not even notice that she had not taken the drink, and he simply waved her good night, or perhaps was signaling across the room in a gesture, meaning something quite other, and not intended for her, that she took as an appropriate one.

"I'm so sorry, but if I don't go to bed now, I know I'll never be able to get up in time tomorrow. You will forgive me—"

Mrs. Ardendyck grinned into the apology with warm indifference, interrupted in the middle of an exchange in which the second half of each sentence was exploded in laughter and clutchings: "All I could do was—" "True as God, I couldn't—"

She got up and led Freda quickly down the long passage. "There's the bathroom, lav next door, I s'pose the kids've left the bath filthy. Here's the room." She opened the door on a neat, dank spare room with a strip of mat between two beds covered with chintz. She cut short Freda's thanks, standing for a moment, hands on her hips, one foot turning on the pivot of its high heel. Her hair seemed to spring up from her head with a gaiety of its own, her neck was ruddy, her strong nose shone, and the outer corners of her eyes were rheumy with laughter. "Well, I hope you don't freeze, that's all," she said jauntily, and she was gone.

Freda Grant stood, aware only of the small weight of the toilet bag hanging from her fingers. The chill of the room was like peace. But the noise came back, warmth to a numb limb; the clash of laughter against an engine-room hum of talk, the thumps and bumps and scrapes of movement. She lifted her overnight case—Alfred Ardendyck must have brought it into the room at some point—onto the bed and took out her night things and Duncan's. She opened the toilet bag and, still standing in the middle of the room, slowly creamed her face. The children ran in a posse down the passage and up again, smothering giggles and thudding against walls and doors. While she was in the bathroom, one of them turned the handle of the door, which had no key, and she said in the indulgent, sporting voice she used for children, "What is it?"—but there was only a spluttering sound and a clattering race away back to the party. She spread her coat over the bottom of the bed and wound her watch and put it on the stool that stood between the two beds, and slid her hand between the sheets: there was a good weight of blankets, after all—she would not be cold. A spatter of clapping followed laughter; some sort of performance must have been concluded at the party. She took a pot of handcream from the toilet bag and got into bed, taking note that she would have to get out of bed to switch off the light when she had finished reading. And then she discovered that she had no books.

She must have left the books in the living room beside her chair, or wherever they had been pushed by people's feet. She had a start of painful anxiety at the thought of the books, underfoot, sifting away somewhere inaccessible, lost in a crowd. She jumped out of bed at once, struggled into her dressing-gown, and then stood about before the door. How could she go down the passage and hang about, hoping to catch Duncan's eye? How could she march in, before them all, to go scratching about under chairs for her books? But the sense of anxiety persisted. The books were not part of the essential library of reference and scientific books, or even the new books brought along for entertainment, that she and Duncan had left locked up with all their other equipment, in the jeep, but were simply her own personal things, an old novel, a book of poems, and a missionary's chronicle of early travels in Africa, that she kept with her always on field trips. If there were delays, if she and Duncan were stranded, she always knew that she had these, her hardtack, to sustain her.

No harm could come to them, of course. How could they be lost, in a room? No one would touch them. No one would even look at them. They would be quite safe. All she had to do was to go into the living room in the morning, and pick them up. She had a vivid picture of the living room by the light of early day; the chairs cast like husks, the ashtrays, the bottle tops and dirty glasses. Under a thick lid of ash, the sleepy eye of the fire still alight. But the books, somehow the books were not there.

Suppose she should forget them, in the morning?

Irritated with herself, she closed down sharply on this fantasy. She took off her dressing-gown determinedly, folded it ready to pack away, and went to turn off the light. But with her hand on the switch she hesitated again, and suddenly went swiftly to the overnight case and felt for something in one of its worn silk pockets. She took out a small leather diary and, opening it at an empty page belonging to a month of the year that had already passed, she wrote, "My books," and underscored what she had written. Then she looked about her, picked up the pot of cream, and propped the open diary against it, on the bedside stool. She got into bed. She shifted the cream pot and the diary so that they faced her line of vision. Her lips moved slowly, shaping two words. Her hand went out almost secretly and she took up the diary and scrawled, this time in big, untidy block letters, MY BOOKS, and again underscored the words.

When she had turned out the light she pulled the covers up to her neck and closed her eyes and lay, all alone, listening to the party.

Little Willie

She was eight when Little Willie first began to take notice of her. Her brother had taken a photograph of her with the box camera he had been given for his birthday. She showed the picture—a small streak of a face, a darker streak of the dog in her arms, a reeling blur of garden behind, like a scene glimpsed on a switchback—to Uncle Basil. He was one of those courtesy-titular uncles of childhood, a great intimate of the house. He gave the picture the serious attention of his pince-nez and his considering mouth, and said, begging a singular favor in the manner of someone who knows his privileged place, "May I have it?"

"Uncle Basil's going to have my picture!" the child shouted to her brother, in the next room.

"So what?" came back the jealous voice.

The child went and stood behind the man's chair, looking,

with him, at herself, in that concentration that only females give to themselves. When her mother came into the room, the child said, suddenly shy with pleasure and triumph, "Uncle Basil wants to take my picture to keep."

He put the photograph down on the table beside him, took off his glasses, put them on again, twitching them into position on his nose, then propped the picture against an ashtray. "The only thing is, I know who'll never be satisfied until he's got it away from me."

"Who?" said the child, wary, not yet curious.

"Ah, Denise," said Uncle Basil, sounding the connotations of the name, as he might have said, ah, Cleopatra, ah, Delilah.

In a rush, curiosity came over her, a pleading frenzy. "Who? But who? Oh please, please, tell me who will take it?"

"Little Willie," said the man, implying she might have known it.

"Who?" She screwed up her face in an urgent snarl of incomprehension.

"Little Willie, of course."

"Who's little Willie?" she said, scornfully.

He raised his eyebrows, drew her to his knee. "My dear Denny, you must know Little Willie."

"But who is he? Where did I see him? How does he know me?"

"He knows you," said Uncle Basil. "He never talks about anything else *but* you."

She was silent for a moment. Then she said, "Is that his real name?"

"That's the only one he's told me."

"Is he grown up?" she said quickly. "Is he big or is he a child?"

Uncle Basil measured the air round her head with his eyes. "In between," he said.

She nodded, as if she saw what he was describing.

"Where does he live?" she asked, warming. The man looked her straight in the eyes, as if to brace her for it. "In Railway Avenue," he said, and raised and lowered his eyebrows in a fractional movement of confession.

She slid off his knee and landed, standing, between his spread legs. "He doesn't!" she said.

The man nodded his head slowly.

In the gold-mining Transvaal town where her father was town clerk, the poor whites of the town were the railway gangmen and their families who lived in one mean street of corrugated-iron cottages between the station and the black dump of a disused coal mine—Railway Avenue. The name of the street was not only the synonym of poverty, it was a name-calling epithet for all standards that fell below those of the town clerk's family and the friends who lived and thought as they did. Because she had never been poor, and had never known anyone who was really poor, Denise was deeply imaginatively aware of the shame and disgrace of poverty—just as, because she had never been rich, or known anyone who was rich, she knew that wealth was a blinding glory of jewels and palaces. Poverty, in her mind, was a state compounded of the sufferings of children like Hansel and Gretel, wandering hungry in the woods (she had never seen a wood, and she thought of the rustling plantations of gum trees planted to provide timber props for the gold mines), and the sight of the Railway Aveners, coming once a month from the Welfare Society office with their paper carriers of charity groceries. There were the grandmothers with bandaged legs and old, battered straw hats, like the hats the town clerk's children had in their dressing-up box, the mothers with the sucked-in mouths of women who have lost their teeth young, and the silent innumerability of children: children carrying smaller children, children dragging other children along, children being pushed in go-carts—children with the sharp, wicked, gleeful faces or the dull, closed, stoic stupidity with which nature had hurriedly armed them far ahead of the time of their lives when such choice of front is usually made. "It's a disgrace," she would overhear her mother say of a neighbor's child. "He behaves like something out of Railway Avenue!" Or to Denise's brothers: "Now don't come home from the barber's looking like Railway Avenue."

Railway Avenue boys wore their heads shaved almost clean, for reasons Denise's mother didn't like to think about; no doubt the schoolteachers had to insist on it, or even to do it themselves. Denise used to see the boys running about the town on Friday afternoons and Saturdays, when they sold the local weekly paper. Their skinniness, brownness, and generally wild and spare look were accentuated by the bony outlines of their skulls, showing so clearly through the faint pile of shaven bristle, which, if it was fair, caught the light like spears of new grass. They darted and skimmed through the people—the miners were paid on Fridays, and so the streets were full—and their startling faces would surface the shoppers' attention at waist level—" *'Tiser*, sir? *'Tiser?*" They never wore shoes, and somehow they always looked cold, winter and summer.

"He can't know me," she said, in a voice that had already given in in acceptance of the fact it was in the act of denying.

"He's always said you'd feel like that about it," said Uncle Basil, "but what can he do? That's where he lives. And his mother. And his father. And his *oupa* and *ouma*—"

At the casual use of the Afrikaans words for grandma and grandpa there came at once to mind one of the old women with the swollen legs—Little Willie's grandmother. And in her hand, the paper carrier with the bag of mealie meal, the sugar and coffee that the Welfare people doled out—some of these families have lived off Welfare parcels for three generations, and proud of it, Denise's mother sometimes remarked, just to show you what they were, these poor whites.

"You remember that time, after Christmas, when we went to the regatta?"

"What was that again?" the child asked.

"The time when we saw the boats racing, and we had a picnic."

"Oh yes," she said at once. "I'd forgotten what it was called."

"Well," he went on, "you remember the boys who stood around the landing-stage, where the cold drinks were sold?"

"Yes?" she said, apprehensively. Those boys had gone quiet with the approach of people to the refreshment stall, the way monkeys in the zoo drop their distractions of scratching and swinging and sit, their eyes fixed on the bag of peanuts in your hand, as you come up to their cage. There was one boy who had got a Coca-Cola from somewhere, and the others had immediately fallen upon him, snatching and punching. He was one of the dirtiest, with round patches of ringworm showing on his head.

"That's the first time he saw you."

She tried to remember the gang better; tried to search their faces in her memory, to identify this boy who had been watching her.

"And now always when you go to town with your mother on Saturday mornings. He looks forward to Saturdays so much."

Denise's mother had been standing with her back to the window, listening to all this. With her hands on her hips, smiling, she said, fondly, "Basil! You are the limit!"

He raised his head and looked at her with prim inquiry, then with the meticulous air of returning to a matter that concerned him greatly, he said to the child, "You won't mind if the poor chap gets the picture of you, will you? I don't see how I can promise to prevent it."

She rushed at him and buried her face in his lap, hammering at his chest with her chapped, scratched fists. "He doesn't know me!" she cried. "He doesn't!"

But he did. A few weeks later, Denise went with her mother to an afternoon wedding reception. Uncle Basil was out of town that weekend, but the first time he visited the house after his return, he remarked, "I hear you looked very pretty at the wedding on Saturday. Though you didn't smile to left or right as you went into the Town Hall, just held your mother's hand and looked straight ahead. Little Willie was disappointed."

"He wasn't there!" she said derisively.

"Oh, he wasn't *invited,* he couldn't expect that, of course" —and Uncle Basil lowered his eyes and paused a second with his teeth on his lower lip. "But he saw you outside. He was waiting."

Whenever there was a wedding or a dance in the Town Hall, the Railway Avenue urchins spoiled the whole look of the thing by hanging round the doors; sometimes, if the drinks went freely and the party seemed likely to be too preoccupied to notice, the barefoot brats even managed to slip in and filch some food from the tables nearest the exits.

The child was confused with annoyance. "I wish he'd mind his own business," she snapped.

Uncle Basil looked pained. "Oh, he knows it's a fearful cheek. But he does admire you so much. I've told him to put it out of his mind. I've told him how you feel about Railway Avenue. But it's no good."

Sometimes, when Uncle Basil took the family out in his car, he would slow down incomprehensibly. When he had crawled along for half a block, someone would say, "What's the matter? Are you going to stop here?" Then, putting his foot on the accelerator and sending the car leaping ahead with a flourish, he would say casually, "I thought I'd give poor Little Willie a chance to get a look at Denise."

There would be a flurry, Denise bridling, her brothers jeering.

"Where was he?"

"Soppy thing!"

"I didn't see him."

And Denise would slide down in the back seat until she was well below the level of the window, and remain there in sulky exasperation, like a celebrity who has just escaped her importunate fans, while the grownups in the front seat laughed and made oblique comment.

When Guy Fawkes' Day came near, and Uncle Basil was helping the town clerk's children, as he did every year, to make their effigy for the bonfire, he brought along a shapeless khaki-colored felt hat and a pair of veldschoen as his contribution to the Guy's clothes. "They're Little Willie's father's," he explained cheerfully, "but he's had them a long time and Little Willie feels"—with a glance at Denise—"Little Willie feels he should get something better. So he persuaded his father to sell them to me."

Denise did not seem to be so enthusiastic about the Guy Fawkes preparations that year. She would come into the garage, where the effigy was being made (of straw packed into old clothes, with a liberal seasoning of crackers to ensure that his would be a sizzling and noisy incineration) and after standing about for a minute or two, wander off again. "Denise is getting to the stage where the things that interest the boys are not the same as the things that interest her," her mother remarked to her father.

But on the night itself, the night of the Guy Fawkes celebration, the child seemed seized by a mood of exceptional gaiety. The bonfire lit up her fiercely laughing face as she stood, right in the liquid-feeling heat of it, watching the effigy burn up. When the effigy's hat took flame and fell, curling in frenzy, from the straw head, she shrieked and swaggered with joy, a cue that the other children took to join in a general expression of the wild pleasure of destruction.

Denise felt the eye of Little Willie upon her wherever she went. She tried to remember never to smile in the street; it was her way of showing him his place. Unaccountably, she begged to be let off her solo tap-dance in the pupils' display given by her dancing class. Her mother decided she must be "outgrowing her strength" and put her onto a course of pink tonic medicine.

To Denise, her mother's attitude to Little Willie was a surprising one. She seemed to be on Little Willie's side. Denise had thought—or rather accepted—that forever, in everything, her mother would be on her side. But now, when Uncle Basil came to dinner and reported on Little Willie to the unwilling but fascinated Denise, her mother would take up the anecdote with her guest. Freshly powdered for dinner, and with the scented cream on her hands that she liked to use when she had finished cooking, her mother would watch Uncle Basil's face with her chin lifted, lips parted, eyes smiling. "Why don't you bring Little Willie over one day, Bas?" she said once, as if she'd suddenly had a good idea.

"I'll shut myself in the shed," Denise said fiercely.

"Oh, the little madam!" "What a snob your daughter is, Josie!"

"But Denny darling, he's such a nice boy and we could always lend him some of Dick's clean things."

Denise's father did not join in this baiting; but then he never joined in any sort of family diversion—he was the sort of man who brings his work home and carries it about with him, always looking for a corner to settle down with it, like a cat looking for a place to lie down with her kittens.

The fact that her mother was no longer with her produced a hardening in Denise that became her armor against, and finally defeated Little Willie. She did not care, any more, if he saw her smile in the street. She did not care if he was watching her. She despised him. What a cheek he had, a hopeless cheek, to look at *her*. All her embarrassment fell away; she scarcely thought about him.

When Uncle Basil began, "I saw Little Willie yesterday—" she would interrupt, "Horrible dirty thing, why doesn't he have a bath? Haven't they even got any soap and water in their house?" And her mother and the man would laugh delightedly.

In December, just before Denise's ninth birthday, the town clerk's family were to go for a holiday. "Little Willie's quite envious," said Uncle Basil. "He's never seen the sea; still, he's glad you're going." Denise felt glad he had never seen the sea. Nearer the day when the family was to go, Uncle Basil, writing trunk labels for them, said, "Little Willie's very keen to come to the station." And, on the day they were to leave, Uncle Basil telephoned to say good-by and left a message for Denise that Little Willie would be there—the three-thirty for Durban, platform eleven. "He won't come," said Denise with apathetic derision. "Don't worry, he won't come."

Yet as they drove to the station, a sudden apprehension turned turtle in her belly. Platform eleven was crowded; she felt reassured: she would never see him among all those people. He was quite out of her mind (she and her brothers were hanging out of the train corridor window, watching for the wave of the green flag which would signal their departure) when the office boy from Uncle Basil's office came up through the crowd with a large oblong parcel in his hands. "What is it? What is it?" The town clerk leaned out of the train impatiently, as if he felt himself (inevitably) pursued by the bulky minutes of some meeting of the town council. He took the parcel, and at once said, "It's for you," and handed it to his wife. "Miss Denise Howle," she read. "It's not for me—it's for Denise." The boys pressed round; she lifted it over their heads, waving it. "Denny! Denny!"

Denise sat down on the seat in their carriage, surrounded by importance. She had no idea why she should get a parcel, or from whom, two minutes before the train left to take her on her summer holiday. She dragged the string off the hard edges of the parcel and tore away the paper. Underneath, a layer of tissue paper took off in the gust of live air that came in the window as the train began to move. On her lap was a toffee-colored padded satin casket with a big gold tassel hanging from the lid. A gasp rose from the children, along with the sound of the train rattling comfortably into its stride. Denise lifted the tassel. The inside of the lid, as it was raised, was seen to be satin-covered, too; the box was filled with chocolates shining in gold paper. Her brother Dick thrust his finger down the side. "Two more layers underneath!" he said excitedly. "Oh, she's *lucky!*" wailed the smaller brother. "Wait a minute," said Denise, and took a card from the band of ribbon that was stretched across the inside of the lid. They all read it at once. "It's from Little Willie, it says from Little Willie!" someone shouted. She swatted her brothers' hands away like flies. "Get off!" she cried. And then she read the card herself, in peace. The train was going quite fast now; they were well out of the station. "Have you ever seen such a big box, Mummy?" she said, aware that the present was outside the range of a child's experience.

"It must have cost two or three pounds," the father said to the mother, with a note of reproach.

"Well, you know what he is," said the mother, half admiring, half conceding the reproach. She said, smiling, to Denise, "Little Willie must have saved for months to buy you that."

The child slid the golden tassel through her fingers. The casket lay on her lap, a chorus-girl's trophy. She was looking out of the window, without attention, and her cheeks were sleepily flushed. She thought of a group of ragged children; of a bony-headed boy, looking on at her pleasures and triumphs. A dirty boy without shoes. She was ashamed of him. She would never speak to him or look at him; and he knew this. But the present in her lap was not to be resisted. No one whom she had loved, been kind to, or tried to please had ever rewarded her with something as fine as this. Earned by scorn and disdain, it was like nothing she had ever been given before; she held the box recklessly tight, and when she peeled the gold paper off the first chocolate and put it in her mouth, the cherry inside was the fruit of knowledge on her tongue.

A Style of Her Own

They envied her her dignity. It gave them something to talk about as they sat on the veranda (on fine days) and (on rainy days) in the lounge of the private hotel. "Money, that's it," one of them always said. "It's easy to go about like a queen when you can afford it."

Most of the other old ladies disagreed with this view. One look at the poor old thing who had said it—they thought of one another as poor old things but each exempted herself from this generalization—that was enough to convince you. Rothschild's millions couldn't make a queen out of *her*. She was one of those who had bad legs and whose board and lodging were paid by the contributions of her children.

"It's got to be born in you," said another sagely. She had always mixed with what she called "a better-class type of person," and she felt she knew. "She's got the looks, too, you must remember," another one always reminded them. She herself had a large, fat face that had never found room for a wrinkle, though her body had gone inert under the weight of age, and she never got farther than the five yards from the lift to the sofa that stood between the reception desk and the door.

"She looks every day of her age," said one who believed she herself didn't; under two nets, her rich red curls never dulled, and she even powdered the old lady's hump of flesh at the back of her neck, where the diamanté clasp of her pearls rested.

They sat beached, with their feet crossed on the maroon carpet, and watched Mrs. Clara Hansen come in from the street. "Have a nice afternoon, dear?" The enormous, smiling face of the woman at her usual seat on the sofa at the entrance, called out her inevitable greeting. But Mrs. Hansen only smiled slightly, and murmuring an acknowledgment, passed on to the dim maroon vista of the passages. Her ankles were slim; she wore narrow, laced-up shoes that they thought were old-fashioned, and she wasn't painted that you could see. Her face beneath one of her pale, expensive hats was exactly the color and texture of the well-washed, white doeskin gloves that she wore. It was a beautiful face, with the rather bloodhound look that comes with the sagging of even the finest tissue; the eyes were gray, speckled, commanding, the bridge of the nose was high, and the mouth was weary. (It was said that she still had her own teeth—no one dared ask her whether this was true.) There was nothing at all like her, in the bilious corridors beneath naked bulbs outside the numbered rooms, where chintz curtains hid the washbasins and the air was a patchouli of old clothes; in the dining room with the slimy-stemmed asters in a blue glass vase on each table; in the lounge where the gilded cane basket of pink gladioli stood over a worn patch on the mustard and green carpet, and the springs of the sofas and easy chairs nudged your flesh.

Of course, the hotel was not her sort of place at all—she did not stay at "private" hotels but at old, large, expensive public ones, intimidating as museums to those who had not been coming to them for years, as she had, all over the world. She had been led to come to the private hotel in Johannesburg "by misinformation," as she quietly put it, her eyelids drooping and her voice dying away. She had not liked the large Johannesburg hotel she had stayed at on her last visit to the city ("It was full of American tourists with their cameras and their children—both bumped me about constantly in the lifts") and she supposed all the others were as little to her taste. The man at the tourist agency in London had been stumped, and then, looking through his files, had produced, with special references, the Barret-Tromp. She had not cared much for the sound of it, but then she did not care much for Johannesburg anyway (she really liked only places that she had been visiting since she was a child, and that she felt knew her very well) so she gave in quite suddenly and said it would serve. Once she arrived at the place, she realized that it would scarcely do that, this complex of old houses joined by passages where the electric lights had to burn all day, and the patchwork of worn carpets, each laid to hide the baldness of the other, might be suspected of cosily harboring cockroaches. She was appalled at the rows and rows of old ladies, creeping or puffing or stooping about ("It is disgusting," she wrote to Europe, "to see how we fall to pieces while we are still alive") and the nasal voice of the little Indian who went through the public rooms with a sandwich board, calling out the names of people who were wanted on the telephone. But she had come to Johannesburg to make some complicated arrangements about her mining investments that would take a month or two, at the most, and then would release her once and for all from the necessity of coming to Johannesburg, or even South Africa, for that matter, ever again, and she decided that it was not worth while to move to some other hotel. The distastefulness of the Barret-Tromp Residential Hotel along with the irksome visits to lawyers and revenue offices seemed to her a fitting end to her connection with South Africa—a last and therefore almost pleasurable trial wrought upon her by the subcontinent where she had stood so many, and through whose plaguy fingers she was finally slipping.

There was something else to it, too, her decision to bear wryly with the Barret-Tromp. The old ladies whom she found repulsive and with whom she had nothing whatever in common—they attracted her in some secret, reluctant part of herself that she wouldn't explore. They appealed to some imprisoned whimperer inside her who wanted to be the old lady that she herself could never be, the old lady sunk into the mumbling, gossiping, repetitive consolations of old age, the gerontic nursery rhyme to which all the meaning and passion of life is reduced. So while she let the old ladies admire her, while she paused, occasionally, to let them talk to her for a few minutes, she was flirting with the perverse, anarchistic, almost tempting desire to abandon herself to them as if to a vice. Nothing of this rocked the pedestal of her dignity, of course; it is doubtful if, in her well-disciplined mind, the rumor of it ever got beyond the anterooms of her own consciousness, where, to maintain sovereignty over herself, she kept hanging about in the half-dark so much that she refused to recognize.

"That hat suits you too beautifully, darling," Mrs. Green, the one who sat on the sofa in the entrance, said to her for the twentieth time since her arrival at the hotel. The "darling" was like a pawing caress; Mrs. Hansen thought, with a faint thrill of horror, would she live to find the language of endearment debased from the communication of lovers to the small talk of old widows whose glands, like the true occasion for the words, were withered?

"All my hats are the same," she said.

"Oh, I know, that's just it, you've got your own style. You can carry it off, never mind what the fashion is," said the fat woman, a schoolgirl whispering in a corner. "That's what they all say about you, my dear. There's some's jealous of you in this hotel, I don't mind telling, either. Some that's not much themselves, and jealous, of course. I watch them all, going in and out. With all their feathers and flowers and what not, it doesn't help. Not one of them's a patch on you, believe me, Mrs. Harris and I were saying only just now, before lunch. You've got real dignity. That's born in you, that's what I say. Not one of them's got that dignity you've got, every line of you."

"You looked like a queen this morning, honestly," said Mrs. Harris, turning her good ear to the talk and settling her bad legs, stuffed into her shoes like the legs of a cloth doll.

Mrs. Hansen sighed, a little beyond them. She never quite talked *to* them. "Dignity?" she said, and the one corner of her mouth went down in a slight smile, weary, hinted at. Her voice was always low, as if she wondered if they would understand her, anyway, even if they happened to hear her. "You people talk about it as if it were something you could buy, in a shop. I've lived in a lot of places, I've seen . . . My life has taken me"—she paused, and the word that followed took on a reference other than geographical—"about. You begin to look a certain way, just as a country person looks a certain way in a city—the opposite way, of course. I don't know about being 'dignified.' . . . But you don't find these

ving on trees, you know." For a moment, she was
n, an old lady herself, mouthing the familiar plati-
perience—"Dignity doesn't grow on trees."

Not on trees. No, no. She knew very well where it had come from, that look on her face, that tone in her voice, that presence. She knew where and when it had been bought, as one is always able to find again, in one's mind, the exact circumlocution of back streets by which chance led to the little shop in a foreign town where, on a certain day, a particular piece of jewelry was discovered. And as if it were an old trinket, or a letter never thrown away, she knew, under the accumulation of years, just where to put her hand on the—memory? (It was too weak a word for it.) No, no, not on trees, or in shops, or in the sort of experience that for these poor old creatures no doubt had passed for life. (What would an unfaithful husband have meant to one of them? A return to mother, and the children to bring up on her own.) No, no, not here, not nearer dying than loving, nearer the dark grave than the dark bed, nearer the weight of earth on one's breast than the weight of a man; not here in a boarding-house that outside smelled of cat, and inside of old people.

Far away from this. Nearly thirty years away. She was not young, even then. Almost middle-aged. Forty-three. (But then women only begin to feel, after they are thirty; when she was a girl she was nothing.) Carl Hansen, her second husband, had come home from his office at half-past four or five, one afternoon, and had told the driver to go. "We won't need you, tonight." "But aren't we going to the harpsichord recital?" she said. They were living in Durban at the time—she could put the memory of the place, like a shell, to her ear, and hear forever the majestic clanging of the lighted trams along the front at night.

"Shall we?" He sat down in his big chair as if he never

wanted to move again. "Won't we get all the concerts we need, in Europe next month?" He smiled at her; he was rather an ugly man, really, but who would have dared to think of him that way? You had only to see the strap of his watch holding the quick, strong tendons of his brown wrist above his masterly black-haired hand, you had only to get that impatient glance sideways from under his brows as you opened a door and disturbed him, to feel the irrelevance of good looks.

"All right. I thought you were so keen to go."

He shook his head, yawned, and settled himself with the paper, his whisky, and his cigar. It seemed clear that he was there for the evening. She felt again a sense of security that ridiculously did not belong; as if everything were all right. Like many women who are desperate, she had reached a state of mind when the desire to have things other than they are provides toeholds of credulity in the most doubtful of assurances. The wife of the drunkard cannot stop herself from believing that the one night on which he stays sober is the reality, while the other nights were the nightmare from which she was awakened; Clara Hansen, every time her husband came home and read his paper in the evening, like any other man, could not help succumbing to the feeling that he had never, so to speak, left the fireside. He had, of course, time and again. Once, she herself had been one of his women. She had left her husband in order to marry him. It had not occurred to her that by marrying him, she was simply exchanging one position for another; now someone else would be one of his women, and she would sit at home and be his wife. Her mother, of all people, seemed to have understood this, and more. "For God's sake, don't marry him. I tell you he's mad," she had said. "There's something wrong with that man, you'll see. He doesn't want you or anybody else; he wants everything —and that's something different, that's a madness. You'll see."

Clara was thirty-three when she married Carl Hansen and

she did not speak to her mother for nearly ten years after that. The conversation had horrified her so much that she flew into a rage at the mention of her mother's name. And in ten years with Carl she learned to understand that she had merely changed positions; that there were weight and counter-weight, and there could not be one without the other. But she never accepted the situation. She began with suffocating jealousy, weeping, and anger.

"I don't think I'll ever leave you," he said.

She grew, by torturous processes, forcing herself to hold her hand in the candle flame of her passion for him, to cold reproach and the fear that after all, he never would. And she came, at last, to begging him for decency's sake, in the name of the ten-year marriage, to give himself some peace from women.

Whichever way she chose to do it, she had never stopped fighting him. At first she fought him because she wanted him, and later she fought him because she didn't see why she should let go, anyway; he was the torn and bloody rag of something whose original form and identity had been forgotten, but which was guarded, in that name, even more savagely than it itself had been.

She did not know what woman it was with whom he was spending his nights, that particular summer in Durban. She had tried to narrow down his field of opportunity, God knows; she had learned long ago that it was not possible for her to have women friends, because, inevitably, her husband found new lovers among them, and the only woman who came to the flat was a plain, timid, middle-aged spinster who spent a day there once in two weeks, sitting at the sewing machine doing the household mending and repairs, and alterations to Mrs. Hansen's beautiful clothes. But who was to know what women he managed to meet outside the flat, as he went about the town on affairs of business? She had no way of controlling this. She only knew that since just after Christmas, he had begun not coming home from the office at all, in the afternoons, and on those days when he did come, it was merely to tell her that he had to have dinner with some business acquaintances (the old lies, worn smooth, still served him). This time, of all the times there had been, she was exasperated. He looked so old, so past that sort of adventure. He looked like a man who is haggard with financial worries, plagued by reverses in his business plans. He looked like that. And it was nonsense, there was no need for it; he was an extremely clever businessman and he and she were the sort of rich people who have their eggs apportioned between many foreign baskets, and are secure in the certainty that if some break, there will always be others, intact, elsewhere. There was no *need* for him to have that harassed air, the nervous, greenish shine on the line of his jowl, the wavering sigh as he sat down. It was simply some woman, that was all; Clara Hansen thought of her as she might have thought of the return of a chronic ailment that beset her husband.

The evening of the harpsichord recital to which they were not going, he sat on comfortably in his chair until dinner, looking up from his paper only once, to ask, "What did you say we are eating tonight?" She had not said; but she answered inquiringly, "Duck. Braised duck." "Ah, that's fine, then. Ask Alfred to take out a bottle of red wine—the Château Mouton." This small self-indulgence—like many rich people who have no need to be, they were careful with money, and usually drank only South African wines when they were in South Africa—was somehow reassuring, was a pleasure in keeping with the dignity of a man in his late fifties. They ate slowly, and the bottle went fairly evenly between them; the candles burned softly and she had about her, absolutely unchanged, the remote, hooded regard, calm and fascinating, that he had seen and immediately taken for himself, when she was somebody else's wife.

What happened, then, to change this mood? As usual, as always, she did not know. But suddenly, between hesitating about his emptied cup and the second cup of coffee, he got up, put the cup absently down, and went into his bedroom. He was gone only a minute (could he have telephoned without her hearing the croak of the dial or the sound of his voice?) but when he came back to the living room, his manner was changed. "I must go out for a while," he said; his face was the face of a man walking quickly along the street. She was never one of those jumpy women who react sharply. She turned splendidly, moving her whole full-bosomed body, from the waist. Her lips were just parted, as if she waited for something —but then she closed them, and the right side of her mouth quirked once, in a disbelief of its own, before she said, "What is it now?" "I have to go out. There's a man I've got an appointment with in town. He's sailing tomorrow."

"Oh yes," she said.

He came over to the chair where he had been sitting before, took two cigars from the box on the arm, and put them carefully into his breast pocket. She saw that he had brushed his hair, but his face looked heavily lined.

"Clara," he said from the door, "good night."

"Good night."

She heard his footsteps, with the heels coming down hard along the corridor, for a few seconds, and then they were lost in the sounds of the seaside place on a summer night that came in at the open balcony doors and seemed to settle around her silence. The sound of the sea—dark out there, two hundred yards beyond the balcony—was always in your ears in the flat. It muted other noises akin to it, the sound of your own blood, the purr of a cat, and the noise of water running in the pipes.

But at night, and in the absence of talk in the room, it brought with it, as the tide itself carried sugar cane from the rivers, ice-cream cartons from the beach, and all sorts of refuse from the ships in the harbor, all the sounds of the living town that were adrift in the warm dark. First of all the gliding grind and rattle of the trams on the front, and the clang as they swayed round the corner; then the voices of the barkers at the amusement park, twanged and stretched and pulled apart by the wind. The hooting of young joy-riders; the laughter of children up late, going for a walk with their parents after supper. The shouting of the big-voiced Zulus who cleaned the hotels; the tender pizzicato of their monotonous guitars as they strolled and played; the soft, nasal putter of a phrase in some Indian dialect, caught up from the conversation of two Indian waiters. A wisp of song from the promenade concert on the beach.

Clara Hansen took her second cup of coffee and let all these come to her. Somewhere, if you could separate the great rippling, bobbing tide of sounds, one from the other, you would find the one small note—a door opening, a woman's voice—that was her answer. She sighed. She took up the evening paper, where he had put it down on his chair; she never read the Durban papers—to her they were the local gossip sheets of a foreign town, and nothing happened in the world until she read of it in the Swiss and French and German papers that came to her every week. The paper sank to her lap, under her hand. She did not see the beauty of her hand, either, with its long plump joints and sapphire ring; she did not know where she had lost the ability of a young woman to find a moment of distraction in some example of her own beauty.

She sat there a long time. The servant Alfred cleared the coffee things away, washed up the dinner dishes, and locked the kitchen door behind him; the city hall clock struck its wavering nine blows across the town, and presently struck again, ten. She let her mind zigzag down into the past, matching this experience with that, finding this fragment in relation to that picture. And while she saw herself in the roles of the past, and sometimes dreamily recast herself in the course of some vanished afternoon, a thought stingingly of the present was formulating itself in that same mind. She ignored it wearily, it was an interruption she couldn't be bothered with, but it came again. And each time it was more insistent, more reasonable; more incredible.

At last, she got up, rather awkwardly, and went into her bedroom. It seemed she did not know what she had gone in there for. She took her dressing-gown off its hook; and put it back. She stood quite still a moment, looking round the room; the bunch of sweet-smelling, short-lived roses from the Indian vender who hawked them up and down the front, all day, the picture of her child, in a little old silver frame—suddenly she began to breathe fast, as if something inside her were racing. She went over to her wardrobe, took out a silk coat, and, after the briefest pause (you could not keep your hair in place in the wind from the sea), a small hat. She put the hat on very quickly, looking at it but not at her own face, in the mirror, and as she put on the coat, she appeared to remember something, and stopped to examine, with interest, the place where a tuck had been stitched to shorten the fine, thin lining. Then she went out of the flat leaving all the lights burning.

Outside, on the front, the night air was so soft that it was a shock. It laid itself lightly, moistly, muffedly against her face; she breathed it and it was not there, so that, breathing it, you would wonder how you lived on something so meltingly substanceless. It swam around the looped lights of the front like glycerine, making them look like their own reflection in water; it drowned the glitter of the city in balminess. She did not feel it blowing but it blew, sculpting the silk of her coat against her thighs and legs, spreading the escaped tendrils of her hair against her hat. She went to the taxi rank on the corner and got into the first car. "Take me toward the docks," she said. "I'll tell you where, from there." She did not know the address exactly, of course—who would bother about such a thing?—but she knew which part of the town it was in, and she had some idea of the name of the street. Haddon or Addo, something like that.

The inside of the taxi smelled like a tired old sofa. She sat forward, watching the streets. It was not far to the dock area. "Do you know a street named Haddon?" "There's Addno Street, madam," said the man, uncertainly. "That's it"—and with the name of the street, the rest came to her too—of course, Addno Street, 7a Beryl Gardens. "That's what I want." They drove quite far behind the dock area, into a suburb of semi-detached houses and maisonettes, with old, ragged palms struggling past the wooden balconies. When they found Addno Street, she suddenly said to the driver, "Drop me here." As he drove away, she began to walk quite briskly up the street, past a little crush of shops in darkness and plastered with advertisement signs of the chipped enamel kind, past the bar of an old, small hotel, and along the double row of houses. She found she was on the side of the even numbers, and crossed. She came to 7a Beryl Gardens; and instantly it all seemed so unlikely and impossible that she walked on, right past the house, and round the block.

It was a tall narrow house, divided down the middle. On either side of the dividing wall, there were a small veranda, a double window, a front door, and a concrete path leading a few yards down to the railings. Number 7a had half an old motorcar tire, made into a fern basket, hanging on its veranda. The double window downstairs, and its replica above it, were not lit up, but through the fancy stained glass of the upper half of the door, there was a glow that showed that there was light in some room within. As she walked her brain tingled with a sense of recovery from unreality; she felt as if a slap had brought her back to her senses. Carl in that house! How could she have made such a fool of herself as to think it! No, it was not possible; those ferns on the veranda. And what could there be inside such a house?—some poor soul sitting peacefully over the evening paper.

When she rounded the corner onto the third side of the block, that would bring her back into Addno Street again, she was on her way not back to Beryl Gardens, but to find another taxi and take herself home. There was a car parked in this side street; it was empty, and the lights had been left on. As she came on into the glare, hurrying now to the thought of the taxi, she half closed her eyes against the brightness, and then, as she came out behind the orbit of the lights and level with the car itself, she saw that it was her car—Carl's car—their car. There were Carl's old driving gloves, in the open cubbyhole. There was the yellow duster that the driver always threw onto the ledge under the back window. Yet she went slowly round the back of the car to look at the number plate; and she spelled the familiar number over to herself. A fit of trembling seized her. All the sanity and purpose of a minute ago were sucked violently out of her. I could have died, people said of certain moments, I could have died then and there, in the street. For her this became a rational statement instead of an exaggeration not really meant to be taken seriously. A hideous vertigo of the heights of emotion made her feel that she could fall dead in the street. It seemed that it was only the corrective of commonplace that saved her; two Africans came round the corner from Addno Street and passed on the other side of the street, chattering to each other, ignoring her. At once she began to walk steadily and fairly fast, but without haste, past the car that shone on into the empty dark, into

Addno Street, and up to the gate of 7a Beryl Gardens. The quirk of the corner of her mouth, which belonged to her particular kind of smile, was hardened into a tight downward pressure of disgust and unbelief. She opened the gate and went up the cracked concrete path. She had no idea what she would say. In all the other times there had been, she had never shown herself to the women, never spoken to them, acknowledged their existence, except through her husband. If they had happened to be former friends of hers, she had never received or greeted them again once she had come to know of the existence of the affair.

She was aware of only one thing: the wish to be confronted with—this. To force herself to look at it; to believe it. She rang the bell. Nobody came. She knocked, first on the wood of the door, then a sharp tat-tat-tat on the colored glass. The light behind it brightened; another light had been switched on somewhere in the house. A woman's footsteps came slowly, paused on the other side of the door. Clara Hansen lifted her hand and knocked at the glass again. The door opened. Behind it, there was the mending-woman, the dressmaker. Yes, her face. The pale, plain old maid who had blackheads in the creases of her neck, and who sat bent over the sewing machine twice a month, in the flat, mending sheets. When she saw Clara Hansen she stood gaping as if the punishment she had expected from God had come. She was unable to speak.

Mrs. Hansen took her in, from head to foot, a licking flame of a glance; and then it was out, and cold. She said, "Tell my husband he has left the lights of his car burning."

And jeering, mourning, she turned and walked out into the street before the eyes of the dressmaker, like a queen.

The Bridegroom

He came into his road camp that afternoon for the last time. It was neater than any house would ever be; the sand raked smooth in the clearing, the water drums under the tarpaulin, the flaps of his tent closed against the heat. Thirty yards away a black woman knelt, pounding mealies, and two or three children, gray with Kalahari dust, played with a skinny dog. Their shrillness was no more than a bird's piping in the great spaces in which the camp was lost.

Inside his tent, something of the chill of the night before always remained, stale but cool, like the air of a church. There was his iron bed, with its clean pillowcase and big kaross. There was his table, his folding chair with the red canvas seat, and the chest in which his clothes were put away. Standing on the chest was the alarm clock that woke him at five every morning and the photograph of the seventeen-year-old girl from

Francistown whom he was going to marry. They had been there a long time, the girl and the alarm clock; in the morning when he opened his eyes, in the afternoon when he came off the job. But now this was the last time. He was leaving for Francistown in the Roads Department ten-tonner, in the morning; when he came back, the next week, he would be married and he would have with him the girl, and the caravan which the department provided for married men. He had his eye on her as he sat down on the bed and took off his boots; the smiling girl was like one of those faces cut out of a magazine. He began to shed his working overalls, a rind of khaki stiff with dust that held his shape as he discarded it, and he called, easily and softly, *"Ou Piet, ek wag."* But the bony black man with his eyebrows raised like a clown's, in effort, and his bare feet shuffling under the weight, was already at the tent with a tin bath in which hot water made a twanging tune as it slopped from side to side.

When he had washed and put on a clean khaki shirt and a pair of worn gray trousers, and streaked back his hair with sweet-smelling pomade, he stepped out of his tent just as the lid of the horizon closed on the bloody eye of the sun. It was winter and the sun set shortly after five; the gray sand turned a fading pink, the low thorn scrub gave out spreading stains of lilac shadow that presently all ran together; then the surface of the desert showed pocked and pored, for a minute or two, like the surface of the moon through a telescope, while the sky remained light over the darkened earth and the clean crystal pebble of the evening star shone. The campfires—his own and the black men's, over there—changed from near-invisible flickers of liquid color to brilliant focuses of leaping tongues of light; it was dark. Every evening he sat like this through the short ceremony of the closing of the day, slowly filling his pipe, slowly easing his back round to the fire, yawning off the stiffness of his labor. Suddenly he gave a smothered giggle, to himself, of excitement. Her existence became real to him; he saw the face of the photograph, posed against a caravan door. He got up and began to pace about the camp, alert to promise. He kicked a log farther into the fire, he called an order to Piet, he walked up toward the tent and then changed his mind and strolled away again. In their own encampment at the edge of his, the road gang had taken up the exchange of laughing, talking, yelling, and arguing that never failed them when their work was done. Black arms gestured under a thick foam of white soap, there was a gasp and splutter as a head broke the cold force of a bucketful of water, the gleaming bellies of iron cooking pots were carried here and there in the talkative preparation of food. He did not understand much of what they were saying—he knew just enough Tswana to give them his orders, with help from Piet and one or two others who understood his own tongue, Afrikaans—but the sound of their voices belonged to this time of evening. One of the babies who always cried was keeping up a thin, ignored wail; the naked children were playing the chasing game that made the dog bark. He came back and sat down again at the fire, to finish his pipe.

After a certain interval (it was exact, though it was not timed by a watch, but by long habit that had established the appropriate lapse of time between his bath, his pipe, and his food) he called out, in Afrikaans, "Have you forgotten my dinner, man?"

From across the patch of distorted darkness where the light of the two fires did not meet, but flung wobbling shapes and opaque, overlapping radiances, came the hoarse, protesting laugh that was, better than the tribute to a new joke, the pleasure in constancy to an old one.

Then a few minutes later: "Piet! I suppose you've burned everything, eh?"

"Baas?"

"Where's the food, man?"

In his own time the black man appeared with the folding table and an oil lamp. He went back and forth between the dark and light, bringing pots and dishes and food, and nagging with deep satisfaction, in a mixture of English and Afrikaans. "You want *koeksusters,* so I make *koeksusters.* You ask me this morning. So I got to make the oil nice and hot, I got to get everything ready. . . . It's a little bit slow. Yes, I know. But I can't get everything quick, quick. You hurry tonight, you don't want wait, then it's better you have *koeksusters* on Saturday, then I'm got time in the afternoon, I do it nice. . . . Yes, I think next time it's better. . . ."

Piet was a good cook. "I've taught my boy how to make everything," the young man always told people, back in Francistown. "He can even make *koeksusters,*" he had told the girl's mother, in one of those silences of the woman's disapproval that it was so difficult to fill. He had had a hard time, trying to overcome the prejudice of the girl's parents against the sort of life he could offer her. He had managed to convince them that the life was not impossible, and they had given their consent to the marriage, but they still felt that the life was unsuitable, and his desire to please and reassure them had made him anxious to see it with their eyes and so forestall, by changes, their objections. The girl was a farm girl, and would not pine for town life, but, at the same time, he could not deny to her parents that living on a farm with her family around her, and neighbors only thirty or forty miles away, would be very different from living two hundred and twenty miles from a town or village, alone with him in a road camp "surrounded by a gang of kaffirs all day," as her mother had said. He himself simply did not think at all about what the girl would do while he was out on the road; and as for the girl, until it was over, nothing could exist for her but the wedding, with her two little sisters in pink walking behind her, and her dress that she didn't recognize herself in, being made at the dressmaker's, and the cake that was ordered with a tiny china bride and groom in evening dress, on the top.

He looked at the scored table, and the rim of the open jam tin, and the salt cellar with a piece of brown paper tied neatly over the broken top, and said to Piet, "You must do everything nice when the missus comes."

"Baas?"

They looked at each other and it was not really necessary to say anything.

"You must make the table properly and do everything clean."

"Always I make everything clean. Why you say now I must make clean–"

The young man bent his head over his food, dismissing him.

While he ate his mind went automatically over the changes that would have to be made for the girl. He was not used to visualizing situations, but to dealing with what existed. It was like a lesson learned by rote; he knew the totality of what was needed, but if he found himself confronted by one of the component details, he foundered: he did not recognize it or know how to deal with it. The boys must keep out of the way. That was the main thing. Piet would have to come to the caravan quite a lot, to cook and clean. The boys–especially the boys who were responsible for the maintenance of the lorries and road-making equipment–were always coming with questions, what to do about this and that. They'd mess things up, otherwise. He spat out a piece of gristle he could not swallow; his mind went to something else. The women over there–they could do the washing for the girl. They were such a raw bunch of kaffirs, would they ever be able to do anything right? Twenty boys and about five of their women–you couldn't hide them under a thorn bush. They just mustn't hang around, that's all. They must just understand that they mustn't hang around. He looked round keenly through the shadow-puppets of the half-dark on the margin of his fire's light; the voices, companionably quieter, now, intermittent over food, the echoing *chut!* of wood being chopped, the thin film of a baby's wail through which all these sounded—they were on their own side. Yet he felt an odd, rankling suspicion.

His thoughts shuttled, as he ate, in a slow and painstaking way that he had never experienced before in his life—he was worrying. He sucked on a tooth; Piet, Piet, that kaffir talks such a hell of a lot. How's Piet going to stop talking, talking every time he comes near? If he talks to her . . . Man, it's sure he'll talk to her. He thought, in actual words, what he would say to Piet about this; the words were like those unsayable things that people write on walls for others to see in private moments, but that are never spoken in their mouths.

Piet brought coffee and *koeksusters* and the young man did not look at him.

But the *koeksusters* were delicious, crisp, sticky, and sweet, and as he felt the familiar substance and taste on his tongue, alternating with the hot bite of the coffee, he at once became occupied with the pure happiness of eating as a child is fully occupied with a bag of sweets. *Koeksusters* never failed to give him this innocent, total pleasure. When first he had taken the job of overseer to the road gang, he had had strange, restless hours at night and on Sundays. It seemed that he was hungry. He ate but never felt satisfied. He walked about all the time, like a hungry creature. One Sunday he actually set out to walk (the Roads Department was very strict about the use of the ten-tonner for private purposes) the fourteen miles across the sand to the cattle-dipping post where the government cattle officer and his wife, Afrikaners like himself and the only other white people between the road camp and Francistown, lived in their corrugated-iron house. By a coincidence, they had decided to drive over and see him, that day, and they had met him a little less than halfway, when he was already slowed and dazed by heat. But shortly after that Piet had taken over the cooking of his meals and the care of his person, and Piet had even learned to make *koeksusters,* according to instructions given to the young man by the cattle officer's wife. The *koeksusters,* a childhood treat that he could indulge in whenever he liked, seemed to mark his settling down; the solitary camp became a personal way of life, with its own special arrangements and indulgences.

"*Ou Piet! Kêrel!* What did you do to the *koeksusters,* hey?" he called out joyously.

A shout came that meant "Right away." The black man appeared, drying his hands on a rag, with the diffident, kidding manner of someone who knows he has excelled himself.

"Whatsa matter with the *koeksusters,* man?"

Piet shrugged. "You must tell me. I don't know what's matter."

"Here, bring me some more, man." The young man shoved the empty plate at him, with a grin. And as the other went off, laughing, the young man called, "You must always make them like that, see?"

He liked to drink at celebrations, at weddings or Christmas, but he wasn't a man who drank his brandy every day. He would have two brandies on a Saturday afternoon, when the week's work was over, and for the rest of the time, the bottle that he brought from Francistown when he went to collect stores lay in the chest in his tent. But on this last night he got up from the fire on impulse and went over to the tent to fetch the bottle (one thing he didn't do, he didn't expect a kaffir to handle his drink for him; it was too much of a temptation to put in their way). He brought a glass with him, too, one of a set of six made of tinted imitation cut glass, and he poured himself a tot and stretched out his legs where he could feel the warmth of the fire through the soles of his

boots. The nights were not cold, until the wind came u
two or three in the morning, but there was a clarifying chill
to the air; now and then a figure came over from the black
men's camp to put another log on the fire whose flames had
dropped and become blue. The young man felt inside himself
a similar low incandescence; he poured himself another brandy.
The long yelping of the jackals prowled the sky without, like
the wind about a house; there was no house, but the sounds
beyond the light his fire tremblingly inflated into the dark—
that jumble of meaningless voices, crying babies, coughs, and
hawking—had built walls to enclose and a roof to shelter. He
was exposed, turning naked to space on the sphere of the
world as the speck that is a fly plastered on the window of
an airplane, but he was not aware of it.

The lilt of various kinds of small music began and died in
the dark; threads of notes, blown and plucked, that disappeared
under the voices. Presently a huge man whose thick black body
had strained apart every seam in his ragged pants and shirt
loped silently into the light and dropped just within it, not
too near the fire. His feet, intimately crossed, were cracked
and weathered like driftwood. He held to his mouth a one-stringed
instrument shaped like a lyre, made out of a half-moon
of bent wood with a ribbon of dried palm leaf tied
from tip to tip. His big lips rested gently on the strip and
while he blew, his one hand, by controlling the vibration
of the palm leaf, made of his breath a small, faint, perfect
music. It was caught by the very limits of the capacity of the
human ear; it was almost out of range. The first music men
ever heard, when they began to stand upright among the
rushes at the river, might have been like it. When it died
away it was difficult to notice at what point it really had gone.

"Play that other one," said the young man, in Tswana. Only
the smoke from his pipe moved.

The pink-palmed hands settled down round the instrument.

The thick, tender lips were wet once. The faint desolate voice spoke again, so lonely a music that it came to the player and listener as if they heard it inside themselves. This time the player took a short stick in his other hand and, while he blew, scratched it back and forth inside the curve of the lyre, where the notches cut there produced a dry, shaking, slithering sound, like the far-off movement of dancers' feet. There were two or three figures with more substance than the shadows, where the firelight merged with the darkness. They came and squatted. One of them had half a paraffin tin, with a wooden neck and other attachments of gut and wire. When the lyre-player paused, lowering his piece of stick and leaf slowly, in ebb, from his mouth, and wiping his lips on the back of his hand, the other began to play. It was a thrumming, repetitive, banjo tune. The young man's boot patted the sand in time to it and he took it up with hand-claps once or twice. A thin, yellowish man in an old hat pushed his way to the front past sarcastic remarks and twittings and sat on his haunches with a little clay bowl between his feet. Over its mouth there was a keyboard of metal tongues. After some exchange, he played it and the others sang low and nasally, bringing a few more strollers to the fire. The music came to an end, pleasantly, and started up again, like a breath drawn. In one of the intervals the young man said, "Let's have a look at that contraption of yours, isn't it a new one?" and the man to whom he signaled did not understand what was being said to him but handed over his paraffin-tin mandolin with pride and also with amusement at his own handiwork.

The young man turned it over, twanged it once, grinning and shaking his head. Two bits of string and an old jam tin and they'll make a whole band, man. He'd heard them playing some crazy-looking things. The circle of faces watched him with pleasure; they laughed and lazily remarked to each other; it was a funny-looking thing, all right, but it worked. The owner took it back and played it, clowning a little. The audience laughed and joked appreciatively; they were sitting close in to the fire now, painted by it. "Next week" the young man raised his voice gaily—"next week when I come back, I bring radio with me, plenty real music. All the big white bands play over it—" Someone who had once worked in Johannesburg said, "Satchmo," and the others took it up, understanding that this was the word for what the white man was going to bring from town. Satchmo. Satch-mo. They tried it out, politely. "Music, just like at a big white dance in town. Next week." A friendly, appreciative silence fell, with them all resting back in the warmth of the fire and looking at him indulgently. A strange thing happened to him. He felt hot, over first his neck, then his ears and his face. It didn't matter, of course; by next week they would have forgotten. They wouldn't expect it. He shut down his mind on a picture of them, hanging round the caravan to listen, and him coming out on the steps to tell them—

He thought for a moment that he would give them the rest of the bottle of brandy. Hell, no, man, it was mad. If they got the taste for the stuff, they'd be pinching it all the time. He'd give Piet some sugar and yeast and things from the stores, for them to make beer tomorrow when he was gone. He put his hands deep in his pockets and stretched out to the fire with his head sunk on his chest. The lyre-player picked up his flimsy piece of wood again, and slowly what the young man was feeling inside himself seemed to find a voice; up into the night beyond the fire, it went, uncoiling from his breast and bringing ease. As if it had been made audible out of infinity and could be returned to infinity at any point, the lonely voice of the lyre went on and on. Nobody spoke, the barriers of tongues fell with silence. The whole dirty tide of worry and planning had gone out of the young man. The small, high moon, outshone by a spiky spread of cold stars, repeated the shape of the lyre. He sat for he was not aware how long, just as he had for so many other nights, with the stars at his head and the fire at his feet.

But at last the music stopped and time began again. There was tonight; there was tomorrow, when he was going to drive to Francistown. He stood up; the company fragmented. The lyre-player blew his nose into his fingers. Dusty feet took their accustomed weight. They went off to their tents and he went off to his. Faint plangencies followed them. The young man gave a loud, ugly, animal yawn, the sort of unashamed personal noise a man can make when he lives alone. He walked very slowly across the sand; it was dark but he knew the way more surely than with his eyes. "Piet! Hey!" he bawled as he reached his tent. "You get up early tomorrow, eh? And I don't want to hear the lorry won't start. You get it going and then you call me. D'you hear?"

He was lighting the oil lamp that Piet had left ready on the chest and as it came up softly it brought the whole interior of the tent with it: the chest, the bed, the clock, and the coy smiling face of the seventeen-year-old girl. He sat down on the bed, sliding his palms through the silky fur of the kaross. He drew a breath and held it for a moment, looking round purposefully. And then he picked up the photograph, folded the cardboard support back flat to the frame, and put it in the chest with all his other things, ready for the journey.

Check Yes or No

On the afternoon of the first matinee performance in Johannesburg the circus drew a great crowd. The day was hot, the traffic was thick, and those families who had reserved seats arrived all at once, a little late, and pressed in from all sides upon those who were queueing to buy tickets. More and more people came stumbling over the humpy grass from the car park; the arms of grandmothers were clutched high by younger relatives as if the old ladies were in danger of drowning; children were swung over guy lines; from inside the tent the band struck up and gathered the confusion into one vast blare.

One family among many others, a young woman with three children about her, and a man, rather older, with a face so fine and well made that even while he was chewing a cigar and screwing up his eyes against the glare it was distinct in that bobbing of many faces, stood in the press round the entrance to the big tent. The woman smiled at the man and shrugged. He held five green tickets in his hand; with the same hand he took the cigar out of his mouth, waved it purposefully, said, "Don't budge, darling," and pushed deep into the crowd. She watched him go. Hers was a face that, after being roused to smile or quicken in speech, quickly sank back into its preoccupation: this afternoon, a compliant content. Even when he could no longer be seen behind the tweed shoulders and floral backs, she seemed to be looking at him still. She roused herself to say aside, in a voice of controlled irritation, to the tallest of the three children, a ten-year-old boy, "Don't *do* that, Neil! Do you hear me?"

He was pulling at a tent peg, boasting to the other children, "The whole tent may fall down. If I do, if I pull this out—" They bent over, with interest. "Mary, Davey, come here," the young woman said politely. The two smaller children came and stood at her side; the eldest remained, looking at but not quite touching the tent peg. At that moment the husband reappeared, swept them together with the one word "Come," and got them through the crowd, past the frantic, besieged doorman, and into the tent.

They stood huddled together for a moment, dazed, as if they had found themselves in the ring and the eyes of the amphitheater of faces upon them. A long shaft of dusty sunlight struck down from the top of the tremendous tent; it was criss-crossed out by the white brilliance of spotlights. They had missed one act already; in the ring the iron bars that are strung up for the appearance of the lions were being dismantled while clowns shouted and tumbled in the entr'acte. The great, warm, dusty circus smell came to the family; and as they stood in the main gangway between tiered planks full of people, the dimness of the interior beyond the splash of light in the ring cleared as their eyes adjusted to it and they saw that it was quite light, indeed it was afternoon inside the tent as well as out, and they could see everyone, recognize anyone, just as they could be recognized. So they stood, unembarrassed, triumphantly in, and hoped to catch the attention of one of the usherettes who raced by.

As far as anyone could see the tent was completely full already. The people who had come early and bought cheap, unreserved seats had simply taken themselves up and moved, when their section had become uncomfortably crowded, into the reserved seats. The young woman left the situation to her husband, who clearly was equal to it, or any other; she stood there, looking quietly round, waiting, her hand lightly on the head of the youngest child, while the husband importuned the usherettes with their melting, painted faces. They shook him off. Other people were after them; indignant, pleading—where were they to find their seats? How were they to get usurpers out of their seats?

"Ask the manager! Ask him! Don't expect me to know!" said one of the usherettes furiously, cornered.

"All right! I'll do just that," said the husband. Which was the manager, anyway? "I saw a theatrical-looking old man hanging about the entrance," said the young woman. Her husband went off, a grimace of determination hardening his face. As he left her, she glanced up at the stand on her right, perhaps idly, perhaps because the attention of someone up there drew her. Looking over the knees and faces, she saw the bright face of a woman turned to her. She recognized her at once, and the man beside her, and the little girl on his lap whom both were indicating with grins and viola-gestures.

They were the couple who had lived in the flat next door to hers three years ago, before she had remarried. That awful flat. The Dunns, Mr. and Mrs. Dunn and Angeline—only, of course, Angeline was a baby, then. Mrs. Dunn with her kind, young red face that didn't improve with make-up and the passage of the day, but, on the other hand, didn't look any worse, or less fresh and shiny when she put out her tousled head and arm to bring the milk round the door in the morning.

That awful flat.

Mornings in that awful flat. Hard words in the small hours. The lovers, the would-be lovers, the good friends who wanted to sit and talk about their problems half the night—all let out when the stars were guttering, to creep like alley cats past the Dunns' door with its brass Scottie dog knocker. (Quietly, don't wake the people next door.)

There in that flat, the young woman, long divorced, young as she was, had lived alone with her child, two, perhaps three years before these Dunns moved into the building. She had not wanted to get to know them, let alone get friendly with them; how many nights had she lain awake in a kind of horror, imagining the outer wall of the building swung back, like that of a doll house, and the two sets of box-size rooms, the Dunns' and hers, revealed side by side. The newlyweds' varnished furniture, embroidered tray cloths, frilled chintz bedcovers, and display cabinet where the sugar ornaments from their wedding cake had a place among the silver-plated sweet dishes, separated by only a six-inch wall from the shabby divan, the painted tile table that didn't show glass rings, the Beardsley drawing she'd never returned to its owner, the piles of dusty records and the piles of dusty books, the endless trays of bacon and eggs on unmatched plates—her possessions, thrown together by whim or necessity from the pickings of a past life. She had lain in the dark and wondered, Is this all? Only their way, on the other side of the wall, and mine, on this? Nothing else? For something in her filled her with a distaste for her own way of life almost as strong as that which her tastes, her intelligence, and her needs made her feel for the Dunns'.

The Dunns were kind, of course. A ghastly kindness, it had seemed then. (How emotional she had been about everything at that time; unable to take any human exchange at its own value.) The life she led was something beyond not only their range of experience but also their understanding, and so they treated her partly as if she were someone just like themselves (because they hadn't the imagination to conceive of anything outside themselves) and partly as if she were sick (because they must explain away the things she did that they would never do).

They had got to know her through Neil, naturally. Neil was her son, then already seven years old and born of that marriage so far off, and at nine years' distance so preposterous that she often found herself thinking of him as a natural child she had got herself somewhere under a hedge from a stranger on an irresistible summer's day. She would have preferred it to have been that way, in reality; she might have liked the boy better. Of course, the Dunns—the Dunns didn't know that she didn't like him; how could they know that such a situation could exist between mother and child? The Dunns thought it was such a pity that Neil's mommie had to work and leave him alone with the native nanny after school. When his mother couldn't stand what the psychologist told her were plus gestures—the overcompensation with which he tried, poor irritating little devil, to atone for his "subconscious guilt at being there when you don't want him"—and she screamed at him, in imprecations larded with "darlings," to get out, to get out of the flat, *quick,* the Dunns chose not to hear through that six-inch wall. But Mr. Dunn, just happening to go out into the public corridor, would happen to see the boy hanging about, not playing with the expensive toy in his hand. Then Mr. Dunn would ask whether he wouldn't come up to the corner shop to buy milk or cigarettes.

It was the Dunns, too, who had found that unspeakable note

that Neil had left the time he ran away. Left it on a milk bottle, of all places, and (typical of Neil) the wrong milk bottle, too; the Dunns'. The child had been abominably naughty, in a way that no damned psychologist could persuade her to let him get away with. There had been a row, he had been punished, and then he had run away for a couple of hours. Mrs. Dunn had found and brought over the open note. It said: "Do you want me to go away for ever or do you want me to come back. Check yes or no." (This last was a puzzle. Where had he got the curt Americanism from? Then his mother remembered his friendship with an American child, and the American magazines he must have read at the child's home.)

The Dunns, father, mother, and daughter. Well, there they were, grinning down at her delightedly from the tenth row at the circus. Check yes or no. Oh my God. Well, here was Neil beside her, fatter (This youngster could do with putting on a bit, Mr. Dunn used to say from time to time), obviously gay, and here she was herself, also a little fatter, both her manner and her dress blessedly without the necessity of bravado.

There's Mrs. Van der Camp, they must be saying to each other, there's the young woman who used to live next door to us. Phoebe Van der Camp—and what a change in her! Indeed, only the name, like an old address label on a suitcase that has come to rest in entirely another part of the world, remained of Phoebe Van der Camp. Phoebe Secker, as they could see, with her husband, conventionally shepherding her son and the two small children of a friend to the circus on a Saturday afternoon, was a different person. As she smiled and waved, slowly, as if giving them a chance to take her in, she suddenly saw that they knew all this, it must be conveyed to them merely by the way she stood, in the particular context of that afternoon. And while the three children craned and tugged at her in an effort to see the waltzing elephant that came into the ring now with all the extraordinary lightness of a fat man on the dance floor, there came to her a sweet knowledge that she had not, even in her happiness, actually tasted before: there was something other than the choice between the Dunns' side of the wall and Phoebe Van der Camp's, and she had found it. Made it, in fact. The racier term, with the stronger connotations of dangers, ugliness left behind, was more accurate. I have made it, and with ease, and with nearly all of myself to spare, she thought with serenity. The Dunns, exclaiming in dumb show over the size of Neil, smiling, waving, gave her this proof of herself with simple surety.

The elephant act was nearly over when her husband, Victor Secker, came back after a fruitless search for the manager, or *somebody* in charge. "Now we're going to find those seats for ourselves, and push out whoever's taken them," he said. Phoebe and the children passed before him along the gangway beside the ring, where a hoarse-voiced man in blue and silver livery was shouting about something being unique and extraordinary.

Of course, the Dunns were up there, directly above them, for a moment; looking down on their heads, on Victor's head. One didn't have to wonder if the Dunns noticed Victor, noticed what he *was*. Victor's strength and nervous determination, the overt qualities with their implication of the private, covert ones of tenderness and self-confidence, were sensed (were, perhaps, present in his face) at a glance. Rather different from the others, eh—the pretty, weak boys and the undiscovered great souls who went about the world uncertainly as creatures blinded by long confinement underground—those others whom the Dunns used to see slinking into her flat, to prey upon her, when she summoned them, slinking out when she was sick to death of them.

Phoebe was tempted for a moment to lift her hand—a salute

to the Dunns up there once more; but she did not. She followed, instead, as if it were the most natural thing in the world, the path indicated to her by her husband between the stands. "Where now?" she turned and said, at last. "Well, this is block E," said her husband. "Our seats are in F. I presume F's over there, near the band." "Has Victor found the seats yet, Mum, has Victor found them?" Neil kept asking. She ignored him, but her husband said, "Just a moment, boy. We'll find them."

". . . positively the first time in Southern Africa, straight from New York, Paris, and Vienna . . ." the hoarse voice from the ring went on, rising to a bellow.

"THE BICYCLING BERNADOS!"

The flock of bicycles, wheels twirling like silver parasols, seemed to start up from the Seckers' feet; F block of chairs was right beside the broad lane that opened into the ring from the performers' dressing rooms, the stage entrance. Inevitably, the five seats for which Victor had the tickets in his hand were occupied. The people in them, challenged, refused to move by the simple expedient of not answering Victor and staring stonily away. He began to get angry. Phoebe heard from the quiet, intense reasonableness of his voice that he was getting angry. "What is it? What're they doing now?" The smaller children kept up a bleating whine. Neil tantalized them by being just tall enough to see what was going on in the ring.

Phoebe saw that her husband, who was not precipitate in anything, was now very angry. He did not know the childish rages of outraged vanity that she had been used to, in those others who had gone by the name of men, in her old flat. His anger had to rise above years of self-control. Now he saw a young man with an exquisitely combed golden pompadour and a blue and gold uniform, standing a few feet away in the lane opening into the ring, and he walked over to him and said, "I insist that you provide some sort of place for my wife and these children to sit. Here are our tickets. Our seats are occupied by somebody else, and we've been standing about here for half an hour." The young man turned a vain, self-conscious face upon him and said, "Nothing to do with me. I'm assistant ringmaster. You can't stand here, this is for artists only."

Phoebe did not hear what her husband said then. Only saw, happening quicker than she could take it in, the golden-headed one grab or push her husband's arm, her husband thrust himself out of the grip, the other stagger back under the impetus of his withdrawal, and then, unbelievably, another man, a tall dark man in the same uniform, lift his fist high behind her husband's turning back and bring it down in a crashing blow between his shoulder blades. There was Victor, for a moment, flung in the sawdust, a creature washed up in a wave of violence. Almost at once he was up again, the two liveried men standing tall and threatening about him; at the same time the bicyclists must have reached a peak of sensation in their act, for the people were applauding, there was some sort of gasp, a vast breath drawn in unison—was it for the cyclists or the glaring scuffle in the sawdust? There was a trailing-off of voices—Victor's and the others'—in altercation, but Phoebe was no longer looking there, where it was happening. She was looking away, straight ahead of her into the lights and the faces, and the hideous pounding of her blood made her vision throb, so that the outlines of the objects—the painted platforms, gleaming wires—on which she fixed her eyes, swelled and shrank, swelled and shrank.

Then Victor was beside her; she heard him panting. She turned. His hair, tousled, showed that it was thinning. The bones of his face came up under a damp pallor like the face of an old man. There was a fleck of saliva at each corner of his mouth. The bicyclists were whirling out of the ring; a fat old woman was beckoning with extravagant jerks of her head. "Shame, shame, the poor kids! Sit here, lady, you can sit here," she called from the tiered planks above block F. She pushed and crushed her large family together and made room. The little girl Mary was crying silently. Phoebe thrust the three bewildered children before her, after Victor. There was sawdust on his jacket, and his shoulders seemed bowed.

They were squashed together on the hard plank, closed in with the heat and the clothing odors of the people pressed against them, but at least they had sunk out of prominence into the anonymity of the audience. For the first few minutes Phoebe, blinded, as it were, by the glare of attention that had been on them, was scarcely aware of this sanctuary and felt still the heat of everyone's curious eyes puckering her very skin. The faces of the Dunns—even at this distance she could make out which white blurs were theirs—she felt turned on her as if they would never look away again. Up there, on the other side of the ring, they had, of course, watched everything. They had seen—she knew it—with their round, innocent faces curious, shocked but not surprised, Phoebe Van der Camp (that used to be) in one of those situations again. Remember that fuss with the doctor coming, that time when some chap tried to cut his wrists in her bathroom? And what about the poor little boy, and that note he left? No, they would not be surprised that the new husband, mature, distinguished-looking man though he'd seemed to be, got into a brawl at a circus.

Phoebe spoke for the first time, saying to her husband without looking at him, "I'll go to the car till it's over." She knew that he would not leave because he wouldn't deprive the children of their day: the circus. He looked at her but did not answer.

They sat close together, like enemies chained to each other. I didn't lift a finger to help him. They might have killed him while I wouldn't even look, she kept thinking fiercely, proudly to herself. He's the only person I've ever loved, but I wouldn't lift a finger.

She hated the circus but she couldn't leave. Though she longed to go she could not walk out alone, before everyone—before the Dunns—providing a sequel to the incident that had gone before. She had never liked circuses, ever, even as a child, and now she felt hotly that *this* was the reason, this hateful and ridiculous scene this afternoon. Somehow she must have sensed, long ago, that *this* was coming to her some day at a circus; the dusty arena, the wild beasts shamelessly anthropomorphized, the human bodies contorted till they were something less than human, were marked out to provide the setting for her humiliation. Now one act followed another in what seemed to her a tawdry succession. The principal woman acrobat's thin, strong, aging neck strained above the gold cloth that covered a worn body in which muscle had defeated age, sex, and whatever there might have been of beauty; she did not move, she articulated. She had once been blond and her still-blue eyes, hard-looking as the eyes of a dead man over which no one has had the grace to draw the lids, seemed propped wide open by lashes spiked with mascara. When her act was over she trotted obediently out along the performers' exit lane, like an old horse making for the stable. A bear rode a motor bicycle, its paws strapped to the handle bars, and shambled off with the bowed gait of a long-term prisoner. A man in a Buffalo Bill outfit, with the bearded, fanatic face of a Gothic saint, hurtled knives to outline the figure of his wife, a woman who, with her shining, curly red hair and drum majorette's high-stepping legs, looked like a chorus girl from the back and, when she turned, had the gleaming, hook-nosed face of a witch. What nonsense it was—what affected nonsense of the sophisticated pretending to be little children at heart—to talk about the enchantment of the circus! But of course, the fat woman who had made room for the Seckers was enjoying it; she and her family had their own special approach to it. Theirs was the spirit of the cockfight or perhaps even the public hanging; during the knife-throwing act two male members of the family scrambled up and down between the ringside and their places on the crowded plank, reporting the progress of the act to the old woman, who kept her eyes closed and held her hands open, raised apprehensively before her, as if she were playing blindman's buff. "Oh my God, he'll take her eye out, he'll kill her," the woman keened in the broken English of a Lithuanian Jewess. One of the men darted delightedly back to her, hopped up beside her. "The knife's got her ear." He giggled. "Open your eyes, look, there's her ear hanging off." "Oh, for God's sake! I caught such a fright! Whad'you wanta tell me such things?" And the woman giggled in terror and delight. The little girl Mary, feeling the same emotions, clutched fast at the stranger's skirt in instinctive sympathy.

Phoebe slowly became aware of the warmth of Victor's side. He was resting against her and she against him. They did not speak, but she felt a sober twinge of anxiety about him: had he perhaps really been hurt, in some way that would only show itself later? She lived again the moment when he had risen from the sawdust, looking as he might look when he was old, when she had lived with him for many years. She sat very still against him. After the knife-thrower, a wire-walking act had come on, and she had been following, without realizing the sight, two women and a man riding bicycles and drinking tea up on the high wire. But now her preoccupation, turned blindly upon the figures moving against the summit of the tent, where the sun came goldenly through the canvas like light seen through a brown paper bag, drew into itself consciousness of a figure on one of the platforms who was slowly getting himself into a great brown sack. He climbed into it just as if it were only a sack, but then it appeared that it had places for his arms, closed in over the hands like a child's snowsuit. When he had enclosed his arms he paused a moment, then hunched his shoulders and pulled the thing over his face and held the top of it clumsily over his head. One of the two women came up behind him onto the platform and drew the top of the strange garment together with a drawstring; all the way below, from the crowded plank, Phoebe could see her tie a double knot, firmly.

And now he stood there, the man in the brown sack. The usual moment of the crowd's apprehension, when the wire-walker is about to set off upon his bright thread, did not happen because there was not the sight of a recognizable human figure gazing, measuring the way he had to go, aiming himself at the other side. The man in the brown sack, looking, apparently, nowhere, because he had no face, poked out the bottom of the sack with the tentative, nervous, hesitant movement of some delicate animal's paw and took the wire. There was another slow, prehensile movement and he was out there, above everything. His inch-by-inch progress along the wire was uninformed, utterly lost; as the man had disappeared inside the sack, so the existence of the wire, the platform on the other side, even the net below that would save him, and the crowd who watched, must disappear from him. There was nothing for the man inside the sack; no way to be seen, forward or back, up to fly or down to fall. He was alone up there, in the middle of nothing; with only his feet, a man's ordinary feet that can do limited things—run just so far, so fast, carry just so much—to find a way.

As he balanced up there, pausing in an immense crisis of decision each time before he put his groping foot down, his figure became for Phoebe the focus of a strange and suffocating recognition. She *knew* him, not in the usual sense, but as if she had come face to face with the embodiment of part of the vast, common human state. All that she had been afraid of, all that she had sought was in his darkness, all that she had found was in the length of wire traversed, astonishingly, behind him, all that she had secured to herself was in those particular inches of wire that held his weight at that particular moment.

The Lithuanian woman, mouth open, wincing as she watched the figure on the wire, pressed her old heavy body close on one side; on the other side there was Victor. Phoebe put her hand on Victor's wrist. Then, on impulse, she smiled and said to the old woman beside her, "It's all right. He does it every day."

The Gentle Art

In the heat of the day the huge, pale silky width of river put out your eyes, so that when you turned away from it, everything else looked black and jumped. There was a one-room square reed house on the bank, with a reed-mat door that rolled up and let down. Inside was a camp bed with an animal skin on it, and a table with an enameled teapot, an assortment of flowered china cups, a tin of tea, and a tin of powdered milk. There was a stool with a battery radio set that played all the time. The enormous trees of Africa, ant-eaten and ancient, hung still, over the hut; down on the margin of the river, in the sun, the black-and-lemon-checkered skin of a crocodile made a bladder of air in the water, and, right on the verge, the body of the creature lay in its naked flesh, stripped, except for the head and jaws and the four gloves of skin left on its claws. The flesh looked pink, fresh, and edible. The water stirred it like a breeze in feathers.

At night there was nothing—no river, no hut, no crocodile, no trees; only a vast soft moonless darkness that made the couple giggle with excitement as they bumped along the river track in the path of their headlights. "Shall we ever find it?" said Vivien, and her husband knew that he must. "This is it, all right," he said. "Do you think you're on the right path, Ricks?" she asked, ignoring him. Just then they heard the intimate, dramatic, triumphant, wheedling voice of the radio, finishing off a commercial in a squall of music; they were there, upon it, at the very hut. There was the dull red of a campfire, an oil lamp came toward them, Ricks's torch leaped from branch to branch, figures emerged like actors coming onto a stage.

"We been waiting for you people since half past seven!" said a large blond man, half-challengingly.

Vivien broke into the exaggerated apologies of a woman anxious to make good in a world other than her own; at home in Johannesburg she was never punctual, and disdained any reproach about it, but here, in the bush, she was really abject at the thought that she might have kept the crocodile-hunters waiting. She was sorry; she was terribly, terribly sorry, the hotel was so small, they couldn't upset regular meal hours by giving dinner a little earlier. . . . She really was *terribly* sorry. "I should jolly well think so," said the blond man, no longer challenging, no longer even listening. Although the night was warm as milk he had a muffler round his neck, and his blue-eyed, red face wore the perpetual bright smile of short temper. The other man, in shorts and ribbed stockings, stood about with his hands on his hips. "Ruddy motor's been kicking up hell," he said. "Jimmy and I've been friggin around with the damned thing best part of the afternoon." In the light of the oil lamp he had piggy good looks; handsome turned-up nose, bristling mustache, narrow, blinking eyes.

A man's voice called, "Davie? Davie, old man? You all

ready?" and another oil lamp came out of the hut, circling with light a stripling and a woman. As they came nearer, the stripling became a forty-year-old man whose thin, hard body stored up nothing; simply acted as a conductor of energy. He was skinny and brown as an urchin, and he had dusty straight brown hair and large, deeply recessed black eyes in a small, lined face. He looked like one of those small boys who look like old men, and the others watched him come toward them.

He was the host of the couple and the boss of the two men. Vivien followed his approach with parted lips; each time she saw him, since they had met by a miracle of accident on the river bank three days before, he materialized to her unbelievably out of all the stories she had heard about him. "Mr. Baird!" she called. "Hello there! I'm so terribly sorry . . ." and she went off into her elaborate obeisance of apology, all over again. "That's all right, that's all right." His voice was quick, light, and friendly. "Only I want you people to enjoy yourselves and see some action, that's the idea, isn't it? Haven't you got a coat along with you, Mr. McEwen? It gets pretty chilly on the river at night, you want to wrap up. Mike, can you spare a jersey or something for Mr. McEwen? Nothing of mine'd go near you, I'm afraid."

Vivien spoke up for her husband. "Oh Ricks's fine, Mr. Baird, he's tough, really, he never wears a thing, even in winter. He spent his childhood running wild in Rhodesia, he's not really a soft city boy at all." He was one of those huge, thick-set young men who have gone almost bald by the time they are twenty. He passed a hand over his head and said, "Oh Vivien . . ."

"He c'n have my coat," said the smiling blond man, over his muffler.

Jimmy Baird turned to him with quick concern. "No, no Mike old man, you better hang on to that, you're not yourself yet. Give him one of your jerseys, there's a good chap."

"I'm not comin'," said Mike. "I don't need it."

Vivien drew back, her head on one side. "Not coming? Oh but you must, why, we wouldn't think of you staying behind alone."

"He can keep me company," said Mrs. Baird. She stood beside her husband, her arms folded across her body, that was young but made soft and comfortable with frequent childbearing. She had the air of the wife who, as usual, is walking down the garden path with her husband to see him off to work. Vivien turned to her. "Mrs. Baird! *You're* coming?"

"No, I think I'll just stay here. There's the children and everything." She moved her head in the direction of a tent that was pitched in the shadowy darkness beside a truck.

"Aren't they asleep?"

"Yes, but the little one might wake up, and it's so close to the river . . . I don't like the idea of one of them wandering round. It's strange, to the little one, we usually leave her at home, you see, it's her first time camping out up here with her daddy."

Jimmy Baird, talking, giving orders, making suggestions all the time, disappeared into Mike's reed hut—this was Mike's headquarters, of the three that belonged to Jimmy Baird's river concession—and came out shaking himself into a pair of overalls.

"Doesn't he look wonderful?" said Vivien. "Doesn't your husband look wonderful, Mrs. Baird! That's how I like a man to look, as if he's really got a job to do. It drives me mad to see poor Ricks shut up in a blue suit in town. Isn't that a wonderful outfit, Ricks? Is that the sort of thing you had on the night the hippo overturned the boat, Mr. Baird? I can imagine it's not too easy to swim in that, unless you're a terrifically strong swimmer."

But Jimmy Baird was not so easily to be led to repeat, firsthand, as she longed to hear it, the story of one of his exploits famous in the territory; one of the stories out of which she had built up her idea of what such men are like. That idea had had to go through some modification already; she had always loathed "tiny men"—that was, any man under the standard of six-foot-one which she had set when she married Ricks. But although her picture of a man had shrunk to fit Jimmy Baird, three days ago, other aspects of it had not changed. Everything he said and did she saw as a manifestation of the qualities she read into his exploits and that she admired most—ruthlessness, recklessness, animal courage.

She said to Mrs. Baird, "I still can't believe this really is the famous Jimmy Baird. Oh yes, you know it. Your husband is the most talked-about man in the territory; wherever we've been on this trip up here, it's been Jimmy Baird, Jimmy Baird. And now we're actually going crocodile hunting with him!"

"*Ag*, yes." Mrs. Baird came from South Africa and had the usual offhand, careless way of speaking, putting in a word of Afrikaans here and there; tongue-tied and yet easy, shy and yet forthright. "The Bairds have lived in the territory for donkey's years. Everybody knows them."

"We're off now, girl," said Jimmy Baird, coming up to her and putting his arm round her.

Out on the river, the boat kicked and roared and puttered into silence again under the experimental hands of Davie; he brought it back into the submerged reeds with a skidding rush. "Right-o," he yelled.

"Enjoy yourself," said Mrs. Baird.

"It's awful your not being able to come. Are you sure you won't? But I suppose you've been dozens of times before," said Vivien.

Mrs. Baird held her arms and looked round the limit of the campfire's light as if it were a room. "I don't like water," she said. "They say if you don't like it, that's a warning to keep away from it."

At the last moment, the man Mike got into the boat with them after all. He wore an old army overcoat in addition to his muffler—Ricks put the borrowed sweater round his shoulders as a concession to Jimmy Baird's insistence. Davie handed Vivien into the boat, while she called out, "Now where do you want me to sit? Don't let us be in the way, please." The light of an oil lamp ran over their faces like liquid; the boat grated heavily in the mud. Two Africans, enclosed in a sullen cocoon of silence, pushed and shoved beneath the shouts of the men in the boat. "Ricks, you're too heavy," said Vivien, laughing excitably. They began to argue about the distribution of weight, changing places with each other. "No—wait—" Jimmy Baird rolled up the legs of his overalls, kicked off his shoes, and jumped out of the boat. "That's it—that's it—" His strong, thin hands spread in a straining grip on the prow, his head was lifted with effort. With one last concerted shove, along with the Africans, he freed the boat and jumped in.

They saw the two black men, for a moment, gasping, leaning forward with hands hanging where the boat had been wrenched from their grasp, they heard the reeds hissing away on either side, they felt the sky open, enormous, above them. The black water took them; between one moment and the next, they left the downward pull of the land and were afloat on an element that made nothing of their weight. "Oh!" said Vivien, like a child on a swing. "Oh, it's lovely." And at once remembered that she was on a crocodile hunt, and fell silent.

They were drifting without sound or sensation in the dark. Far away already, there was the small glowing center that was the campfire, throwing up a fading orbit of light that caught the trees architecturally, here a branch, there the column of a trunk, like the planes of a lost temple half hidden in the jungle. They were out in deep water; the middle of the river offered them to the sky.

The oil lamps had been left on shore and Mike, who was to

steer, switched on the long, stiff, powerful beam of a portable searchlight. It shot through the dark and plucked out of nothing the reeds of the opposite bank, rose like a firework steeply into the sky, plunged, shortening, down into the water. "Okay," said Mike, and Davie started up the engine at the first kick. They began to cleave smoothly up river at a steady pace.

"Now we let the light travel all over the show, like this," Jimmy Baird was explaining, "along the reeds and so on, specially when we get further up, in the shallows, and we watch out to pick up the eyes of a croc. You can see them quite distinctly, you'll see, Mrs. McEwen, you can pick them up quite a way off, and then when you do you just make straight for them, keep the light on them all the time. They're like rabbits, you know, in the headlights of a car. They seem to be fascinated by the glare or something; so long's you keep the light full on them they don't move. Then we go right close up, right up, and shoot them at about two yards—bit lower down, Mike, that's it. There you are, Mrs. McEwen, you can see the mudbank over there, that's the sort of place the old croc likes, nice and soft for his belly."

"Two yards!" said Ricks.

Jimmy Baird turned sympathetically. He was standing up in the boat with his gun in his hand. "Yes. Two yards or even less. It's not sport, you see, Mr. McEwen. You must get them, and you must kill first shot. Then we usually give them another one, anyway, just to make sure. It's pretty nasty if you get one coming alive in the boat. We've had some scares, eh, Mike?"

"I'll say," said the blond man, bright-eyed, grinning into the night.

"Yes," said Jimmy Baird, "you must be quite sure they're knocked right out. Can you see, Mrs. McEwen? I'm sorry to be standing right here half in front of you like this. But I promise I'll skip out of the way the moment there's anything to see. Are you comfy? Wait a minute—there ought to be a cushion down here—" "Oh no, please, I'm wonderful," protested Vivien, rapt. "Davie," Jimmy Baird called to him, "isn't there that old leather cushion down there?" "Oh please, Mr. Baird, don't worry—I am—perfect—here!"

"Over there," said Mike's voice dryly.

Jimmy Baird, excusing himself, slipped past Vivien and came up behind her so that he could direct her. "There you are! Yes, there he is, fair-sized chappie, I should say. See those red eyes?"

The long beam of light led across the dark to a small reedy island. Vivien half rose from the box she had been huddled on. "Where?" she whispered urgently. "Where?"

"There, there," Jimmy Baird said soothingly. "There he is."

Ricks said, "I've got it. Like two little bits of coal! I'll be damned!"

"Oh *where!*" Vivien was desperate.

Jimmy Baird took her hand and pointed. "Straight ahead, my dear. Got him?"

Then she saw, low down in the dank tangle, two glowing red points. The boat bore down upon them. Nobody spoke except Jimmy. He kept up a quiet running commentary, a soothing incantation to keep the crocodile unmoving. But as they reached the reeds, there was a movement quicker than a blink. "He's gone!" said Jimmy. "There he goes."

The boat kicked, turned, made for open water again.

"I saw him!" said Vivien. "I saw his tail!"

"Never mind, lots more to come," said Jimmy Baird, promising.

"I think you'll find 'em a bit shy, down this way," said Davie. "We been giving 'em hell the last week, Jimmy. I think we ought to go right up a bit."

"Okay, Davie, if you think so," said Jimmy politely.

In a few minutes they caught another pair of eyes in the beam of the searchlight; but again the unseen creature got away without even a splash. To the two visitors, the unlikelihood of the whole business—that men should earn a living on a tropical river, at night, shooting crocodiles in order to sell their skins—seemed the answer. They could not believe that they themselves really were *there;* so it did not seem strange that there was no crocodile lying dead in the boat. Then Jimmy Baird said in his encouraging, friendly voice, "On the right, Davie, please." As the boat swerved neatly and closed in, Vivien said, "Oh yes, I see it"—although she could see nothing.

"It's a babe, I'm afraid—yes, just a babe," said Jimmy, who had explained earlier that they did not shoot crocodiles below a certain minimum size, though they took them as big as they came. "You can see how close together the eyes are, that's a little head, that one." The boat nosed into the reeds and the engine cut out. Suddenly Jimmy Baird said, "Bring her right in, Davie! Right up!" and as the boat shot by the mud bank where the light had settled, he leaned swiftly out of the boat and with a movement of incredible balance and strength, like a circus performer, he brought up in his hands a struggling two-foot-long crocodile.

Vivien was so astonished that she looked quickly round the boat, from one to another, as if she were afraid she had been fooled. "There you are," said Jimmy Baird, with both small hard hands rigid as steel round the long snout of the frantic creature. "Now you can have a good look at him, Mrs. McEwen. Ah-ah, you wicked one," he added to the crocodile in the special voice of admonishment you would use for a young child. "Look at him, look at him trying to lever himself loose with his tail." The crocodile had slapped his strong tail round the man's slender right forearm and was using a wrestler's muscular pressure to free himself.

The young woman put out a hand. "Go on," said Jimmy Baird. "He's all right, the little blighter." And she touched the creature's cool, hard back, a horny hide of leather medallions, fresh, strange, alive; from a life unknown to the touch of humans, beneath the dark river. In the light of the searchlight, turned upon the creature and the faces of those round it, she saw the scissor jaws—parted a little as the man moved his grip a shade back toward the throat—with the ugly, uneven rows of razor-jagged teeth. In the light, she met the eyes; slits of pale, brilliant green, brilliant as fire; in their beast's innocence of such things, they held, for humans, the projection of hate, cunning, and evil. There was a moment when the eyes saw her, of all the others. She felt that the thing knew her, as God knew her; there was an incomparable thrill of fear.

The creature suddenly bellowed hoarsely with the yell of an infuriated and desperate baby; and they all laughed.

"Ma-ma! Ma-ma!"

"Jesus, how he'd like one of your fingers!"

"Could he really?" asked Vivien.

"You bet," said Mike, "just like that. Clean as a whistle."

Jimmy Baird bent over the water, with care. Then his hands sprang back like a released trap. "That's the last we'll see of him," he said, wiping his wet hands down his overalls.

Vivien was excited and boastful. "Oh I'm sure you'll get him. You'll get him next year, when he's bigger."

Davie was using a pole to shove the boat off from the mud bank.

"They live a long time. Their lives are slower than ours. Probably he'll be lying here in the sun long after I've finished banging away up and down this river or anywhere else," said Jimmy Baird. His face was serene, in the light, then the light left him and went out over the darkness again.

"We should have put a mark on him," Vivien went on joyfully. "Couldn't we have branded him, or something, so that you'd know him if you caught him?"

Mike turned with his perpetual ill-tempered grin. "We got six hundred last season and we didn't know any of 'em by name."

"Sure you're okay, Mike?" Jimmy Baird asked, and touched him on the shoulder.

"Fine, fine," he said, looking out into the dark with his eyes wide open, like a blind man.

"Isn't he well tonight?" said Vivien.

"He's had a nasty temperature all day," said Jimmy Baird, concernedly. "Bit of malaria—he says it's flu, old Mike."

In an hour the haze had cleared from the sky and although there was only a thin new moon, the stars were bright; their faint silvering, that is put out by the glow of cities in countries where there are cities, came out in a night silence hundreds of miles away from even the most distant sound of a train. The mere touch of light lay on the water, a membrane upon the darkness; touched the reeds; penetrated nothing of the great massed mansions of wild fig trees on the banks. There were low calls and whoops, a snatch of far-off human laughter from the jackals—the behind-the-hand noises of the river's secret life. Awe invaded the heart and took the tongue of Vivien McEwen; at the same time, she wanted to giggle, like a child watching a Hollywood adventure film. At one point, where the right bank of the river opened out on what must have been treeless scrub, small glowing points jumped about; it looked as if, out there in the waste where no one lived, someone was throwing cigarette butts away in the dark. Jimmy Baird explained that they were the eyes of spring-hares, who had a big warren just there.

"Slow down, Davie old man, perhaps we can spot them."

The searchlight swiveled obediently and made slow sweeps on the bank, but it was too far away; they could see nothing but the light itself, the color of strong tea, reaching out.

They went on and twice they entered a water-maze, where the river closed in to alleys and lanes and passages enclosed by high walls of reeds, but to the crocodile-hunters these were the streets of their own neighborhood. They glided by narrow mud-bars where heavy wet bodies had made resting-places like the places in long grass where a dog has made a bed. The propeller was lifted clear of the water, bearded with debris, and their progress was silent, as Davie poled them along. Jimmy Baird held back the reeds that came to splatter and hit at Vivien's face. This was a closely inhabited place; like a ghetto or a souk, it had the atmosphere of an interior, of the particular quality and kind of life lived there. It was a closed saurian world of mud, dankness, sun, unmeasured time.

The boat emerged again, into the broad main flow and the power of the engine coming to life like a great fish carrying them along on its back. The big blond Mike sat hunched in his place, his face turned smiling into the dark, not following the purposeful wandering of the light his hands directed. There were stretches where he whistled piercingly and professionally, tunes that had gone round in people's heads exhaustively, then died, like spinning tops, of their own repetition, over the past twenty years. When the young woman heard a tune that was recent enough to have pleasant associations for her, she asked him what it was called. "I wooden know," he said, not looking at her. "I pick 'em up from the radio." The searchlight pushed aside the darkness from the reeds, first on this side, then on that; occasionally, as you might lift your eyes from a trying task in order to rest them with a change of focus, it ran lightly over the bank, discovering trees, caves of undergrowth, sudden clearings, and the crook of the terrible finger, gray and fifteen feet high, of an antheap.

"What d'you think?" Davie called.

"Well, yes, I suppose we should think about getting back, you know Davie," said Jimmy Baird, and paused to consider a moment. "What d'you say, Mike?" It seemed that it was not out of an inability to make up his own mind about things that he consulted his companions with great care, on every point, but rather out of a fear that, always knowing exactly what he wanted to do, he might impose his will thoughtlessly.

"Nothing up here tonight," said Mike, as if someone were arguing with him. "This's where I got those two big fellers yesterday."

"Oh we'll raise something yet," said Jimmy Baird. "We'll go back down slowly and see what we can find. I must say, this's been disappointing for you so far, Mrs. McEwen—are you sure you're warm enough? Hands not too cold?" He added to Mike, "You missing your teatime tonight, Mike, eh? Mike always pumps up the old primus and gives us a cuppa tea round about this time, it makes all the difference, you know, specially when it's cold—you just long for that cuppa tea."

Mike looked at his watch. "Half past ten. Yes, just about time."

"We'll have something hot when we get back, to make up," promised Jimmy Baird. Vivien and her husband protested that they were not thirsty, needed nothing.

Davie, who could not always follow what was being said, because of his closeness to the noise of the motor, suddenly called out, "Mike! D'jou forget the tea tonight? 'S half past ten."

"He didn't bring the primus."

"Well, of all the lousy chumps . . ."

"We're not working," said Mike. "That's why I didn't think of it, man, just fooling around."

While the discussion about tea was going on, Jimmy Baird, still talking, spotted a crocodile with that third eye of alertness that was constantly awake in him. He had been telling Vivien and her husband how Davie and Mike always argued over the cups—Davie had a flowered china cup, the last of three he had brought with him from town life two years ago, and he didn't want Mike to risk it on the river. "I must say, it is a very pretty cup, Royal Doulton or something posh like that—" he was saying, when he suddenly changed his manner beneath his voice, which went on in exactly the same tone: "On the left there, Davie. Come on, now—" and he bent down and picked up his gun. "Excuse me, Mrs. McEwen," he said with concern, because he had brushed her shoulder as he moved—and he was looking at the two red eyes fifty yards ahead, and he was loading the gun that he insisted must always be kept unloaded the moment it was not in use. Mike thrust the light into the hands of Ricks McEwen, saying, "Keep that dead steady, eh?" and picked up the gaff.

With the numb swiftness of a piece of surgery it was accomplished; Vivien seemed to hear Jimmy Baird's voice through ether, kind and confident, the voice of the doctor doing what has to be done, without the futility of pity and with the mercy of skill.

"Right up, now, quickly, Davie."

The boat bore down fast on the reeds and the two pencil-torch eyes glowed nearer, and there it was, in the space of a second, the horny-looking, greenish-black forehead with the frontal ridges over the eyes above the water, and the nostrils breaking the water again at the end of the lumpy snout—there it was, gazing, in the eternity of a split second, not three feet away, and Jimmy Baird's calm, compassionate voice saying,

"Right," and the gun swiftly on his shoulder and the crac beside her where he stood. Then the pale gaze coming from the dark forehead exploded; it blew up as if from within, and where the gaze had been there was a soft pink mess of brain with the scarlet wetness of blood and the mother-of-pearl sheen of muscle. There was violent threshing of the water, and although the crocodile was dead—had been completely alive one second and quite dead the next—Jimmy Baird shot it again and the great gaff swooped down and hooked it out of the pull of the river. The men heaved it aboard. "All over. Okay. Okay. Let's get him down here, that's it." Jimmy Baird saw the creature laid out carefully on the bottom of the boat, out of the way, but so that Vivien and Ricks could see it well. It was about five feet long, less than half grown. The broad, soft-looking belly part, which was the part for which it had been hunted, was beautifully marked in lozenge-shaped plates, cream-colored with tinges of black, that were as perfectly articulated as the segments of a tortoise-shell. The lizard legs and the belly twitched occasionally, as if the blown communications had left some unfinished message of impulse.

Vivien McEwen was on her feet. "Oh my God," she cried, grinning, laughing, "what a man! Wasn't that wonderful, Ricks? Did you ever see anything like it! What a man! Oh Mr. Baird that was terrific. Terrific!" She was in such a state of excitement that she was unsteady, like a drunk; the boat rocked and her husband had to hold her elbow. "That's the most wonderful thing I've ever seen." She appealed from one to the other. "Wasn't that splendid? Oh my God, what do you think of him? The way he simply goes up and blazes the hell out of that thing— Those eyes! Staring at you! Crash— Whoom— Finished!"

Mike took a look at the crocodile. "Just a teen-ager, eh, Jimmy?"

"Well, not too bad, Mike, he'll pay for the petrol."

Ricks McEwen said, as one man to another, "You certainly don't give yourself time to fumble. Hardly a chance to aim, even."

Jimmy Baird gave him his attention. "You're so close, you don't have to aim, really. It's instantaneous, you know. The old croc doesn't suffer at all. I don't like to kill. I haven't shot a buck, for instance, since just after the war. But I often think these old crocs have a better end than most of us will ever have. We come up so close, you see, it's only a second—"

"Ricks, look at this!"

Davie had taken a spanner and knocked off one of the crocodile's teeth for the young woman. She was a dark woman, rather plain, with a very small head; the scarf she had worn over it had fallen back and now, bared, with its smooth brown hair in a bun, her head emerged, rather reptilian itself—the little black moles, one beside her left eye, one beside the corner of her mouth, and two on her cheek, added to the suggestion. She might have come out of the night river, a creature cunningly marked for concealment in the ambiguous, shifting, blotchy light-and-dark of reeds and water. "Just look." Her teeth and small eyes shone in the light. "Imagine that crunching into your leg! And if he breaks this one, he's got another inside!" She showed her husband how the big mossy yellowed tooth held a spare one wedged within it.

At last they all settled themselves in the boat again, and Davie poled off from the mud bank where a cloud of blood, suspended in the shallows, was slowly threading away into the mass of water.

Vivien McEwen sat back, plumping herself with sighs of triumph. She could not control her excited laughter; it rippled over with everything she said. "Ricks? Ricks? How do you feel about Johannesburg now?" She wrapped the crocodile tooth carefully in a handkerchief and put it in among the cigarettes and cosmetics that made a perfumed jumble in her handbag.

"Oh fine, Vivien, fine."

Her brow wrinkled, she drew her head back on her shoulder with intensity, as she confided to Mike, "This'll make my poor husband just impossible. He loathes cities, anyway. This is a life for a *man*."

Jimmy Baird had unloaded the gun and put it away and was squatting next to Ricks McEwen. He took out his pipe and began to fill it, but McEwen said, "Oh come on, try some of this." "May I really? That's jolly nice." Jimmy Baird took the proffered pouch, a pigskin-and-suède affair that Vivien had had made for her husband last Christmas.

The two men sat feeding the tobacco into their pipes and tamping it down. The light of matches opened and closed on their faces, and a spasm of muscle made the dead beast at their feet nudge suddenly at their shoes. "Sometimes when I've got five or six big crocs in one night, I look at them spread out on the river bank and I think, that's a thousand years of life, lying there. It seems kind of awful, a thousand years of life," Jimmy Baird said.

The night river closed away behind them. It went back where it came from; from the world of sleep, of eternity and darkness, the place before birth, after death—all those ideas with which the flowing continuity of dark water is bound up. And the boat came back; brought them within sight of the light of the campfire and the shapes it touched, and then back to the camp itself, existence itself, a fire, the reed house, the smell of food, and a human figure. A moment, between boat and bank, when each one of them saw the dark water beneath them, wriggling with light from the oil lamp an African held—and then they were on land, lively and stretching. "Are you all ready for us, my girlie?" said Jimmy Baird, putting his arm round his wife and looking at her tenderly. "Yes, yes, there's coffee there, and sandwiches," she said, making as if to put him away, but staying within his arm. Mike stamped around, hunching his shoulders and hitting the fist of one hand in the palm of the other, and Davie kicked the big logs closer into the fire so that sparks flew. "I didn't see you coming, you know," she said, smiling. "You gave me quite a scare. You can't see beyond the light of the fire, when you're sitting there in it."

Vivien McEwen was glowing, even panting a little. "Ah Mrs. Baird," she said, "your husband! It was sensational! I thought I'd die! Oh you should've been there! You should've been there, really!" She stood dramatically, as if the other woman, who was smiling at her kindly with a polite smile, might catch alight from her. "I'll bring you a cup of coffee, eh," said Jimmy Baird's wife, and as Vivien, who had followed her to the table, stood beside her while she poured the coffee out of a big enamel jug, Vivien looked at her and suddenly said, curiously, "What did you do, all the time we were gone? Did you read or something?"

"I waited," said Mrs. Baird.

"Yes, but I mean how did you pass the time?" Vivien had taken the cup and, although the coffee was boiling hot, was taking quick, darting sips at it.

The other woman looked up from the coffee jug a moment, apologetic because her visitor hadn't caught what she had said.

"I waited," she said.

For a moment, Vivien looked as if, this time, she really hadn't heard. Then she gave the woman a big, brilliant, dazed smile, and wandered off back to the company of the men.

The Path of the Moon's Dark Fortnight

Manuel de Vos began to think about Sunday's lunch four days ahead, and three days ahead, began to prepare it. He bought artichokes from the Indian greengrocer who always had the best of everything. He inquired about inkfish at the Greek provision place. He put a saddle of Springbok in to marinate. Before he went to town on Thursday morning, he shouted for Simon, the gardener. "Hey! The small beans? The young ones? You know? You know the ones I mean? Pick me plenty. Big basket." And Simon, black as gunpowder, with the savage face that gentle Nyasas seem to have been saddled with by mistake, mumbled, "I know, master," and spent an hour of the cloudy afternoon stripping the vines of their young peas. So there would be none of the pickled French-bean salad for which Manuel was famous.

"That one ith one of God's living idiots," said Carola Bonheim, his neighbor, when he mentioned it to her that evening. "I watched him, this afternoon, and I wondered, Now what on earz ith he doing? Not one zingle pea ith left on."

Manuel answered so distantly, he might suddenly have been speaking from another planet. "It doesn't matter at all." He was annoyed, again, at the idea that this woman watched his garden while he was not there; it was even worse than her surveillance when he was there. In the early evenings and at weekends, she was always coming through the slack wires of the fence that divided her property from his, as she had done now, her slow progress unavoidable as a guided missile as she came over the soft clods in the high, cork-soled mules into which her bunioned feet were always thrust.

They were lumped together, Manuel and his neighbor, in the Afrikaans rural community where they had chosen to live, as exotics. It was maddening to think how someone so different from oneself, toward whom one felt an uncontrollable antipathy, should have the same ideas as oneself on how to live. *He* had hit upon the brainwave of buying up two or three plots in an area of poor and unfashionable small holdings considered undesirable by those Johannesburg people who could afford rural estates. *He* had had the notion of converting an existing *pondokkie*—a shack without a bathroom or electric light—into a studio-cottage. Why should she have thought of the same thing? All around them poor Afrikaners in whom there was an unresolved conflict between the farm and the city, lived in *pondokkies* with great numbers of barefoot children. Their dogs were of no known breed and their chickens raked and pecked a peevish living where they pleased.

Carola Bonheim ran a dress shop in the city. But she left the shop at five o'clock every day and changed, the moment she got home, into her black linen shorts and her cork-soled mules.

She was fifty-one, her hair was cut short and dyed the color of the nicotine stains on the first and third fingers of her right hand, and she was well preserved, so that the hard flesh of her sturdy legs had the thick, bruised look of frozen meat. She kept three horses and bred rabbits, scientifically, in patent tin hutches, where their food came down to them only as they pulled at it and their excreta rolled away into channels provided for perfect hygiene and thrifty manure. In her little house she kept a small collection of pornographic statuettes in velvet-lined boxes specially made for them. They were the work of a Polish friend, a woman who had suffered—oh, God knew what she had suffered—from the Communists: these dark reflections, with which Mrs. Bonheim accompanied the opening of the boxes, produced in those who were being privileged with a viewing of the statuettes, a peculiar confusion, as if they had found some holy relic to be an unmentionable part of the saint's anatomy.

It was the legs, his neighbor's legs in her shorts that Manuel de Vos could not stand. He felt he could have forgiven her anything else; but perhaps they merely provided a focus for the sum of his irritation with her. "That old woman with her trousers up to her thighs! All the little veins round the ankles! As if someone has scribbled them on with a ball pen! I want to say to her, Woman, for God's sake, cover yourself with a skirt." Manuel hated ball-point pens; they belonged indiscriminately along with all substitutes for, or "advancements" on what had been familiar to men's use for a generation or two. He loved to do the things that men had always done: make love, grow vegetables, fashion pots. He had been born in South Africa, but his mother was Portuguese and he had lived in France for many years (one of his wives—now both divorced—was French) and he thought of himself, as people thought of him, as a foreigner. He had failed with a number of enterprises, in the city, and with the two wives; now he had business interests which did not interest him, but his interest in women was unflagging. He was not in the least content, and he gloried in his lack of contentment. He made pots in his studio-cottage. He made wine out of his own sour Catawba grapes—those grapes that pop in the mouth like outsize globules of caviar—he bottled in brandy the fruit from his trees, he grew herbs as well as vegetables for his elaborate home cooking. He was exactly fifty-one, exactly the age of his neighbor, the old woman with the horrible legs.

If he could not escape her sharp eye for the welfare of his property, and he could not prevent her from popping in, at least he never invited her for a meal; Manuel had always cooked for his friends. It was so clearly to be understood that she would never graduate from the category of neighbor, that he sometimes described a proposed menu to her, and, after the occasion for which it had been devised had passed, she would ask, with her air of having been, for herself, better occupied, "Yes? And how wauz za dinner? All right?"

So it was that he could say to her now, "Maybe I'll make a pea soup, use up those peas and forget about the artichokes. They looked a bit too big, the ones I bought this morning, anyway. A thick pea soup, with little smoked sausages in it. No, perhaps that's too heavy for lunch—a thinner one, with a little cream and sherry. I've got some chicken stock, luckily."

"You can make for twenty people, I'm zure," she said, indicating a superfluity of peas. It was not a hint that some might be passed on to her; she too, it had to be admitted, loved to grow vegetables. She had plenty of young peas of her own.

On Friday, the menu for Sunday's lunch went through a further modification to circumstance. Manuel met a friend in town at the license office, where he had gone to renew the license disk for his car. It was Yvor Lennox, an old friend; Manuel never lost an old friend, except through death or departure to another country; he was never estranged from them, as it seems almost impossible for most of us not to be, by taking sides in their divorces, scandals, and general fluctuations of fortune. He was so tolerant, in fact, that he sometimes forgot that certain people, through past association with each other in these things, would rather not meet, and they would find themselves sitting next to each other at dinner. In any case, he regarded jealousy, illicit passion, and frustration as as much a condition of living as breathing. How else would one love or make pots?

Lennox was twelve years younger than Manuel but Manuel had been through it all with him; touched upon Lennox's life through its many stages and vicissitudes. When Lennox was a youngster and had wanted to paint; when, just after the war, his family couldn't get him to stick to a job; when Lennox fell in love with Ruth, in England, and after he had come back to South Africa and had sent for her to follow, wondered if he really wanted to marry her after all. Of course, there had been months, years, almost, when he and Manuel didn't see each other, but when they did meet again there was always the immediacy of Manuel's response to whatever was going on in his friends' lives at the moment of contact.

During the last year he had seen very little of the Lennoxes. At the sight of each other, Manuel and Lennox had the sharp impulse of regret that the reminder of time passing brings between old friends. "We've thought about you so often, lately, honestly," said Lennox. "I know," said Manuel. "I've said to myself a dozen times, What's happened to Yvor and Ruth? I've been meaning and meaning to phone you." After they had talked a little longer, he said, "Come to lunch on Sunday.

Bring the children to lunch." The gap was bridged, the breach of time closed emphatically as a mouth. "This Sunday? We'd love to."

Manuel lifted his foreign-looking hands, with their parchment-colored nails. "Come as early as you like. The Tollmans will be there. You remember Skippy Tollman? And Luigi Rossa and Thelma Brown—a charming girl, I don't think it can go wrong this time. Give Ruth my love—"

"Oh Manuel, before I forget—" They had been moving away from each other, two men in a hurry, but now Lennox drew them together again. "There will be a salad or something, so that Ruth can eat?"

Manuel assumed one of his pondering frowns. "My dear fellow! A salad? There will be calamari and venison and whatever I can think up for you!"

"Oh I know, I know, I can guess. But you'll remember that Ruth doesn't eat meat or fish any more—just so there's something for her, anything, cheese and fruit will do."

"Doesn't eat meat? Since when?" Manuel looked skeptical.

Lennox smiled a patient, husbandly smile, designed to convey that he, as least, saw nothing out of the way in what he was explaining. "Don't you remember last time we saw you, you and she were talking about religion?"

"We were talking about God," corrected Manuel.

"Well"—Lennox gave the layman's culpable shrug at technicalities he shouldn't be expected to understand—"she was talking to you about some books she'd been studying, Yoga and so on. Now she's taken it up properly, and one of the things is, she doesn't eat meat or eggs or anything like that."

"Is that so," said Manuel eagerly. He was a Catholic, but he was drawn to all forms of the occult. "She was busy with Gurdjieff and Ouspensky then, I remember. Someone had just given her *All and Everything* to read. That was it."

Lennox's expression slowly deepened into that of the clumsy parent describing the prowess of its child at dancing class. He shrugged and said modestly, "D'you know, she gets up at half past four every morning to meditate."

"Ruth!" said Manuel. "Ruthie used to like to go to bed about that time!"

"Not these days," said Lennox, as if giving testimony to a cure. "You'll find us in bed before half past ten, mostly."

"And you," said Manuel, "have you taken it up, too?"

"Oh no," said Lennox, exactly like one of those rich men who explain that they know nothing about pictures; the art collection is entirely the wife's department. "The only other member of the family who's interested is William—he often goes along with Ruth to the what-you-call-it, the Guru."

"William!" said Manuel in a get-away-with-you voice. "How old's that little devil now?" And went on to remind Lennox how his small son had once stolen a duckling from the pond at the "farm" and had hidden it in the napkin bag that Ruth had brought along for her younger child, Roderick.

Manuel had a busy and harassing day in town, but as he came into his house, he threw his briefcase down on the veranda and went straight to the pantry to have a look at the Springbok. He poked at it with his finger and it bobbed, sending up a smell of wine and blood; a bay leaf floated to the surface of the marinade. Good. Good. But now what about this woman and her lunch without fish or flesh? Asparagus, that was the answer. He would give her fresh asparagus, with butter—no, vinaigrette sauce. The cherry dessert? Well, she probably couldn't have that, because of the brandy in it—no doubt she'd given up alcohol, too. But he'd leave a pretty bowl of plain iced cherries for her. And she could have the soup, of course—the pea soup. Vegetable soup, asparagus, fruit. Quite adequate. And for the rest of the guests, as planned: soup, ink-fish, venison, dessert.

He worked on the luncheon all Saturday afternoon. The inkfish was a big one and the devil of a job to clean. Simon and the houseboy, Jacob, were never sober from Friday till Monday, and they stood about the kitchen looking giddy, as if they'd just stepped off a roller-coaster. But Manuel didn't mind; he didn't really want any help, just so long as they didn't break anything. And they never broke anything, washing up while they were drunk; they were dreamily extra-careful.

On Sunday morning there wasn't much to do that didn't have to be done at the last minute. Manuel came out onto his little terrace in his dressing-gown and looked out over the freshness of the morning garden. It had rained in the night and the homemade swimming pool, which was under a jacaranda tree close to the house, was full of leaves and bits of twig. There was something else in the water, too. He went down over the sparkling grass to see. The thing turned out to be a drowned rat, already swollen; as he prodded at it with a long stick, it bobbed against the weight of the water, and some leaves eddied to the surface; he was suddenly reminded of the venison, lying in its embalming fluid. He went into the house to get himself a cigar, and, looking along the book-shelves, on his way back to the terrace, picked out a paper-back copy of the *Bhagavad Gita* someone had once given him. He lay in the delicate morning sun and read, skipping, turning pages, his mind flitting to arrested glimpses of Ruth Lennox in contexts he didn't remember—her pious smile, somewhere, when she was pregnant, her way of following a conversation as if it were a tennis match; a party (how long ago that must have been, in the old days when Lennox still painted and they were Bohemians) when she had taken off a black velvet dress in a stifling room, and danced a tango in a black bra and a petticoat that had no bodice. He read:

There is the path of light,
Of fire and day,
The path of the moon's bright fortnight
And the six months' journey
Of the sun to the north:
The knower of Brahman
Who takes this path
Goes to Brahman:
He does not return.

There is the path of night and smoke
The path of the moon's dark fortnight
And the six months' journey
Of the sun to the south:
The yogi who takes this path
Will reach the lunar light:
This path leads back
To human birth, at last.

"These two paths, the bright and dark, may be said to have existed in this world of change from a time without any beginning. By the one, a man goes to the place of no return. By the other, he comes back to human birth." Of course, he had read the whole thing through once before; bits of it came back. A choice of destiny after death; good God, that was too much! It was bad enough, in life, that whatever you chose implied a rejection of something else. How could you decide? Oh, to live again, I suppose, he thought, with one of his swift desperate moods. Capitulate, be born again—he imagined it happening, with horror and deep longing, it was given to him again, all that he had done, all that he had not done. He imagined himself a child, an old child, one of those old, old children beginning again from the beginning—if you believed this business, how terrifyingly patient, ancient, and wise children were!

His mind, with sure homing instinct, left the Way and turned back to the faint paths it had made for itself; he sank into a dream, wandering the emotional woods of his life with a caressing palm of the hand for every name carved on the trees. But the thought of lunch brought the present before him abruptly as an alarm clock. There had been too much time; now, as usual, there was none too much. He bellowed, "Simon! Bring the net and clean up the pool! There's a rat in it"—and went into the kitchen, firm with purpose.

The Tollmans came first—Skippy's complaining voice (he did not always complain, but his voice made everything he said sound dismayed) giving warning of their arrival before they came into sight round the side of the house. They had just returned from Japan, and they had brought their spoils with them to show to Manuel—they carried scrolls, silk, netsukes, and jewelry. Skippy was a rich man's son bewildered by the freedom of his money; without necessity it seemed there was no virtue to be found in life. He was a slight, slim man with a thin lock of prematurely gray hair blowing disorderly over his forehead. He had, quite genuinely, the noble, harassed refugee face of the twentieth-century man; looking as if he were perpetually in flight, he had had nothing to flee from—in all his life, nothing had threatened the security of his home, his person, or his stock. His wife Vida reinforced this air of personal drama; like Manuel, she was a South African, but she looked unmistakably and mysteriously foreign. She was beautiful, with a thick, shiny olive skin, gray eyes and black hair coarsely streaked with gray. Bracelets seemed to grow up her arms like creeping plants. She kissed Manuel, threw her head back, smiling magnificently, to look at him, while her husband droned on, putting his treasures down among the bottles set out on the table under the jacaranda: ". . . all this muck. God knows why . . . can never leave anything where we find it . . . some of it's all right, I suppose, look at this, Manuel—not that thing, that's Oriental kitsch . . . this, look at those colors . . ."

Vida and Manuel exclaimed over each other. "But you look wonderful!" "Darling, what a bear-hug, I see your arm hasn't begun to fail. . . ."

"Do I really begin to look much older?" Manuel was suddenly serious, feeling over his jaw with his fine hand. *"Ag, man, Manuel, ou skat."* Vida embraced him again, dropping roughly into a coarse, tender Afrikaans manner—an affectation of earthy simplicity that she had tried on Manuel many times before, and always with unvarying success. At once there was a look of excitement in his eye; he was a man again, and a vigorous one, he need have no doubt about it.

When Skippy had run down everything he had brought, and, gins in hand, they had looked at everything, all talking and nobody listening, he gave Manuel his present—an exquisite silk obi in gray, black, mauve, and silvery-lemon. "Now let's get it all away before anyone else comes," said Skippy. "Get it into the car or somewhere, before everyone begins pulling it about. I can't bear to go on talking about it the whole day. Who's coming, anyway?" "All old friends," said Manuel, still taking in his silk with half-closed eyes and deep breaths, as if it were a perfume rather than an object. "Luigi Rossa and girl-friend, the Lennoxes and their kids." Skippy began bundling everything together. "There you are! They've got children! For God's sake, Vida, they'll paw everything!" "Nonsense," said Manuel tranquilly, "Yvor and Ruth's children are delightful. Beautiful boys. You can dump it in my bedroom, if you like," he added to Vida.

When she came back from the house, the two men were talking about Luigi Rossa. "How's the fragile Bella?" said Vida, lifting a stiff old boxer bitch off the most comfortable chair and sitting herself down. "Manuel's just been telling me," said her husband. "She isn't. There's a new one." "Well, nearly," said Manuel. "They aren't married yet. You'll see her. Charming girl, I like her tremendously." "You always say that," said Vida grudgingly. "They're *all* charming. Then what's the matter with him, or them? You said Bella was charming, the other one, what's-her-name, *she* was charming—" Skippy ostentatiously did not listen when his wife talked, as if he were sure, in advance, it would be something he had heard her say before. Following his own line of thought, he interrupted, suddenly asking, "Is the old Bonheim bitch still next door?" But at that moment the Lennoxes and Luigi Rossa and Miss Thelma Brown arrived, all at the same time, and conversation took to the air, a paean of cries, greetings, laughter, that seemed to set off the hens, for, out of coincidence or rivalry, they set up a whooping and cackling echo from their quarters.

"My God," said Skippy to Manuel quickly, under the cover of the noise, as the new arrivals bore down upon them, "Ruth Lennox has got that Secret Under My Heart look again." "I know, but it's not the secret you're thinking of," hissed Manuel, before turning away in welcome.

Yvor was in tennis shorts with a badge on the pocket of a striped blazer. Ruth, a large blonde with slow eyes, had grown her hair into a bun and wore a pink silk dress that, as Vida Tollman said afterward, seemed to have been as much calculated not to do anything for her as her previous styles of dress had been calculated to do things for her. The children *were* beautiful; especially the elder boy, the nine-year-old William, who was dark and graceful, like his father, and had, perpetually in shadow under prematurely heavy brows that almost met, his mother's slow blue eyes. They were well-behaved, unobtrusive children, who greeted the grownups shyly, prodded on by Yvor, and then sat on the grass with their bottles of Coca-Cola, eyeing each other silently in communication of their eagerness to drink up and be off, exploring. Luigi, unchanged Luigi with his young man's body that did not yield an inch to the forties, and his contented, well-balanced, considerate manner that had come unrattled through a series of nerve-shattering marriages, kept Miss Thelma Brown under his sheltering arm, as it were, while all the old friends met. Then Manuel drew her away and introduced her and settled her with a drink, and all the while she watched, with the pleasant smile of one who is ready to learn, she watched Luigi and his friends, as if she were confident that she could recapture for herself the way he was all the years when she had missed knowing him. She wore already the few pieces of delicate jewelry—encrustations of semi-precious stones and blister pearls pressed like barnacles on thin gold, all made by the same man—with which Luigi had always marked out his choice.

"My dear Ruth!" said Skippy, next to whom Ruth Lennox had been given a chair. "You've put it on a bit since I saw you. Yes, indeed." Ruth had always been a little afraid of him, and he had always taken advantage of it, flirting with her, in their Bohemian days, when there was plenty of opportunity for such things, with an edge of rudeness to his attentions that suggested that he could not think why he should waste his time with her. "About ten pounds," she said, with a smile. He looked critically at her bosom; she'd had a very sweet pair, once upon a time, no question of that; why, that time when she'd taken off her dress and danced . . . There was nothing provocative about her breasts now; he felt disgusted with her: nothing but a complacent mother, that cow-eyed look had come out in her, all right. "You'll have to diet, my girl," he said, and added in irritation, "Soon put the roses back in those cheeks."

"She does, that's the whole thing," said Yvor, just as, in the old days in their set, a husband would make a point of saying, of a man whom people suspected to be his wife's lover, "I'm enormously fond of old So-and-So; he's in and out of the house all the time." "Since she hasn't been eating meat or eggs or fish, she's just kept putting on pound after pound. It's amazing. When you think of it, you'd wonder what's left to get fat on."

"Doesn't eat meat?" said Skippy, frowning. "But that's stupid. It's the other things you must cut out, the starches."

"She's given up eating flesh," said Manuel, with a gesture large as it was explanatorily vague.

"But she feels wonderful. Don't you darling?" said Yvor, smiling, and she smiled back, nodding her head, and repeated, "I feel wonderful. I've never felt so well in my life." Attention rested on her a moment, and she lifted her smooth throat and gazed out through the leaves with conscious unselfconsciousness, as if she were a demonstration of something.

Yvor had picked up his drink, but he did not put it to his lips, wanting to be sure of getting in, on cue, what he wanted to say.

"What is this diet of yours?" Vida asked Ruth, amusedly.

At once, Yvor said, "It's not a diet. She's taken up Buddhism, and one of the things is, you don't eat meat."

They all started questioning Ruth about her new preoccupation; all, that is, except Skippy. As soon as he heard the word "Buddhism" he let the whole conversation drop away from him; Buddhism indeed! A nice discussion with her about the difference between the Left-handed and the Right-handed Tantra. What a piece of impudence!

Ruth had the look of bashful pride of the successful convalescent, describing an operation. "I've really never felt so well. Nothing seems to make me tired."

"Up every morning at four!" insisted Yvor, eager for their incredulity.

"I honestly never miss it at all, any more. Just at first, you know, when I saw Yvor eating oysters . . ."

Yvor looked round, noted that the children were safely out of the way, and said, "But listen to this—the funniest thing is the way our kid's taken to it. Ruth's never said a word to him, of course, but he's terribly keen. For months now, he's even stopped eating meat."

"Which one's that?" said Vida, a childless woman to whom all children looked much the same.

"The big one, William," said Ruth. "I never suggested anything to him, you know, but he suddenly asked me one day if he could come along to the Guru."

"That's a beautiful child!" said Rossa. "The best features of both parents, in that face. I noticed when we arrived."

"Oh, do you think so?" said Ruth, warmly accepting, as an aside, the compliment.

"It started one morning when he must have heard Ruth get up, and he came creeping down the passage to the room where she goes to meditate," Yvor was telling Manuel and Rossa. "What was it again Ruthie? He thought you were a burglar, didn't he?"

"The poor little chap, you know," said Ruth, laughing. "He

came into the dark room, scared stiff, and then he found it was me! He flung himself on me crying and almost hitting me, he was so scared."

"And then Ruth explained to him why she was there and so on, and it was just after that that he began to be interested."

It was not only his wife whom Skippy could make a point of not listening to. He said now, clearly and unconcernedly, as if no one else had been talking at all, "Manuel, I was asking you before whether old Carola Bonheim's still next door?"

"What's that?" Manuel turned to him. "Oh, of course, of course. Still poking her nose over the fence."

"Oh my God. Well, I hope she keeps it on her own side today; that's the last encounter I want, at the moment."

Luigi Rossa smiled. He said to Thelma Brown, "You remember the woman we met at the Hungarian Relief Cabaret? That's the one they're talking about." Miss Brown had been playing with one of her rings, and now she slipped it back hastily onto the wrong finger, caught out in inattention. "That baroness?"

The others roared with laughter. "She still goes around playing the baroness!" said Vida. "This town never changes."

"She was telling me about three old horses she keeps for a French friend who has gone to claim his estates in South America. His wife's mother sends the money for their keep. It was a long story, quite sad. She sat next to me for ages. She asked me to come and see her, as a matter of fact," said the girl, whom being in love had obviously disposed to kindness to aging ladies.

This brought another great shock of laughter. The gin slopped over Skippy's glass, and Yvor, throwing back his head, almost tipped himself out of his chair.

"That's rich, oh, that's rich!"

"Christ, that's a good one!"

"Perrault's *mother-in-law,* if you please!"

"Now who could that be?"

"But was he ever married to any of those women, the old fox?"

"Get away!"

Vida shook her finger at them, arm extended and bracelets sliding. "He was! Yes he was! I beg your pardon! He was! That must be the mother of the poor Pinski girl, the daughter of those big printers or whatever they were. Don't you remember, he married her and ran that Rhodesian hotel combine thing that flopped, and always lived at Carola's all the time anyway."

A guilty intoxication of gossip carried them away; even Manuel was caught up in it, could not resist the temptation to contribute to the crackling effect. "Well, you'd better not take advantage of her invitation today, my dear," he said to Thelma Brown. "She always tells everyone she's not at home on Sundays, not at home. Except, of course, to a certain fat pale Englishman in a beige car. If I saw her house on fire on a Sunday I wouldn't even dare to go over and tell her!"

Skippy had risen from his chair, and was standing, holding up his glass under the tattered shade of the tree; with the animation and good humor that he always displayed when he was being malicious, he set off his companions in pursuit of another victim, while Manuel slipped away to put the finishing touches to the lunch. Manuel was a little dazed as he entered the dark of the house; gossip left him feeling as if he had got his head caught down in a rugby scrum.

The asparagus lay green and tender in a silver dish; Manuel would never have had the white kind in his house. The vinaigrette was ready in a blue bowl he had made himself. The aroma from the Springbok was indescribable; after one whiff, one could no more resist it than go into a convent; still. He remembered that he must not put sherry in two of the soup bowls, Ruth's and her son's. As he put them aside, there was a sudden dislodgment of something that had been stuck, and now fell into place in his mind: the pea soup is made with chicken stock. He actually touched at his own brow in token of striking it. Why hadn't he thought of it before? Idiot! How many times had he run through Ruth's vegetarian menu: vegetable soup, asparagus, fruit? Vegetable soup, indeed!

It never occurred to him simply not to serve her any soup; once it was included on his menu, the deception was already made. He put a spoonful of cream in one of the portions, stirred and tasted. It was delicious. Young, young peas, nothing in the world so fresh and sweet to taste. There was no hint of the chicken, no one would ever dream that there had ever been any chicken; it was as if the essence of the chicken had evaporated, gone completely. The soup was entirely innocent. He stifled all the soup bowls quickly, with their lids, and went out of the kitchen.

There were cries of pleasure when the guests straggled into the dining room. No one ever set a table quite like Manuel; such perfection of taste and imagination in the execution of the commonplace produces a positively emotional effect on people—they are seized with regret for their own daily habits of living. "Come, sit down, sit down," said Manuel gently, disposing his guests in order, and opening the wine. The gossip had died down but, in combination with the gin, had brought them gleefully closer; they felt that, surprisingly, they all got on particularly well together. Only the children, who had been called in from some private absorption behind the house to wash their hands at the last minute, sat rather out of it, parted by Luigi Rossa and Thelma Brown holding his thigh under the table.

Even Ruth, on tomato juice, was animated as if by infection. As Manuel passed behind her chair with the wine, she half turned and murmured, interrupting the giggles with which she was punctuating one of Skippy's stories, "This is all right for me?" And Manuel, seeing her bowl of soup at that moment placed before her by Jacob, looked straight into her large eyes, that always looked dazzled, and said, without betraying the inward flinch that came to him, "Perfectly. Pea soup, with some lovely asparagus I've got for you, to follow." There was a moment when he would not have been surprised by a thunderclap and a patriarchal accusation from the heavens; perhaps the house would fall in. But it didn't, and he thought to himself with a kind of pleasure, All the things she's taken up, the pottery, the gay life, the simple life, one can't even remember them all.

Manuel slid into his place at the head of the table, and they all began to eat. Thelma Brown, quite overawed, murmured, "Delicious!" and Manuel smiled, to indicate that it was nothing, really, a simple pea soup. Vida, who, from overmuch traveling had come to believe that there was no good food to be had at home, was moved to raise her eyebrows. Ruth spooned up the creamy green liquid regularly as she listened to Skippy.

But the child William, not listening perhaps to things he would not have understood anyway, but looking dreamily over the faces and hands and movements of the grownups, had hesitated after the first spoonful. No one noticed, but he paused, then slowly let the spoon sink down through the surface of cream, and fill up, like a sinking boat. Then he held it, just above the bowl, and his whole body seemed to prick up, as a dog's does in the moment of concentration of the senses just before it gets a scent. Bringing his thick eyebrows together, nervously, puzzled, he drank the second mouthful.

And then, suddenly, the whole table was made aware of him because he had gone. His spoon clattered off the table and fell onto Thelma Brown's dress and his chair grated back over the stone floor, and he ran from the room, all so quickly that they only had time to notice he wasn't there any more.

"What's the matter with William, Ruthie?" said his father, believing he had missed something.

"Why nothing; he was perfectly all right," said Ruth.

"Have you been teasing him, Roderick?" Yvor turned accusingly to the younger boy.

"Don't be silly, Yvor, we were sitting between them," said Luigi.

Ruth got up, begging everyone's pardon, and put her napkin down on her chair, ready to be taken up again. "I suppose I'd better go after him," she said.

But she couldn't find him. She was back in a few minutes, standing awkwardly in the doorway, and saying plaintively, "I don't know where he's got to." Soon the whole table had broken up in search of the child. The little boy Roderick sat alone on the floor and cried, "My brother's lost, my brother's lost!" They looked all over the house (he might have come in again through the side door), and the garden and the vegetable garden and the henhouses. At last Luigi Rossa, hardly aware that he had crossed the boundary of Manuel's property, the fence was in such poor repair, found the boy lying beside Carola Bonheim's rabbit hutches. Rossa called, "Here he is!" and Manuel heard and came running, under the slack strand of wire. The boy was lying face down, with his head hidden in the frame of his arms, and he would not speak to the two men, or get up. "Shall I go and fetch Ruth?" said Manuel. But Rossa unthinkingly assumed the manner he had learned in his long experience of the moods and hysterics of his wives, and instinctively said, "No, leave it." Gently he knelt on the earth, and without any further coaxing or entreaty, lifted the boy and sat him up. "There you are, William." The boy's mouth was smeared with earth, as if he had been trying to eat it, and he turned on the two men a face of blazing despair. "Now you tell me," Rossa kept saying monotonously, "you tell me, William." And "It's all spoilt, it's all spoilt"—the child gasped and sobbed. "Everything's spoilt! I'm unclean! It's all spoilt again!"

Our Bovary

Once she called to me from her garden, where she was picking dahlias in a leghorn hat, "I recognized you right down the block by your bandy legs. I said to myself, There's Joanie Oldfield." She was smiling her large, consciously generous, winning smile. I was seventeen, I suppose, a spindly girl, possessed by an obsessive secret vanity, who wore very high heels. I have never got over the shame of the moment; it was as if she knew the picture of myself that I had, and she could gleefully compare it with the real sight of me, which I could never see.

She was rather like a dahlia herself. Large, top-heavy, gorgeous. Her lips were curved like a statue's at the corners, her eyes were brown as a cow's, her skin was thickly creamy, and she had auburn hair that looked as silky and luxuriant as an opera singer's wig. She was Sonia Smith, the wife of the lawyer and city councilor, Herbert Smith. Herbert was twenty years older than her, and barely five feet tall. He had married her when she was a poor girl of seventeen, taken her off the hands of her widowed mother. "D'you think I should?" he is supposed to have asked my father, an old friend and a man his own size. And my father is supposed to have answered, with the air of conferred wisdom and good sense with which he always relates the making of such pronouncements, "You must do as you think best, Herb."

Well, Herbert Smith married her. What a picture she used to paint of herself as she was at that time! The thick red plait down her back (as she went into her forties she began to dye her hair and so to remember it as always having been red), the quaking innocence, the touching silliness of a child in a world of grownups. Herbert built her a house and made her pregnant; she produced two daughters, one the year after my mother gave birth to me, the second eighteen months later. She and my mother knitted baby clothes together and exchanged biscuit recipes. Sonia dressed up her house, dressed up her children, and dressed up herself. She looked back on the time, later, as a time when she had been happy; the happiness of not knowing any better. "What did I know? I was such a kid," she would say of herself, lovingly.

I don't remember her much as she was when she was very young; to me she was just another grownup. (Her two children used to come and play with us, great fat girls with plain faces. For, of course, each had Herbert Smith's face, sallow, puffy round the eyes, with the sort of good-natured upper lip that looked as if it should have whiskers.) I begin to remember Sonia Smith as she was when I was adolescent, the time when she emerged into that stage of her middle thirties in which she stayed for at least ten years. It was then that my mother and other contemporaries of hers began to talk complacently about their growing children as "the young people" and to call their husbands "Dad." They were all a few years older than Sonia Smith; not old enough for her not to belong along with them. But this was where she parted from them; at this point in the life that was before her in a town like ours, her foot must have frozen in the air before the next step. She never took it.

Then, when she was no longer really young, she began to be intensely aware of her youth. Then, when her beauty had already earned a way of life for her, she felt the power of her beauty. Then, when she had been mated with little Herbert Smith for years, she saw that she might have been a match for—anybody. She began to feel that the town could not contain her. She bought her clothes in Johannesburg, as if her limbs would burst through the sober, wishy-washy dresses that did for other local women, she went to Johannesburg to have her hair done at a vast beauty salon, she got Herbert to let her redecorate the house in a style that had never been seen in our town before. A mass of minor talents burst out like a rash upon her. She had always been a good needlewoman; now she made eight petit-point chair backs and seats for her elaborately carved and gilded dining chairs. As a girl, she had played the piano and sung; now she had a porch made into a "music room" and in it, hours a day, practiced piercing scales in a big, unsteady contralto. I remember passing the house on my way home from school and hearing the sound pour out; it was strange, like suddenly hearing the jungle cry of some splendid creature that is invariably silent in captivity.

She no longer came to tea, to knit and talk; she was too busy with her work. Later on her work didn't always mean the same thing, for she did barbola-work and she painted, too. She painted me, once. I was fifteen, and at the first sitting she got me rather well—the music room was called the studio by then, and she was a Juno in slacks and a sweater, the red hair wound and curled and piled on her head. But with each successive sitting, she lost me further, and the final portrait, a pastel, showed a good-looking usurper, a cuckoo-image who had pushed me out entirely. Sonia was very cross when my father wouldn't buy the picture; or rather my mother wouldn't let him buy it. "Who does she think she is, anyway," said my mother, doggedly, "calling herself Sonya Necci Smith and asking you fifteen guineas? I can get a set of decent photographs taken for that. Can't Herbert keep his grand wife himself any more?"

But the picture appeared in an exhibition that Sonia held, under what she told my mother was her professional name, in the local tearoom. Sonia used to give singing recitals now and then, too, in the Town Hall. They were always well attended because Herbert's fellow members on the city council felt obliged to come and bring their wives. "Mrs. Smith," they would say, "is a very artistic woman"—and, indeed, among them at municipal functions she did look like all the muses merged into one, with her trailing, shining dresses, her theatrical hats, her great clumps of jewelry.

She had long ago put aside the game of dressing up the two ugly daughters and had sent them to boarding school. They wore the same dresses year after year, for, very sensibly, it must have seemed a waste to Sonia to spend time and money on them, when both were well spent on herself. My mother and I met her in a shop once, where, out of necessity, apparently, she was looking for a dress for the elder one, Isabelle. She was quite unashamedly amused at the idea of getting up Isabelle in green velvet: "Wha'd'you think, Vangie?" she said to my mother in her intimate way, moving her shoulders under their soft weight of red-fox fur and appraising the material with her large, long hands, on which huge rings, which were real, always seemed like stage jewelry, "Will my poor Belle look sick in this? You can't put her in pink, I mean, she'd look like an elephant. Do you know that I can't get a pair of shoes for that girl? Honestly, Vangie—" And she went off into a peal of lazy laughter, her strong perfume blowing out over us.

My mother's hair was full of gray and her body looked sapless; my sisters and I were budding into grownup dresses and permanent waves. When Sonia met my mother wearing a new navy or gray dress and soberly smart matron's hat, she would stop her and take her by the arm kindly. "I want to tell you, Vangie. I said to Herb, I must come over and tell Vangie. I've *never* seen you looking so nice. Now that your hair's going gray you must always wear that blue." "Do you really like it, Sonia," my mother would murmur politely. And Sonia would sweep off, splendid bird of paradise, leaving my mother tingling with insult.

But my mother had her revenge. Untroubled by the women's peccadilloes, my father and Herbert Smith had continued through the years the friendship that had existed before either of them had had a wife. Sometimes the two little men didn't see each other for more than a wave of the hand in the street, for weeks, but when they found themselves both present at any sort of gathering, they gravitated surely and naturally toward each other. "Where are our two Shetland ponies? Whispering in each other's ears?" my mother would call out gaily to Sonia, at a wedding or a cocktail party. Oh the splendid Sonia, half barmaid, half queen, in her ripeness and her elaborate dress that made every other woman look like a molting hen! Who knows how deep the taunt went, and what things, better buried, were released by the piercing! Herbert was increasing in importance and self-importance all the time;

he was chairman of this and that, and twice mayor of the town. His voice had become fruity with the pronouncement of public sentiments, he wore round the big shoulders of a dwarf (which was as far as his picture in the local papers showed him) a purple robe and gold chain of office. Perhaps for Sonia, too, he seemed to be growing, in his own way, to match her. But now, as my mother said it, my mother spoke it playfully, "Where are our two Shetland ponies"—there he was, poor little Herbert, with his self-important little bottom and twinkling little legs and ridiculous three-cornered mayor's hat, trotting along hardly up to the shoulder of the splendid Sonia.

Anyway, it wasn't long after Herbert's second term of office as mayor that Sonia went on a cruise up the East Coast of Africa to Zanzibar and came back with three topazes that would have weighed any other woman down, and the unmistakable air of a woman with memories. She dropped into my father's office one day and apparently they had the sort of kidding, ambiguous conversation that allows a woman to boast of her own self-evident attractions without suggesting unfaithfulness to her husband. "Sonia's had a hell of a good time on that boat of hers," my father said, that evening, putting his feet up on a cane-topped stool that stood before the fireplace. My mother snatched it away from under them; nobody was ever allowed to use that stool for anything, so far as I can remember. "It's easy to have a good time if you can go off when and where you like, on your husband's money," she said.

"You should see how she looks. Must've had a wonderful time in that place—she can't stop talking about it. I think she found herself a bloke. One of the ship's officers must've taken a fancy to her."

My mother looked at him witheringly. "It's funny how everything she does is wonderful. Anyone else, you'd have plenty to say."

After a minute, she returned to the subject, interrupting my father's reading of the evening paper. "It wouldn't be anything new, I must say. What d'you think she's been running to Doctor Naude for all this summer? Don't you believe she hasn't had a fancy for him! Just give her half a chance! Slipped disk! Her disks are as much slipped as mine!"

"Of course she's out for a good time," said my father mildly, ready to pool gossip in a friendly fashion. "Doctor Naude? He's a good-looking chap."

But my mother had fallen into one of her mournful, resigned, martyred moods. "Well, good luck to anyone who can have a good time. What's there in life, anyway. So far as I'm concerned, I wouldn't give you a thank-you for all the men in the world."

Sonia Smith was no longer merely the artist, the beauty; she was a woman of the world. Her traveled air and her secret smiles gave her a kind of calm; with perfect detachment she continued to call Herbert "darl' "—short for "darling"—the way she had done out of habit since the first days of their marriage, when she had believed that all husbands and wives called each other "darling." Unfortunately, the way she pronounced the word, it sounded like "doll"; people had not failed to note how appropriately. Now it seemed that perhaps Sonia noted it, too. "Doll," she would say at some gathering, in her nasal, rich voice, "doll, don't you think it's time we were going?" And her large eyes were lowered over her smile, as if she watched its slow curve on her own face.

Then with violence presaged by the eruption of her talents a year or two before, something else broke out in her. She took to a love affair. Of course, it might have been true that she had had a shipboard affair on her cruise, and the bond between herself and Dr. Naude may not have been purely that of doctor and patient, but these adventures must have been merely a familiar experience with an unfamiliar partner; simply love-making, as she knew it with Herbert, with some man who wasn't Herbert. They hadn't reached her vitally; endangered or changed her. At last that firm and flamboyant flesh, at the equinox between bloom and decay, came to life at the touch of a certain man and savaged all the trappings with which she had counterfeited fulfillment. The studio was shut up, the house was silent, the two plain daughters, when they were home from school, went about lackluster as the nights that had made them.

Sonia spent all her time rushing to Johannesburg, going early and coming home late, or not at all. The certain man was, himself, nothing. Not a mayor, not a councilor, not a lawyer, not a doctor, not the handsome officer on a ship. He was the owner of a small dance band, and, wearing a blue matador jacket and trousers with a red cummerbund, he stood up to conduct his boys, or played the solo bits on a muffled trumpet. It was true that she *had* met him on the ship, or rather when the ship had come home to port in Durban, and she had gone with some other passengers to a night club where he was playing. He wore a gold watch and a fancy signet ring and she had bumped into him again one day in Johannesburg, when she had gone into town to have her hair done. She remembered those hands at once, coaxing the band. He and she had a cup of coffee together; the hands went about the table, passing her things, lighting up a match for her. What those hands, with the gold watch and the fancy signet ring, came to mean to her! She was utterly shameless. In the handsome clothes Herbert had paid for, she sat in the night club where the man had an engagement, alone at a table, looking at him. In the bright sunlight of a

Johannesburg summer, at eleven o'clock in the morning, she went with him to back-street hotels where you could hire a room for the day. She was seen, of course. People at home in our town told where she had been seen, bold as brass, and this dance-band johnny with a thin mustache, not lifting his eyes as he held her arm to cross the street.

At first she was triumphant and superb. She could call to me as I came up the street, "I recognized you right down the block, by your bandy legs, Joanie Oldfield"—the playful strike from the paw of the tigress, arising out of the rippling sensuality of her own magnificent body; not meant to hurt, but careless if it should hurt, in the manner of creatures who have nothing to fear. She must have felt pityingly irritated, in her love-wise sentience, to see a wretched little ill-equipped, self-conscious virgin stalking along on the high heels of femininity and desirableness, more like a woman made out of a boy's Meccano set than a living female.

But the pure state of sensuality could not last long. All the hounds of a town like ours were after Sonia, and they brought her down: her husband should beat her, divorce her, her children should be taken from contamination, she should be stripped of her furs and let loose without a penny, she should be this, she should be that; above all, she shouldn't be allowed to get away with it. Sonia had shown she didn't care a fig if she humiliated her husband and disgraced her neglected children; but I suppose she felt it that *they* cared, the people of the town. She could countenance what she did, but not what other people thought of what she did. She continued as brazen as ever, but she had the hectic, hunted look of one who is always listening for something.

Herbert Smith is supposed to have gone to my father again, and to have asked, "Shall I divorce Sonia? What would you do?" And again, my father is supposed to have answered, with the finality of wisdom, "You must do as you think best, Herb." They were two aging men, then, in their sixties; under their discussion of firmness and practicality and loyalty and the two children, they must have known that nothing had changed: the question and answer were the ones that had been exchanged twenty years before, never spoken aloud but understood between them, then and now—shall a man live? Really live, risking the taking of something not intended for him? To conquer, to be a Napoleon of the heart—if my father could not, did not want to quite enough to attempt this for himself, he wanted it sufficiently to be unable to try to stop someone else: Herb, his mirror-self, that other Shetland pony.

Herb, who had been respected and kowtowed to, but toward whom there had never been any real warmth (people don't often seem really to like a small man, as if his smallness in itself is a power they don't trust), became something of a hero in the town. Even in court, the magistrate and lawyers spoke to him with a special, deferent, gentle politeness, as if he were a very old gentleman, or ill. My mother would cross the street, specially to greet him. "Poor old Herb," she would say in a hushed voice, time and again. "Some people have to know how to take the cracks in this life, all right." She didn't laugh at his retreating figure, any more, and say, the way she used to, "Queer little body he looks, worse than your father—at least, if your father's small, he's in proportion."

When she met Sonia, my mother was cold and appraising; in any case, knowing her, Sonia must have known what my mother thought of her. Yet she came, at last, to my mother.

I had left school, but I hadn't got a job yet and I was taking extra lessons with my violin teacher, to fill in time. I came home from an early lesson at about eleven o'clock in the morning and as I ducked through the broken fence behind our summerhouse, I heard a sound from far back in my childhood—the sound of women's voices over morning tea. My mother and another woman were talking on the side porch, behind the glass and among the baskets of fern and begonia. I crept quietly along the side of the house, close to the shrubs that grew there, because I wanted to slip into the house in peace, without being called in to take tea and be exclaimed over by one of the ladies of the town. And as I reached the big Pride-of-India bush right against the porch, I paused to eavesdrop, thinking perhaps the women might be talking about *me;* I had a passion, at the time, for overhearing people discussing me—such talk, even a chance remark, made me seem an intriguing stranger to myself.

The voice, the other voice, was Sonia Smith's. I couldn't remember when last she had been in our house. I put down my violin case, terribly carefully, on the damp black ground, and, forgetful of myself, now, strained to listen. What did I expect? I don't know. But I felt as if I were about to make a great discovery. My mother was holding the floor; she scarcely let Sonia speak. She wasn't scorning Sonia, she wasn't accusing her and calling her a common whore, as she did when she spoke of her to my father. She was talking to her as if she *were on her side,* as if she were telling her how to look out for herself.

"Look ahead," she was saying, "for heaven's sake, look ahead, Sonia. You're used to a certain way of life, you're used to having everything your heart could wish for—"

"My heart!" said Sonia. "My heart!"

"Listen to me," said my mother, "you've lived half your life like that, with Herb giving you everything you want before you've even opened your mouth to ask. That means a lot to a woman, once she's not young any more."

Sonia said, "You know what I was when I married him. I

was such a kid. What's the good of giving a woman everything she doesn't want?"

"But you're used to being looked after whether it's what you wanted or not. You've got used to it and now you can't do without it, you'll see. And you're used to a position, Sonia, it's all right for two kids to go off and be nobodies, care about nobody. How long do you think it would last, in some cheap hotel or flat somewhere, washing your own dishes? How d'you think it would be to have the children come and see you? Or have one of them marry, and you not even knowing what sort of man he is? Having a good time is one thing. Herb doesn't keep you tied up. You can travel and enjoy yourself, and who's going to know if you have a–" (my mother, suddenly bashful, searched for a harmless-sounding word) "a friendship or whatever it may be with some man you meet? But you've lived all your life with Herb, you're not a child who believes in princes. Herb's worshiped the ground you tread on, when he goes one day, you'll be well provided for–doesn't that count for anything, Sonia?"

I had raised myself just enough to see in without being seen. I saw the woman in a tight silk frock, diamond clips shining at the neck, red hair statuesquely arranged beneath a big black brim, brilliant soft eyes, cheeks with just that look that rose-colored tulips have the day before they turn bluish and fall. "Vangie," she said. She stood up. The weight of her beauty was there, something she had been born with, like genius or a harelip. "You're a woman. Look at me. Remember me. Have I ever been the woman for Herb? Do I look like the woman he should be married to?" She held her arms wide and the rings shook on her hands. "He's trotted beside me like a puppy. I could knock him over. I weigh a hundred and fifty-six pounds. I'm five-foot-ten. I'm a woman. Vangie, he's too small, d'you understand, he's never been anything else, ever, he's too small for me, too small!" Her voice was a shocked, piercing whisper, but her face, as I saw it, full on, for a second, was savage, forcing my mother toward something she refused to see.

I got into the house. I pretended I'd never heard. My mother said to my father that evening, tightly, with private, complacent triumph, "Sonia Smith was here today. I told her what I thought of her."

My father stood in astonishment and curiosity. "Is that so! When did she come?"

"This morning. Walked in just as I was going to have my cup of tea."

"What'd she say?"

"The whole story, everything the whole town knows already."

"Did you put in a word for Herb? I hope you drummed some sense into her."

My mother shrugged. "I told her what *I* thought. I'm afraid women like her are beyond me. I wouldn't give you a thank-you for the finest man in the world." My father said, "How does she look?"

"Blowzy."

"Well, Sonia must be forty-two. Yes, I remember the first time I saw her, at the Williamses' house the night Herb met her, we drank her health because the day before had been her seventeenth birthday."

"She says she's thirty-nine."

"Well, she'd better not say that with me around, I've known her too long. She's no chicken. My, but she was a beautiful girl, then."

It ended, or rather ended by having no end, but merely was worked into the continuation of our lives. Herb talked of divorce but never divorced Sonia; she talked of leaving him, but never did. At some point or other, the dance-band johnny disappeared, to another town and, it was said, another woman. Others said his wife forced him to come back to her. Anyway, there were others, more discreetly managed, for Sonia, and in between times, she queened it about our town, blatantly overdressed now, growing fat, patronizing all our women, looking bored with and amused by our men, as if they were a local *patois* for what the rest of the world knew as men. Her daughters married two of them, and she outshone the poor girls at their weddings, in the shameless resplendence that she had passed on to neither.

She took Herb round the world quite a bit before he died. They went to Rotary conferences and other international gatherings of that nature, where Herb could be a delegate and Sonia could have what my mother called "a good time." I remember my mother saying, once, "She looks what she is." We were looking at Sonia's picture in the social page of the newspaper—she was on a trip to South America with Herb, and there she was, in São Paulo, with a frilly parasol and a wide skirt blowing in the wind, five rows of pearls round her throat under an unmistakable double chin, and her head tilted, smiling. I had married and gone away from our town, but I used to hear of Sonia's moves from time to time, from my mother, although I hadn't actually seen Sonia for years. After Herb died, she was left comfortably provided for, as my mother had predicted, and I suppose she went on traveling about a good deal.

When people sift away out of your life, you lose sense of the length of intervals between hearing of them; years sometimes seem like months. One day when my mother was visiting me, sitting with my third son, Barry, on her knee, she said, "Sonia Smith sends her love. I promised her I'd bring her Barry to see, next time you let me have him for a week-end."

I laughed, knowing that my mother couldn't conceive of anyone who *didn't* want to see the child. "Little children are hardly old Sonia's line, are they? I could think of more appreciative audiences to show him off to." My mother looked at me reproachfully. "Poor Sonia's always asking about you. It would give her such pleasure to see the boy. She hardly gets about at all, nowadays."

I had a picture of her, red-haired, ample, all color and white flesh, looking about her at the last year's hats of other women, as she entered a room. "What's the matter with her?" I asked, wondering if she had another slipped disk.

It was an ordinary horror, one of the three or four ends that await us all; heart disease or a cancer, I forget which. It was taking her slowly, with unexplained halts on the way, when she and her family—Sonia was staying with one of the daughters who was living out the life her mother had refused to live, in the small town—thought she might recover, after all. I discovered that my mother was spending a lot of time with her; she went there to morning tea, and they chatted and knitted together.

"Poor girl," my mother said. "You should see her; you wouldn't know her. Her eyes, and that wonderful skin of hers, all gone to nothing. Her poor legs, too weak to hold her. What a beautiful, healthy woman she was; you wouldn't have given much for the chances of the rest of us to outlive her." Oddly enough, my mother, at this late stage, had taken on a kind of attractiveness she had never had before; her hair, which was an untidy pepper-and-salt for years, had now gone completely white. She wore it very short and tinted pale blue, and her scragginess when she was younger had kept her figure slim and upright.

I said, curious, "What do you talk to her about?"

She looked at me, incredulous, impatient. "What d'you mean, talk about? What do women usually talk about—their homes, you children; Isabelle's got two lovely boys. Weren't we young women together? Haven't we known each other long enough?"

After that, I would ask about Sonia when I remembered; but I never quite believed in her, an aging woman, eager for news of other people's grandchildren, dying in her bed.

When I rang up my parents one evening, my father answered the telephone. "It's been a trying day for your mother, she's lying down. You heard about Sonia? Poor girl. Well, it was a mercy, really. What a tremendous funeral; took your mother and me half an hour to get the car away, afterwards. Yes; I remember her when she was seventeen. Naturally, your mother's upset; when you see old friends go . . . Poor girl. She was beautiful, you know, you wouldn't believe it. . . ." "Oh I know," I said, "I remember." "But my dear child, I'm talking about the early days, before you were born, the time I saw her at the Williamses' the night Herb met her. . . ."

A Thing of the Past

The house in Maadi was as quiet as it had been in the days when they were all out of it, going about their business and their pleasure; yet they were all there. Madame Achilet played patience behind the bougainvillea on the veranda and did not lift her eyes if someone walked past. Irene was writing in the big studio on the roof. Her husband Max was in the darkened library. Even when the children were home from school the great empty garden took their voices like depthless green waters swallowing a handful of coins.

Who was dead? No one—the old man, Achilet Pasha, whose wealth had made the wonderful garden, had died years ago. But the house was dead; the sort of life that had fed it was gone. Irene's husband Max, who had nothing to do all day, sometimes had the fantasy that he was the last white man left in Africa. He sat among the dim shapes behind the shutters and felt himself alone, not only in Egypt, but in the whole continent.

It was not true, of course, that the Achilet family were alone even in Cairo. There were a few others who had missed the exodus of the foreign community that had begun when the King was banished and reached its peak after the Suez Canal was nationalized; but these others were merely stragglers, and they were leaving one by one, month by month. The Alexandria Achilets had gone, and the old Pasha's brother. Of all the big and powerful family, with its French, Greek and Jewish antecedents, only Irene and her small family remained. "I'm a hostage," Irene would explain to infrequent visitors, with her pealing, fidgety laugh that ended or interrupted everything she said. She was a soft woman of thirty-eight, with the special liveliness of an inherited emotional temperament that has been nurtured in an atmosphere of indulgence and privilege. Like many people who have had it too good, she had courage. It took the form, in her, of the show of a refusal to change. She pulled a face at each fresh notice of sequestration; she shrugged her shoulders and laughed over her own efforts to help her children do their homework in the new medium of instruction, Arabic, that they had had to accustom themselves to since the French school was closed; she wore about the house the gay pants and clinging shirts that, other years, she had worn on the Riviera. She was no longer young, and the lines of her pretty, sallow face, with the big black, amusing eyes, had softened and sagged, like the small, voluptuous lines of her body. "Irene feels she can't go while she can do something for the others by hanging on," her husband would explain. Irene hadn't lost *all* her property; there was the house in Maadi among other things. She still had some influence and some connections, too, and as long as she stayed in Egypt she had the chance of getting a trickle of compensation out to her brothers and those other members of the family who had been completely dispossessed. The moment she packed up and left, of course, she would have to leave everything behind her.

It often seemed to Max, her husband (alone in the shuttered library), that, apart from the money, there would be nothing left to leave behind, soon. The old lady, Madame Achilet, had built herself a house of cards to shelter a shadow; the spirit of the children was camping out, without a home—and he, himself, and Irene? It was difficult to judge, with Irene. She was the third generation of her family to be born in Egypt. Even though she did not belong to Egypt—was part of that expendable, exotic life of the cities—she seemed to have been conditioned by the lives of the people, of whom she had never been in the least aware, to something of their acceptance of the passing of kings and palaces and the successive waves of conquering hordes. There could be no other explanation for her wry and yet almost cheerful, unnoticing submission to the silent house. She was writing a play, she said; she had always been writing a play, she had taken it up and put it down like a piece of embroidery, between entertaining, spending the summer in Europe and the winter in Switzerland or Luxor. It was hard to imagine that the play would ever be finished, or could hope to fill the long days. For himself, her husband was an architect, and as a foreigner, no longer allowed to practice his profession. He went on working at home, for a time; he drew plans for all those buildings that no client had ever wanted. And then this sense of freedom went out, no star but a child's rocket. He went to play golf every morning with someone else who was hanging on; a woman as idle as he was, who tried to attract him into the pastime of an affair. Then he began to follow the routine that looked as if it would last. Every morning after breakfast he walked once or twice round

Achilet Pasha's tropical garden, and then he shut himself in the library and pulled the shutters against the heat. Rolls of plans glowed redly, like tunnels in the dimness; they grew brittle as time went by, and the edges were ragged where the servant's duster brushed them. His own hands sometimes touched against them, too. He sat at the desk and smoked. Sometimes he read a little from the middle of any book taken out of the shelf behind him. He dozed. Idleness was a dungeon into which he had been flung.

"Perhaps we'll hang on long enough for things to be all right again, and everyone will be able to come back," said Irene gaily, with one of her eloquent shrugs. "Who knows?"

Her husband looked as if he hadn't heard, but behind his quiet, bored face he was experiencing a moment of passionate horror. They had floated like oil on the thin, poor life of the country—Irene, himself, all of them. Lately he had begun to struggle with a guilt like nausea at the surfeit of the life that he had lived. He turned away his head and swallowed, as if someone had thrust a piece of corpse-meat at his mouth.

Irene came over and picked up his hand. She laughed and her breasts lolled apart under her cotton sweater. "Come on, now," she said cheerfully. "Things just as unlikely have happened here before now, darling. It's not at all impossible, eh?"

Max Leonard was a South African and it was through the war that he had come to marry Irene Achilet. It sounded a pretty brazen sort of story, but it was a common one in all countries that the war touched, and at the time it had happened very simply, without much thinking and perhaps without any real volition on anyone's part. Irene had been married before, very young, to a young Frenchman. He was an archaeologist, and when he arrived in Egypt he had come to Achilet Pasha's house on an introduction from someone in Paris. Irene was eighteen, just back from school in France herself, and in that state of innocent excitability that is often the first and sometimes the strongest state of sexual attractiveness in a girl. She and Jules Sidon walked straight into a trance of delight in each other; he could not possibly have been expected to resist her and the trap she did not even know she had set was waiting to take him. It was impossible for them not to finger each other (she had to pinch the lobe of his clean ear, he had to feel out the bend of her elbow) in a kind of birds' dance of courtship, and old Achilet saw that it was hopeless to oppose the youthful marriage. They were married and Irene trailed off into the desert behind Sidon to love him at night in his tent. He had thought the world consisted of digging and studying what was dug up, before he was confronted with Irene, and now thought that it consisted of digging, studying, and Irene. All day she wandered about the digging site in a pair of Sidon's old khaki trousers, with her hair tied up in a rag of a scarf and her face oiled against the winter sun. She did not worry Sidon but sometimes he explained some shard or carved fragment to her as if he were training some new male assistant sent out from the Institute in Paris. In summer they lived in the house in Maadi that Irene's father had built for them, and often Sidon would put aside his cataloguing and writing and drive out with her to sleep the night in the desert. Sidon knew no human beings other than the ancient Egyptians and Irene Achilet; and then the war came, and all the others crowded in.

Sidon was called back to France and he went into the army. Irene stayed at home in Cairo. She went to meet him once, in Beirut, when they managed to spend two weeks together. And then for nearly three years, while France fell, while he fought now in this country, now in that, they did not see each other. The house in Maadi was lent to the British Army as a convalescent home, and Irene moved into a flat overlooking the

Nile. She wrote letters to Sidon, she drew up a reading plan for herself, to study archaeology, and she took her part in the elaborate social life of the foreign community to which she belonged, and which had received fresh impetus in the entertainment of the men the war had brought to Egypt. She was very young still, and soon Sidon had been away for a longer time than she had lived with him. She was terrified that he would die, but then the years went by and he didn't die, and her terror subsided. There were thousands of people living as she lived; it seemed to be the natural order of things that men should dine and talk and drink not with their own women, but with the women of other men, who, in their turn, were in the company of yet other women, on another side of the world.

She met the South African captain, Max Leonard, in the house of her uncle in Alexandria, and later, when he was in Cairo on leave, he came to see her. She invited him to dinner with other friends, they went out dancing together. The next time he came to Cairo on leave, it was suddenly quite different; he called, and sat stiffly on the terrace, and she did not know what to say. The old tension—the silent whirlpool drawing them to its center—that had existed so uniquely, so extraordinarily between Sidon and her: she felt it again, quite simply, with this man who wasn't Sidon. He wasn't at all like Sidon, she didn't feel any of the other things that she had felt about Sidon, the things that very young girls feel—but she felt this. She went away with Max Leonard for a weekend, somewhere unlikely—Port Said, of all places—and she felt contented, gay and lazy. There were many other affairs like it at the time; they were interludes of peace and happiness in the displacement of feelings that distresses people in war. They were sexual and innocent; and sometimes the partners became friends, as well. Whenever he could get away from the desert, Max lived at the flat with her. Sometimes Max indulged in fantasies about a future life with her, but they were not painful. "If I could take you to South Africa with me, I'd show you some things that'd have you gasping," he said, with affectionate reference to her quick enthusiasms. "I'd take you up the Drakensberg with the pack ponies right over into Basutoland, I'd take you to the Congo. I'd drive you round the Cape Peninsula, we'd get a cottage in a fishing village–" She laughed and wrinkled her nose. "I'd rather have snow. I'd rather take you skiing in Switzerland. Right up to one of the small villages. I bet you'd learn quickly."

When Irene's husband Sidon came back at last, Max was in the Western Desert, not a day's drive from Cairo. Irene and her family met Sidon and went back to the old Achilets' house for a celebration lunch. After lunch Irene and Sidon went into the garden to stroll and talk; it was the first time that they were alone together. Sidon, with his curly fair hair and his glasses that seemed to concentrate his gaze on her, as if she were some beautiful limestone head suddenly freed from the sand of the past, said to her, "Irene, I couldn't write and tell you. For the last eight months I've been having an affair with a woman in England. I must tell you now."

"Oh Jules," she said, "I know! I know!"

"Irene, what's the matter?" Sidon was stiff and pale.

"I've been having–I had something like that myself. I couldn't write, either."

Sidon was silent. He looked up quickly, aware, at the palm trees, as a man does when he has taken an unfamiliar turning and lost himself.

"I can't explain it. I longed for you, Irene."

"I know," she said.

"Was he in Cairo?" said Sidon.

"He's a South African, in the Western Desert. Not far," said Irene.

When he did not speak she said, "He's there now."

He still did not speak.

She leaned toward him, urgingly, and smiled. "Jules, don't let's take it as a tragedy. We're grown up now. It couldn't be helped, could it? We were such infants when we married. Jules, please; please, Jules, don't be sad; just smile at me, just once . . ."

He managed it, though perhaps it broke his heart; really broke that young heart, the moment of freedom from which—essential to attain—is so painful. From that moment on he began to live like a grown man, with the conditional instead of the absolute.

They talked for a few minutes, like old friends in mourning. They were calm, almost confident. Then Jules said, "About the flat—" "I'll give up the flat," said Irene quickly. "We'll get another one, and perhaps we'll get the house in Maadi back, soon."

"Perhaps I shouldn't move into the flat," he said, "for a few days, until you move out of it—don't you think?"

She felt forlorn. "You don't have to see the flat, if you'd rather not," she said, shyly.

Suddenly they felt sure there would be no divorce; they would begin together again, start right at the beginning with a new courtship, even.

"Oh no, it's not as bad as that." He smiled. "I don't mind seeing it."

Unfortunately he came one morning when Max was there. Sidon was staying in the flat of a trusted friend (neither Sidon nor Irene wanted the Achilets to know that he was not sharing the flat with her) and he popped in about eight in the morning to pick up some of his old civilian clothes. The South African, in pajamas, came to open the front door.

The three of them sat on the terrace, drank coffee, and

talked sensibly. Below, the smooth Nile bellied a little with the first of the flood water, like a great sail. Then Max left and Irene and Sidon talked some more. Irene told Sidon the truth, which was that she had sent for Max to explain her feelings to him, and he had slept the night, quite decorously, in the living room. Sidon knew that Irene could not lie to him, and he nodded in acceptance. Suddenly he said to her in French, which the South African could not speak—"But Irene, do you love him?" He watched for her answer kindly, keenly, shortsightedly, as he used to watch to see if she had grasped some deceptively simple archaeological point.

"I loved you," she answered in French, in the tone of something she was sure of. "I thought that was all."

And then he said, speaking English again, "Yes, as you said, it was all so different then. We were children." They agreed that Irene was confused and that they would not rush into a divorce.

But they were drifting to one already—unaware, really; helpless it seemed—and in due time it happened. After the divorce Max lived with Irene until 1945, when he went home to South Africa to be demobilized, and then he returned to Cairo and they were married. It was a very good marriage; Irene was perhaps happier in it than Max, probably because she was by nature of a happier temperament than his—he found life suspect, though he had not yet found it out, and was watchful of it. There was a lot of building going on after the war, and the good connections of the Achilet family brought him scope and success as an architect. Their three children were born to them in the house in Maadi that Achilet Pasha had built for Irene and Sidon, and they lived the rich and comfortable cosmopolitan life that Irene had been born to. Max was able to go to Brazil, Europe, and America to keep in touch with the work of his great contemporaries, and his natural inclinations, given international opportunity, led him to become a man of culture outside the special interests of his work. He went back to South Africa only once, in the early fifties. His brother said to him, "You're not like us at all, any more"; but he himself felt he did not know *them,* for they were preoccupied with a problem that he, with his coin collection, his Turkish glass collection, and his passion for early Japanese woodcuts, did not think of outside the daily glance at the newspaper columns. They were conscious of the fact that they were white men, few, guilty, and unloved, in a continent of black men; the small, warm, fusty context of home to which he had returned was discovered to be an exposed place.

It did not trouble him much at the time; he simply did not go back to South Africa again; there was the whole of Europe, after all.

As frequently happens in a sophisticated community, Irene's first brief marriage had become so much—to use her own slangy phrase—"ancient history" that the former partners quite often met in the ordinary course of social life, entirely without embarrassment. Also, as frequently happens when a romantic marriage has dissolved, the two who it had seemed would do only for each other had quickly found others who would do just as well. Sidon had not left Egypt; he had stayed on and married a nice girl, some connection of the Italian ambassador; they had two children who attended the same school as the Achilet-Leonard children—that was, until the French school closed down. Max and Irene would exchange any tidbit about Sidon quite unselfconsciously along with the other gossip of the town; when Sidon wrote an archaeological treatise that won him some French academic honor, Irene telephoned Lila Sidon to give the Sidons Max's and her congratulations. Irene always referred to her ex-husband by his surname, as if he were some public personality whom she had once met; she remarked to Max, "Who would have thought it?—they say he'll get a decoration from France one of these days. My poor father, how cross he'd be if he knew"—she laughed and pulled a droll face—"he was quite sure Sidon would come to nothing." Two years after Suez, the Sidons were among the few who were still in Egypt; like the Achilets in the house in Maadi, they, too, were hanging on, it was said because Sidon had just begun an important piece of excavation when the ban on foreign archaeological expeditions was enforced, and he was determined to wait for it to be lifted. Irene and Sidon's wife quite often bumped into each other at Groppi's garden, and one would pause at the other's table to talk for a few minutes about a concert, the children's progress at school, or other commonplaces.

Two years after Suez. Irene looked at her husband anxiously when he came out of the darkened library at the sound of the lunch bell every day. "What sort of a morning did you have?"

His face was stiff with loneliness, hours without the sound or sight of anything but his own thoughts. He cleared his throat and smiled. "All right." A moment later he remembered, and said, "And you?" She was off at once, with relief, in chatter, pouring herself a glass of sherry, stretching her short legs, yawning cheerfully; she had written four letters, she had telephoned so-and-so, she had read this or that.

One day she said to him, "How are you getting on with the plans for the villa? Can't I see them yet?"

He drew breath guiltily, let it go again.

Animation and interest, self-forgetfulness dropped from her pretty face; she waited for him to contradict her understanding of the truth, to hide it from her.

"I haven't got far enough yet."

"But three—six months. More." She waited, without hope.

"We won't ever get to Italy," he said gently.

She sat bolt upright. She was suddenly excited, in her way.

"Why do you say that? Don't you *want* to go? Don't you want us to have a house out of this place, in a country we've loved all our lives? Good God, you've always said that the one place you want to build yourself a house is on the hills above Nemi. . . . Why do you say that?"

"We're still here," he said.

"Why do you say that?" she insisted, ignoring him, her eyes challenging with fear. "Why do you say we won't get there? Don't you *want* to get out of this?"

He did not know how to answer her, for he knew he could not tell her that it was not just *this*—the life in which they were without privilege and were allowed to exist only under sufferance—that he wanted to escape; he feared the contingency, however remote, of a return to the life they had lost. The year when he had gone home to South Africa, his brother had said, "You are not like us at all, any more": he had come at last to understand what those men felt, few, guilty, and unloved, in the black men's continent, belonging not there nor yet anywhere.

Directly after lunch she raced upstairs to her studio like a schoolgirl. She did not appear until it was growing dark. "I've been going through everything again," she said, "all the papers. I'll go and see Delbanco again tomorrow. If we could only get some sort of security for my brother's property, and wangle to get Mama's account released, I'd let the rest go."

She was a capable girl, all right, and a good tryer. But it was no good. The money could not be got out; the property was in jeopardy. They stayed where they were, and Max actually did draw up the plans for the Italian villa, to comfort her.

And then one afternoon he was sitting reading in a cool, gloomy arbor of the old Pasha's garden when he saw her flash down one of the paths separated from him by shrubs and the sword-leaves of some rare lily plants. It always touched him to see her run as if she were still a young girl, unaware of her thickened, slackened, woman's body. He thought that she was probably looking for one of the children and he went on reading, but in a moment he heard her calling his name—"Max! Ma-ax?"—and he stood up and called back, "Here! By the pond." She had been out for lunch, quite an event for those days, and he had not seen her all day. "Nobody in the house knew where you were," she said, sitting down with her hands loosely linked between her knees; she had changed out of her town clothes into her usual trousers and espadrilles. "I couldn't have got very far," he said, with a smile. "How was the day?" She did not answer and gave him one of her deep, secret, intriguing smiles, two lines that had once been dimples indenting her cheeks. "Max," she said. "Let's go. That's all. Let's leave everything and go. What does it matter? You'll find work. It needn't necessarily be Italy. Brazil, anywhere. We'll live on what you can earn and look after Mama ourselves."

His heart began to thump very slow and hard. "D'you mean it?"

"Yes," she said, "yes. I've made up my mind. Let's go, Max. We've had enough."

Excitement, release, swept into him like power. Go, and never come back, never come back? he wanted to shout splendidly; but he remembered that this was her home she was leaving, this city, this house, this artificial tropical wilderness kept going by an intricate pumping system from the Nile, this pool covered, as if with a dust-sheet, by a wrinkled green scum of disuse. Instead he said, "Oh God, Irene, I'm sure it's the right thing. I haven't wanted to persuade you, but I've always thought so. It's best for your mother, the children, all of us."

She had the pleased, quavering-faced look of someone who

is trying to be modest about something big that he has done. "You've been so good, darling Max," she said emotionally. "You've been rotting away, in that library."

The next day he went into town for the first time for months. He made to himself the excuse of something he wanted to buy, but the truth was that he simply wanted to feel himself in the world, among people again. About half past one he went into small Groppi's and ordered a vermouth and waited with a sense of pleasure for someone he knew to come in, so that he could tell him: "We're leaving, you know." He greeted an acquaintance across the room, but it was not until his drink was finished that an old friend, Mario Peretti (it was his wife with whom Max had had to curtail his golf games), came over and sat down in the empty chair at the little table.

"So?" said Mario, eyebrows lifting above the line of his thick glasses. "What brings you here? What an occasion!"

"Have a vermouth, Mario," said Max, grinning.

"Okay. And why not? Certainly I'll have a vermouth with you. It isn't many times that I get a chance for you to buy me a drink."

"And what about at my house?"

"Oh that's not the same," said Peretti. "From the cellar it's not the same. It's not cash."

"Well, I suppose you've heard our big news," said Max, when their drinks had come.

"What's that?" said Mario, wiping the rim of his perfectly clean glass with a handkerchief.

"I'm sure Irene's been on the phone to Greta this morning?"

Peretti shrugged. "Greta was with Irene in town yesterday, but she didn't say anything to me. I haven't heard a word. What's it all about?"

"We decided last night. Mario, we're leaving. Packing up and walking out, at last," said Max.

Peretti drew in toward him across the table in admiring intimacy, smiling. "Is that so? So you're going? Well, good luck to you! That's the second lot I've heard about in two days. Did you hear that Jules Sidon is clearing out?"

"Sidon?"

"But Lila Sidon met Greta and Irene yesterday, and told them then. Came up to their table and announced it. Sidon's been given some big job—the South Seas, I think. He's going to lead an American expedition. They're leaving Cairo for good, too. She must have some property; they won't see that again. Shall we eat here? Are you going to have lunch with me?"

Max finished his drink in one long draw and stood up as he put the glass back in its saucer. "Mario, no, I can't. I must get back to Maadi, you know."

"But what for? It's lunchtime."

Max smiled. "Yes. That's it. I must get back for lunch."

It was true that he felt he must get back to Maadi. He must get back there at once. He drove as if it were certain that there would be something waiting for him there in the house, something that would—what? He did not know, but he was sure that he would recognize it instantly for whatever it was, when he got there. The slam of the car door was muffled by the heavy silence that hung about the house. A sprinkler was making shining runnels on the dusty leaves of the bougainvillea; old Madame Achilet must have been resting upstairs and was not at her card table. He closed the front door behind him and entered the big living room where only the two abstract paintings seemed to keep their swirling, changing forms in the fuzzy light that came through the shutters. He went softly and heavily over the carpets and as he was passing out of the room, he realized that there was something—someone was sitting in one of the deep chairs. He turned and went to her. She sat with her legs drawn up tightly under her, like someone in pain. "Max?" she said, as if he were asleep and she did not want to wake him. "I've found out about the formalities, we'll get away without any difficulty. The house may give a bit of bother, but that can easily–" He did not speak, but he made a movement to hush her. She turned her head and the light that sifted into the room round the outline of the window near her lifted her face out of the dusk. He looked at her, fully for a few seconds, but she could not see his face and did not know that he could see hers.

When he had seen her, he sat down on the arm of her chair and put out his hand; it touched her hair once, and then withdrew and instead he began to stroke the back of her hand. There was a strange silence about him, as if it were a struggle for him to do this. She was anxious to explain, asking, perhaps, for an explanation–"I was born here, everything's happened to me here. My whole life. This house–it's the house my father built for me–"

"Yes," he said. "Of course."

"It's all over," she said, and tried to laugh.

"Yes, of course," he said. He sat on, silently stroking her hand. He could feel the set of his face in the dimness. "Yes, of course."

Harry's Presence

My mother's never been much of a one for hospitality. I mean she'll have ladies to tea and bake a whole lot of cakes, but she won't have anyone to stay. I am always surprised to realize that there are some people who actually like to have relations and friends sleeping over at their houses. The fact that we have only two bedrooms in our house is presented by my mother as a triumph—"At least we can't have people landing on us to stay," she says. "We haven't got a room for them and that's that."

She's thinking, I suppose, of my father's relations. My father is a Greek, one of those Cypriot Greeks who run tea-rooms all over South Africa, only he doesn't run a tearoom, he gave his up when he married my mother and he runs a garage instead. George's Garage. Like most Greeks, he has a lot of relations. But as his wife, my mother, isn't Greek, he doesn't see much of them. "What have I got in common with a lot of poker-playing Greeks?" she says. "You go ahead and see them if you want to, I'm not stopping you." And it's true that he used to slip off on a Sunday afternoon to drink tea and play cards in the back of Chris's Café or Nick's Tearoom with my Uncle Christopoulos or cousin Nicholas. But the last few years, he's stopped going. "I don't mix too much with the Greeks," he tells people. "I don't know. They stick together too much. I'm not so keen on it." If my mother doesn't like them, he isn't going to give her the chance to say that *he* likes them.

Perhaps it is the fact that my father is a Greek that has prevented our family from having a real circle of friends among the other people of the town. People simply accept the fact that Greeks stick together, with their poker schools and their tearooms. And it is true that if my father has given up being a Greek, he hasn't been able to become something else. My mother belongs to the Women's Institute but he isn't a member of the Rotary Club; my mother plays tennis at the Ladies' League, but he doesn't play golf with the other husbands at the weekend. At weekends he sits behind the garage workshop, reading the paper and doing his accounts in the little paperboard office full of blue cigarette smoke. All that's missing is the cards and the company.

I don't ever remember my parents' having a party, and, as I've said, no one is ever asked to stay. That was why it was such an event in our lives when, at the beginning of this year, it was agreed that our cousin Harry should come to live with us– "at least until he gets on his feet." Harry is our second cousin, on my mother's side, of course–you couldn't imagine us having one of my father's cousins to stay, we wouldn't know what to say to them. Harry is a boy of twenty-one who never had any sort of a chance–I am quoting my mother all along, now. Uncle Eddie, his father and my mother's uncle, is just too decent a man to make good in business, and what with that fool Emmie for a wife, he hasn't been able to do anything for the boy. As a kid of sixteen Harry had to leave school and work in a sweet factory. He's been pushed from pillar to post all his life. She (my mother) thought it was about time somebody tried to do something for him. My father was able to be natural for once: of course we must take the boy in. He welcomed Harry not so much as Harry as as a sign that our family was relaxing into a Greek family at last; nothing could be more usual, for a Greek, than to include in his household a few cousins and nephews. "He can come into the garage," he said. "Why not?" "Well, we'll see," said my mother, pleased in spite of herself, though she hates what she calls "emotional displays" from my father.

My sister and I (Edith was seventeen in July, and I have just turned fourteen) remembered a dark-faced, curly-haired boy at a railway station; once, when we were quite small, Harry and Uncle Eddie and Aunt Emmie had come to the station of the Karroo dorp where they lived, at the time, to see us as our train halted on its way to Cape Town. But a stooping young man with greased hair and a sallow face, clean, but scarred where he had had pimples, arrived on our doorstep this January. He had a big brown cardboard suitcase with his initials stamped on it in gold letters. He had long hands with square nails outlined in black, and a lovely strong neck in an open-necked shirt. When he grinned he nodded his head as if he knew everything in the world. Although he was only twenty-one his forehead was divided into three layers by deep wavy lines, because he frowned a lot, too.

My mother, Edith, and I walked round behind him most of the first day he arrived at our house. The back veranda had been fixed up as a little bedroom for him, with green canvas blinds to roll down over the flyscreening at night, and the three of us stood about there while he unpacked his case, watching for chances to offer help, and listening to him talk. He talked a lot, although he had not seen us for a long time, and he really hardly knew us at all. He talked about his mother and his father and his various jobs, all in a grinning, shrugging way, saying the sort of things for which my mother always seems to have a remark to match—a way of talking that grown-ups often use: "Well, what can you do?" "Well, that's how it goes, I suppose." "What's the good of squealing, that's what I say." The clothes that Harry unpacked while he talked were terrible. There were silvery stripes on the socks and silvery zigzags on the ties and his shirts were the color of blue that could never go with his greenish skin. I caught my sister looking at the little pile on the bed just the way I was looking at it myself, and we both blushed. I felt that if she hadn't caught me looking at it like that, she might not have noticed how common Harry's clothes were. And I suppose she was feeling the same about me.

When my father came home he and Harry had a glass of beer together, and dinner that night had the feeling of a party, with everyone talking and Harry praising my mother's roast and teasing Edith and me. Then and there Harry began to call me Tin-Ribs, counting my ribs up my back through my summer dress. He started work in my father's garage next day, and in a few weeks my mother was saying to friends she met out shopping, "The poor kid's never known what it was to have a decent home before. People like us can't imagine what it means to him." And by the time three months had gone by, she was saying, "He's just like one of my own. Really. He's always busy about the place, doing things for me." It is true that Harry loves to do odd jobs, to fiddle with broken toasters and sewing machines that won't work, and faulty electric plugs—all the things that we'd always had to call a man in for, before, because my father never does anything with his hands. When the fuses blew during summer storms, Harry stood on a ladder at the fuse box and mended them by the light of candles held up by Edith and me. He grunted and talked in gasps all the time: "Ah, what a blighter. Wait a moment, just-one-moment. . . . That's got it! Yes, that's just about got it!" Some of the things Harry's started to fix have never got finished at all; my cuckoo clock, for instance, was taken to pieces and left on a cardboard box lid, under Harry's bed, and later a bag of Edith's that had a broken clasp, a jammed electric egg-beater, and two leaky fountain pens that he was going to make into one good one, all landed up on the same lid.

Harry's cleverness at fixing things, that my mother has found so useful at home, didn't seem to help him much in his work at the garage, after all, and although my father meant to train him as a first-class motor mechanic under the qualified man who runs my father's workshop for him, he quickly decided that Harry must become a salesman instead—my father deals in second-hand cars as well as petrol and repairs. Harry still wore his grease-monkey outfit at work, though, and sometimes when he felt like it, he would wriggle under a customer's car and fix something. Quite often he hit on what was wrong; once or twice he made a mess of a piece of work he didn't understand. "He's keen, he's keen, all right," said my father, "but it's better for him to keep on the business side."

At once Harry sent off a newspaper cutting that offered a free booklet about an encyclopedia of business management. He is always telling Edith and me that this is a scientific age and that you have to use the scientific approach if you want to make a success. He had already collected a second-hand edition, in five volumes, of the *Standard Encyclopedia of World Knowledge,* three volumes, with all the lettering on the covers eaten off by silverfish, of *Everyman's Practical Electronics*, and a thing as heavy as a doorstop and as full of fingermarks and splotches as a cookery book, called *The Home Encyclopedia of Medical Knowledge*. He is a great talker on healthy diet and clean living (I'm still waiting for someone to tell me just exactly what dirty living may be) and I suppose that somewhere at home in his parents' house, there must be a fat book about that.

Between Harry and me, his being in the house didn't turn out quite like the idea I'd had of it. At the beginning of this year I still had hardly any feelings except those I had read about in the books people give kids to read, and I pretended that he was the jolly, brotherly cousin that my sister and I had a good time with, but what happened in real life—that life that often doesn't seem real to me at all because what happens in it is not the sort of thing that ever happens in the books I read—was queer. I make up games where I talk aloud to myself, and I like to lie on the grass on summer nights with my eyes wide open. I have been doing these things for years and there is no sign that I am growing out of them, even now. Harry used to come up to me like a puppy, puzzled, poking at me with its paw to see what I was. "You're crazy, honestly, talking to yourself like that. I've never seen a big kid like you still doing that." I used to get up and run away, hardly able to see where I was going. In the mirror on the front of the wardrobe in the room I share with Edith, I would look at myself. I am a big girl. I am, as my mother says, developed, and I put my hair in pin-curls every night.

There were evenings, of course, when Harry and Edith and I fooled around together. Harry knows dozens of those trick holds where you have to make the other person do something that looks quite easy but is almost impossible. Harry is good at explaining: "Put your hand here. Look, like this. No, look.

That's it. Now see if you can make me bend my fingers. . . ." Of course we couldn't, and we giggled a lot. But even then, the evening sometimes dragged into light that real life of mine. My way home from school leads past the cemetery, and I often walk through it, reading over to myself the names on the tombstones. There are some names that make me feel that they are not just names, but people; I feel that they want to speak; sometimes I make up what they want to say. One evening I let slip to Harry that I like to walk home through the cemetery—naturally I didn't say a word about the conversations there. Harry got the look, happy, very keen but careful, that I've seen so often on the face of our old tomcat when he's just realized that a mouse has shown itself and disappeared again at the hole next to our sitting-room door. "You mean you go in, to wander about among the graves?" he said. "You'd better be careful you don't go potty, liking things like that at your age. Do you know what it is? It's a sign of insanity. I'm telling you, you can land up mad if you go on being morbid like that. I've read books on psychology and that, and I'm telling you."

"Oh so what? She *is* a potty kid," said my sister, grabbing him by the wrists the way he'd taught us, and they had a tussle, laughing and forgetting about me.

But the clock stopped, for me. What Harry said took me like a hand on my shoulder, found out. I joined in the roughhouse, so as not to think, but I don't forget it. Is that why I find no life like mine, in the books from the municipal library?

Having Harry living with us has made my sister's life much more fun. She and I both went to school at a convent (I still do) and this, plus the fact that we have no brothers and our parents haven't many friends, meant that she got to know only a few boys and scarcely ever went to parties or to a film unless it was with our family. But once Harry had come, there was someone my mother could trust. Edith and Harry walked downtown to the Odeon together at least once a week, and when my father had to buy tickets for the Mayor's Charity Ball, Edith and Harry went, Edith in a yellow net ballerina she made herself, and Harry in tails—my mother borrowed them for him. My father made a bit of fuss over the ball, asking whether a girl's first dance wasn't usually chaperoned by her parents or someone? But my mother said, "This isn't fifty years ago in some Greek village, you know. You haven't done anything to offer the girl any life, have you? Then leave her alone when she's got a chance to be like other girls for a change."

She has a way of making my father confused, so that he finds his anger like a broken stick in his hands. He walks away; he looks as if he can't see or hear beyond the cigarette smoke around his head. My mother says that I am like him, moody. But I go off on my own to lay myself open to clouds, stars, smells, wonderful feelings, and things I'm afraid of; he's like one of those creatures in shells on rocks, that you can break your nails over.

Until Harry came to live with us, my sister, my mother, and I did on our own most of the things that families do together. My father never comes away to the sea with us on our yearly holiday, because there's no one to leave in charge of the garage, but ever since Edith and I were small, we've realized that the holiday is better without him, anyway. As my mother says, he wouldn't want to lie on the hot beach all morning, or go for walks in the afternoon; look at him on family picnics—we always take a folding chair for him, and there he sits, out of it all, dressed in the trousers of his town suit, with the stud taken out of his collar. He never joined in games with us, when we were small; only watched us proudly. And I can remember, when I was three or four, standing a few yards from him, while he tried to persuade me to come and sit on his knee. He would wheedle, singing a song that we used to like as babies, and that we found silly when we were bigger. Since I was ten or eleven, Edith and I have scarcely ever kissed him. When we do, on his birthday or at Christmas, it's on the cheek. The smell of his skin is always strange to me.

Ever since Harry came, he's been doing for all three of us—my mother, Edith, and me—those things that only a man can do, in a family, and that my father has never done. But Harry hasn't been able to do, with my father, those things that men enjoy together without women—as I say, my father doesn't play any sport. Harry can play Klabberyas, a card game that the Greeks here like nearly as much as poker, and once or twice at the beginning he and my father sat down to cards among all those moths that come bumping into our veranda on a summer evening. But my mother discouraged this, for Harry's sake, because gambling is not the thing to teach a young man. So Harry gets the brazier burning for a braaivleis on Sunday nights, and Harry rows us on the dam, and Harry trains our Alsatian not to dig in the flower beds and knock people down. Harry's being here lets my father off family outings—he no longer need sit, uncomfortable, at picnics, he simply stays behind. Harry's being here saves him, too, those reproaches for things left undone—the fixings, mendings, fetchings and carryings that Harry manages now—that used to give my father and mother something to talk about at meals; she scarcely speaks to him at all, now. He's got into the habit of passing up his plate for a second helping without a word. At this my mother gets cross. "What is it you want? I'm not a servant, you know, to have a plate just stuck under my nose."

My mother is a woman who hears noises at night; she's often sure there is someone walking about in the garden, or fumbling with the lock of the kitchen window. She used to make my father go out into the dark at three o'clock in the morning, awakened suddenly out of his sleep. He didn't want to go, and used to come back before he could have had a proper look. She says he was afraid; and perhaps he was. Anyway, now there's Harry in the house, and Harry has a big *knob-kerrie* and a strong, hard-breathing expression like an actor as he goes from room to room, switching on all the lights and flinging the chairs aside, and tramps over the garden waking every dog in the street. My mother says he isn't afraid; and perhaps he isn't.

It certainly is hard to imagine what our life used to be like without Harry; there isn't an hour or a thing we do that Harry doesn't come into. All this year while Edith was still at school, he used to come and lie across the bottom of my bed before supper, while Edith sat on her bed and did her homework, and so I had to hide away my doll Vera, who was expecting a baby and who was married to a very rich, middle-aged man who adored her. In the evenings, Harry and Edith roll up the sitting-room carpet and push all the furniture against the walls so that there is plenty of floorspace where Harry can improve Edith's dancing. My father goes to sit out on the veranda with the paper beside him, as a rule; well, there's a perfectly good light out there, as my mother says. At any hour of the day you can find Harry in the kitchen, beating up a bowl of icing for my mother, talking and eating those biscuits out of each batch that our oven always burns. At weekends, for the past six months, he's been teaching Edith how to drive, and so, since then, if you see our car it's usually being driven by Harry. He's very helpful and ready to give advice about anything; sometimes, in the kitchen, he and my mother discuss how the garage ought to be run, and when Edith gets a new dress, she goes singing at the top of her voice down the passage to the back veranda to show it to him at once. He keeps a nosy eye on me; "Look at Tin-Ribs, hunched up in her corner. Why doesn't that kid bring any school-friends home? That's not the way to get on in the world, sitting around on your own." I stay quite still over the bit of stuff I'm sewing, like a chameleon I once had that, if you teased it, just used to cling to the leafy twig that it seemed to be part of to anyone who didn't know it was there. Then I slip out onto the veranda, where my father is. There's no danger that he would want to handle my thoughts; we don't seem to have anything to say to each other. Sometimes he says to me, "What's your mother doing?" or "Where's Edith?"—but that's all.

Last month, when Harry had been living with us for nearly a year, Edith wrote her matric. My father hasn't written matric, of course, and so he had a great respect for her at this time. He used to wish her luck before she went to school every morning, and in the evenings he used to ask her how the day's paper had gone, although the questions Edith had to answer were always on some subject he doesn't understand, like physics or literature. Edith would say, "It's silly to ask me about it, Daddy, you won't know what I'm talking about." But he would insist, putting on a shrewd face as if he did understand, perfectly; and she would hold forth to the whole table, not looking at him.

Because my father was feeling so particularly considerate toward Edith, then, I was amazed to hear him lose his temper with her the way he did, the Thursday before last. It was the day she was to write her final paper, too. We have only one bathroom in our house and we are accustomed to jostle each other there, every morning, in the hurry to get ready for school and work. Edith and I usually clean our teeth and wash our faces at the bath taps while my father shaves. This year there has been Harry to fit in, too. He usually leans against the door, talking, while he waits for my father to finish, but on this particular morning he was shaving at the same time as my father, peering at himself in the mirror over my father's head. Edith was in a bit of a state; "Oh, get a move on," she said, grabbing the toothpaste from me. My father's foreign face came out under the frills of soap carved away by the razor. "What's the matter, what's the matter," he said, soothing her. Edith was in her petticoat, because she didn't want her school dress splashed. She takes a lot of trouble with her tan, and the smooth nobs of her shoulders and her bare neck shone like my mother's furniture. Edith flashed—when she's impatient her skin actually does flare up, red—"Don't you *know* I'm writing an exam today, do you want me to get there late?" My father wiped his lips with his towel so that he could speak, but I was already grumbling, "Well, you don't have to eat everybody up," and Harry said, in a tone to cut the thing short, "I'll drive you to school, Edith."

"If you know you've got an exam, shouldn't you make sure you get up half an hour earlier, so's you don't have a rush?" my father said to her gently.

"It's all right, it's all right, I've said I'll drive you to school, Edith," Harry said again in a loud voice.

All at once my father turned to look at him. He said, "Since when have you got a car?"

Harry gave a snorting laugh. "I like that! After I've been driving all over the place for you for weeks."

"If you want to be taken to school, why don't you ask your father?" my father said to Edith. "It's my car you're going about in, why shouldn't you ask me? It's your father's car."

Edith's whole body heaved. "Keep your car!" she said. "Keep it! Keep your damned car! You think you're somebody because you can buy yourself a car."

My father started to shout. "Yes, I'm somebody," he yelled, showing the gold in the stumps of his back teeth, "I'm somebody, I'm your father, that's what I am. And is that the way you walk about? Look at you, half naked. You've got no respect. Walk about here half naked."

"Hi now." Harry came forward, calm and bossy. "Hi now, this is not–"

My father's belly is bigger than his chest. Above the drum of his trousers there is a deep wrinkle where his chest caves back from his middle, and you could see it through his thin vest. He turned clumsily and Harry stopped, and suddenly, awfully, Edith giggled. Then my father hit her, quite slowly. His hand didn't seem to understand the unheard-of message reaching it from his brain; he hit her crookedly, across the side of her face. He didn't hurt her at all and she scrubbed at her face with her fist in a dreamy movement. But my mother was there at once, in the open doorway. "What have you done to my child?" she said.

"Oh for God's sake," said Edith, "I'm not a child."

My mother is a pale, freckled woman and she hadn't made up her face yet but her eyes were bright and her lips looked swollen up, as if she were drunk. "What a brave man," she cried in a high, wobbly voice. "Oh go on, Harry, let him see what it's like to hit a man. Go on, Harry."

"With pleasure," said Harry. "Any time he likes, I'm more than ready to let him have it, I can tell you."

I felt them setting on my father; but I stood there, just as I used to when he was coaxing me to him for a kiss when I was small.

My father pushed past Harry, butting him with his belly, and then struck my mother, fumblingly, like a man beating his breast.

She gave a gasp that sounded almost pleased. She didn't seem to see anyone but him. "Now you've lifted your hand to me," she cried as loud as a bell. Harry had caught my father by the thick flesh of his shoulder, that never gets a chance to feel the sun.

"Don't look!" my mother screamed, noticing me. "Don't look!"

But I had seen.

It's over a month ago now, and it's all blown over, though it doesn't sound possible that it could, I know. In books, stories end when something awful happens, so that you believe that life couldn't go on any more. Harry's still with us, but he's taken a job at the estate agent's and he and my father don't say more than good morning to each other. There's a feeling in the house that Edith's being punished, though no one says anything to her, or really knows what for; she's got to go through all her clothes and mine and get the hems put down and the buttons sewn on, while she waits to hear the results of her matric.

It's a funny thing with me. Often lately I find myself imitating to myself the way my mother carried on, that morning—imitating her the way the kids at school imitate old Sister Frances in one of her tempers. I can't understand why I do it. It's mad, really. "Don't look," she yelled in that showy way, waving her arms at me, "don't look."

How idiotic. I'd seen. I'd seen, of course. I've seen everything. There's nothing left to hide from me.

An Image of Success

ONE

When I first got to know Charles Butters he was at just about the age and stage of a man's life that I am now, I suppose. It's queer to think of it. He was a man in his middle fifties, running the small empire of his own prosperous affairs, with a family life of a wife and grown-up children in the background. He was richer, perhaps, than I am; I don't know. It may be that he seemed richer, in my twenty-three-year-old concept of such things. I believe that early in one's life—often in childhood, long before the experience that might give the picture some accuracy—one forms images of various semi-abstract states, poverty, fame, wealth, and so on, past which one never really sees. Just as, in a room where a beautiful landscape hangs and there is an equally beautiful view from the window, one sees the view with the painted landscape always in the corner of one's eye, as it were, as a reservation.

Butters was my image of success, when I was a very young man; I don't know that I've ever been able to change it. I was the most junior of junior partners, then, newly joined, in the law firm, Hodgson, Lellow, and Veysie, in which I have now been the senior partner for many years. Butters was one of the firm's most important clients, and my uncle, old Oscar Hodgson, who was the *doyen* of the firm, had been his lawyer ever since he'd needed one. But I was no ordinary junior partner—I was the son of Oscar's twin sister, to whom he was devoted, and I was called in as the firm's latest acquisition, to be presented to and to pay my respects to all clients of standing. Since I was deputed to be an assistant to my uncle, I had seen something of the complex of files and papers relating to Mr. Butters' account with us—he owned a chain of country hotels, a sheep farm, all sorts of property in Johannesburg itself, and was director of a chrome mine—and I had seen his car, an American car of a make that has long since disappeared from the market—a beige and black sedan with the steel coils of a super-charger sticking out on either side of the bonnet. It always drew its little group of admiring loiterers, black and white, outside our Fox Street offices. I had seen, too, his hat and elegant pale gray raincoat lying in the outer office among the copies of *Punch* and the vase of Cape Everlastings, those ghosts of spring flowers. (Nowadays we have copies of *Time* and the florist on the ground floor of the building sends us up a fresh "arrangement" in a basket, twice a week.) But I had not seen the owner of the car, the hat, the elegant coat, himself.

When I was called into my uncle's office that first time, to meet Butters, he struck just the right note of worldly friendliness that was at the same time a little absent, as if the mind of a man like that had many interests and preoccupations to cut short his courtesy. He had marks round his eyes that suggested those eyes screwed up, looking through field-glasses at the races. His clothes were so expensive and so easily worn that one didn't notice them. He looked as if he had lived well without changing much; he was weathered and stained a little—his mustache with gray, his teeth with nicotine—that was all; like a well-printed book that even in its sumptuous case has taken color with time and the mere effect of the light on its pages.

"How long have you been at this game?" he asked me, somehow suggesting to me, by this one simple remark, that I had been put up for and accepted in some desirable club. I told him that I had been studying law for some years, but had qualified only a few months before.

"I've got a boy who thinks he wants to be a lawyer—this is his last year at school—my youngest boy. Lazy little devil. D'you think he'd stick it out?" "I don't see why not. You get fascinated by the stuff you have to learn, and that keeps you going." "Ah, but it runs in your family," he said, turning his head with a little gesture to Oscar, and, as they began to talk together again, I felt myself to be quite inoffensively dismissed, just as the schoolboy son was. Butters got up from his chair to shake hands with me before I left the room, and said, "We'll be seeing more of you, I'm sure. This firm's had my life in its hands for many years; I'm a constant visitor. Well, good luck to you—and see if you can persuade your uncle to overwork a bit less, now."

I saw him often in the next six months. I did some minor work on his affairs, delegated to me by Oscar, and frequently I was called into Oscar's office with this work while Butters was there. On one occasion, he was just about to sail for Europe, and he had with him a new camera that he had just bought. He handled it as the rich handle their toys, half amused by, half interested in its gadgets; to me it was the sort of superb piece of mechanism about which I had read, and whose features—lens, speed, and what not—I knew off by heart. When I had examined it lovingly, I handed it back to Butters not with envy, but with a feeling of elation, an expansiveness toward a world where the attainment of such possessions was taken for granted.

When Charles Butters returned from Europe, he spent almost a whole afternoon in my uncle's office discussing business problems that had accumulated in his absence, but I did not see him myself that day; I only saw, as I looked out of the window of my own office, the beige and black car, down below in the street. But later in the afternoon—it must have been after five, Butters had left, and everyone but my uncle and myself had gone home from the offices—old Oscar told me that he had found some papers that he had overlooked earlier in the afternoon, and that Butters wanted urgently; he asked me to take them over to Butters' office on my way home.

I was startled that my uncle should have asked me. It seemed to me that he must see the fiery impatience to be gone from the office that was setting my ears and fingertips tingling that evening. Surely my muscles were twitching their message of eagerness to be off—impossible to disguise as the will of a trembling horse? Poor old Oscar, that considerate and indulgent man, he would never, out of disciplinary or other motives, have come between a young man and his pleasure. It was nearly fifty years since he had been going to meet a girl; age came between us, the years wound round his responses an insulation through which the vibrations of my nerves did not reach. And because of this—because he did not mean to be inconsiderate, but was simply too old to understand—I suddenly could not protest. With dismay dancing wildly inside me, I took the packet of papers with a calm hand and left the office.

At that time I owned a motorcycle known as an Indian. In these days of Lambrettas and Mopeds, darting and skimming about the streets as lightly (and, judging from the way some of them are driven, as short-livedly) as dragonflies, it is difficult to remember how dashing the cumbersome Indian was. When it was parked, resting against the curb, it needed a good heave and a strong man to set it upright again; it had to be kicked into action through a starter-pedal that was as vicious as a crank; and it launched itself with a roar that left my ears numbed to sound for minutes afterward. But on that particular evening I did not have my Indian to speed me to Butters' office and then on to my appointment with my girl; I had left it for repairs, that morning, at a garage near where I was to pick her up. I had to catch a tram, and how conscious I was of the racing of the minutes against the tram's slow progress! I ran up the three flights to Butters' offices—although I had never been inside the building where they were housed, it was one of the biggest in town and I knew its façade well—hoping that he would be gone, that nobody would be there at all, and that I could push the sealed packet under the door and run.

Butters himself was still there. He unwrapped the papers, he thanked me for bringing them; he offered me a drink. It was nearly six. I suppose he must have seen the look of anguish that crossed my face at the suggestion; an absolute despair of impatience had broken out in me physically, in a sweat that dampened my hands and upper lip.

"What's the matter? You're not too young to take a drink, are you? You must be twenty-three or four . . . ? I've got a little bar of my own, here, it's very handy when you work late, on your own—" And he got up and went over to a small cabinet near the window. "Oh no—I do drink, of course, Mr. Butters" I said, "But I won't have anything now thank you—"

The doors of the cabinet opened, showing a snug and orderly arrangement of bottles and glasses; he turned and looked at me questioningly, and it seemed that they backed him up, stared at me like an audience, measuring the bought, always available, sophisticated pleasures of substance and middle age against the raw and trembling desires of youth.

"You're in a hurry!" he said, at once. "Of course! You're in a hurry to be off. Quite right, too, it's long past office hours. And I've made you late, bringing these things to me—"

"Well, yes," I said, running into a gabble of relief, "if you'll excuse me, sir—"

"Good Lord, of course. Forget it, man. But look, where are you going? Have you a car? I'm on my way now—I'll take these home with me and read them over after dinner—I can easily drop you wherever you want to go."

I felt quite giddy for a moment, at this sudden resolution of my snarl with time. "Would you? Are you sure you're going now, sir? If you're sure—" "We'll make up for lost time, for you," he said, hustling me out of the office.

"Now where is it you want to go?" Butters, settled in the front seat of the beige and black sedan beside his driver, turned to ask in a tone that good-humoredly suggested he would not flinch at Timbuctoo.

"It's not far," I said, from my seat at the back, "the Technical College." When it was said, it sounded schoolboyish; and I was aware of it—all my talk of an evening that turned out to begin with a rendezvous at the old brown building where young girls went to learn how to be typists and secretaries, and youths went to night classes in commerce and draftsmanship. But Butters gave no hint of being amused. "Right," he said. "The Technical College."

"The girl—that is, the two girls that my friend and I are taking out have a class there at four o'clock, and we always arrange to pick them up straight from class, you see."

Butters had the evening paper on his knee, and he said in the voice of a man who is reading at the same time as he is speaking, "Where do you youngsters go at this time of evening? Isn't it too early for the pictures?" (Cinemas in Johannesburg used to have one show every night, beginning at about eight o'clock.)

"We go to the *thé-dansant* at McDonald's Drift Hotel—on the Pretoria Road," I said self-consciously, not only because of the French word, but because this was in the nature of a confession. But he seemed not to know, or if he knew, not to be concerned about the stories current about McDonald's Drift. I went on excusing myself—or perhaps boasting a little—anyway. "It's become very popular this summer. I've been a few times."

I had been going there at least twice a week ever since I had had my Indian. On Saturdays and Sundays I played tennis at the houses of family friends with whose sons and daughters I had grown up, and went in the same company to cinemas and dances at the country club where my parents had been members since I was a child. But during the week my Indian took me into company and places unknown to family or family friends. The division in my life was one that has existed as long as there has been a middle class; for a time, I wanted something other than my own kind, and that other was sweet, to me, but I was too firmly and comfortably attached to my own kind to want to break away from them, or even to endanger their sound, homogeneous continuity in my own person. So the weekend and the week were kept entirely separate, even in my mind. One day, inevitably (and this, in fact, was what I did), I should go back to the weekend for good, and marry one of the daughters of my own kind, and never see again those other girls, the girls who, when Charles Butters' beige and black sedan drew up to the curb, stood waiting on the steps of the Technical College.

Their description may be surprising; they were not ladies of the town, or wild girls, or even sophisticated ones. They were, in fact, gentler and softer than the girls I knew at home, in whom security, family background, and indulgence had induced an independence and self-confident pride. These were poor, decent girls, whose timid yearning toward some sort of climate of gaiety and attention in which to enjoy a brief blooming had to be satisfied by their own efforts; no proud parents gave parties for *them*. They were ready to go with young men like myself, the sons of richer, better-educated families, to places where the daughters of richer, better-educated families would not expect to be taken. McDonald's Drift Hotel was one of those places. In an oozy hollow beside a muddy Transvaal stream that flowed only in summer and was much fouled by cows, the hotel had colored lights strung up outside, and inside, a cocktail lounge and dance floor decorated with Mexican hats and cardboard palm trees. Among the cow turds and the willow trees of the garden, there were thatched rondavels that were hired for the weekend by couples whose signatures as husband and wife in the register were never questioned. Their illicitness, boldly holding hands or even surreptitiously tongue-kissing in the cocktail lounge, where the smoke, the drinks, and the earth-shaking blare of the eight-piece jazz band had the effect of isolating each table into an ostrich-like illusion of privacy, gave the place an atmosphere. My friend and I drank beer, and our girls drank lemonade and would never have consented to share rondavels with us, even if we had had the nerve to suggest such a thing—yet this atmosphere was an assurance to us that life was an affair in which many rules were broken.

"There they are. Well, thank goodness, they've waited," I said to Mr. Butters as the car stopped outside the college and I saw the girls. "Thanks so much, sir, you've really saved my face."

"Wait a moment—how do you get to your *thé-dansant* from here? Are there buses, or what do you do?" He seemed amused at the ways of the young, and half reluctant to admit that he still felt some responsibility toward my plans.

With sudden snobbery, I felt it impossible to tell him that my girl would sit on the pillion of my Indian, and my friend's girl would sit on his. "Oh, it's all right. We'll go by taxi."

"Taxi!" he said. "Taxi will cost you a fortune, surely? That place must be fifteen miles on the road?"

"It's all right." I grinned.

He sighed, pulled in his lips a moment as if to suppress some objection or distaste, and, dismissing it, said cheerfully to me, "Call your friends over here. Tell them to jump in. I'll drive you out there. No, no, I mean it. Don't waste time arguing, now."

The two girls, who had looked at the splendid car with mild interest, when it drove up, and then with curiosity and bewilderment when they saw me in it, did not come forward when I got out of the car, but hung back, shy and puzzled. These two, June and Lily—there had been many, and many had flower-names or the names of the months—were typical; slender, with pretty legs (dresses were very short, then), rather round-shouldered, with soft hair turning from the fairness of childhood to a pale brown. My one, Lily, put one foot down toward the next step and then withdrew it again. Signaling, I raced up to meet them, and while I apologized for my lateness and explained that we were going to go by car, they stood smiling, looking from me to the car, distrustfully, helplessly, yet happily. "Where's Dennis?" I said, and they told me that my friend had gone to telephone my office. "He's as mad as anything with you," said Lily. And at that moment he appeared, from inside the building, and threw up his hands in a gesture of exasperation at the sight of me.

"All right, all right, change of plan," I said. "I couldn't help it, I had everything in the world to hold me back at the office. This Mr. Butters—he's one of our important clients—wants to give us a lift out to McDonald's in his Cord—look at it, Denny, isn't it a lovely job? I think we should take it because by the time we get to the garage and pick up my bike—and goodness knows if it's been fixed properly, anyway, this is the third time in ten days they've worked on it . . ."

In a moment, we were all getting into the car, and I was introducing my friends to Charles Butters. The girls, with the deliberate look of composure on their faces that I had seen when they had been confronted with an unfamiliar array of knives and forks in a restaurant, sat sunk between Dennis and me on the deep soft seats. Lily kept her warm flank, that my Indian brought so close to me, frozen away from my side, and she and June—always the quieter of the two, anyway—did not speak at all until we were out of town. Then, on the open road, they thawed gradually—Dennis and I had been keeping up an admiring conversation with Mr. Butters, about the car—and began to talk to each other in low feminine cadences that now and then rose into our talk.

In the Transvaal it is in autumn and not in spring that the countryside comes into flower; as we drove along on that early autumn evening, it was still light, and the girls gave little cries of pleasure as they pointed out the thick drifts of cosmos, pink and white, that lay blooming on their tall foliage in the high grass. "Oh isn't it lovely! They've all come out since last week!" whispered June, sitting forward on the edge of the seat to see better. "I wish I could just pick and pick!"

But Charles Butters had heard her; he turned, with a smile, an uncle who is determined that his treat-day shall lack nothing, not even his own inexhaustible patience to go through with it. "Do you want to? Shall we stop?" She was too confused even to answer; it was the first time this impressive-looking man had spoken to her. She slid back down into the seat as if she had been reproached, and looked from Lily to Dennis. "Would you?" Butters said kindly. "Oh, no," she said, unable to keep the affirmative out of her voice. "It's silly, they'll only die," said Lily with finality. But at this, June sat forward in the seat again, blushing. "Of course," said Butters sensibly, "Just pull onto the side of the road here, a minute, Alpheus. That's it. Out you go."

Dennis got out with June and helped her across the ditch at the roadside, but he did not follow her into the swathes of grass and flowers. He stood smoking and frowning, the panes of his glasses and the panes of a little house, far off, exchanging flashes in the last light of the fallen sun. The rest of us waited in the car; yet the cool emptiness of the veld, a plain divided alternately by the rich pile of afterglow and the sunken green of shadow, entered into us. We stopped talking. The cars ripped by on our right. On the left, a few yards from the road, the girl moved through the waist-high flowers like a woman in an enormous, rustling skirt. She picked and picked, stooping with the little pendant she wore hanging away from and then, as she rose to smile at us, falling back on the thin tender place, ribbed like sand with her bones, that, since her breasts were so small, she had instead of a hollow between them. Butters had thrown his cigar away and sat gazing out into the end of the day that was rising, a vanishing emanation, from the earth turning dark. Probably it was a long time since he had watched a day go; one could imagine him among leather-covered armchairs, in the lamplight, rather than outside, at this time of evening. He sighed, pleasantly. His arm and hand rested along the ledge of the open car window, and he blinked regularly, with patience. Perhaps his mind had fallen back into preoccupation with some business problem, far from us, who were so far from him in age.

In less than ten minutes the girl was back in the car ("Really, June!" Lily reproached) and we were on our way again. Close up, in a big, untidy bouquet that overflowed from June's lap onto ours, the cosmos lost much of their charm. The colors were rather wishy-washy, and the petals rather shapeless; the pungent smell of the bruised foliage gave away their origin as a weed, like a cheap scent betraying a lady's origins as a housemaid. "I'm telling you, they'll be dead long before we get home," said Lily.

When the car drew up beneath the strings of colored lights outside McDonald's Drift, and we had all begun to thank Butters, I awkwardly asked him to come in with us and have a drink before he went back to Johannesburg; "Please sir, just one drink. The one you missed because you hurried out of your office with me." I think he wanted to accept as little as I wanted to ask him, but he thought it might hurt a young man's pride to be refused. "Righto, in we go," he said stoically, and the thump-thump of the Charleston beat accompanied by the frenzied sandpaper slither of Charlestoning feet received us into the well-breathed, sweat-, liquor-, and violet-cachou-scented air.

We all felt a moment of constraint at the idea of taking Butters into our haunt, our McDonald's Drift; we were jealously afraid that it might not appear to him as it appeared to us. But this air, like just the right dose of the familiar drug in the addict's veins, at once induced in us four young people its familiar, erotic self-confidence, careless well-being—the arrogance of youth that we didn't feel at home. Butters sat on one of the hard, chipped, enameled folding chairs and sipped the whisky for which his authoritative appearance had even secured him some ice, while I talked to him, Lily sat beside me with her little bottom roundly outlined on her chair, and Dennis and June danced. Butters seemed to enjoy our pleasure in the place. "Well, you young people certainly have a good time, here," he said. "Just look at that!" He pointed to a young man who was scissoring round his partner. "Oh that's not much! We can do better than that. Come, Lily—" and I pulled her up from her chair and, on the dance floor right in front of our table, began to demonstrate. Dennis and June came round then, in the press of dancers, and the four of us showed off our practiced skill at the Charleston. "Bravo, bravo!" Butters said, applauding, and we crowded in at the table again, breathless and laughing. The dance certainly always improved June and Lily; it seemed to shake something loose in them—they were gayer and prettier; even June, who, to my taste, usually lacked animation to a degree that made her positively unattractive. When she sat down after the Charleston, with her hair flying and her eyes lively, she was almost as charming as my Lily with her bold smile and the touch of her boneless, artless hand that made me instantly want to crush it.

Butters finished his drink and left, refusing to let us thank him, and thanking us for showing him what he called our "night life." We understood that, like a grownup leaving the nursery, he would naturally have had enough of our games; and we really thought it remarkably nice of him, when, just after he had gone, a waiter came along and put a large mixed grill down in front of each of us, "with the compliments of the gentleman who left early." We stayed on until the band played "Good Night, Sweetheart," and then Dennis went out to grab a taxi while I went with the girls to get their coats. The bunch of cosmos had been left in the cloakroom, too. "These are yours, miss?" said the old tart behind the counter, dumping them disparagingly on top of the coats. "Oh . . . look . . ." said June, almost sulkily. She stood, lost, with the dead flowers in her arms. "I *told* you, didn't I?" said Lily. "It's no good picking them."

A week later, I was leaving our office building promptly at five o'clock when a uniformed driver came up to me and said, "Mr. Butters wants to speak to you—in the car, over there." Then I recognized the man, and followed him across the street to where, in the heavy afternoon traffic, the beige and black sedan was parked. Butters called out, "I saw you rushing down the steps and sent Alpheus to catch you. How are you?" We exchanged pleasantries, and he inquired after Oscar, who had been at home ill for a few days, and with whom he had had an appointment that had had to be canceled. "Are you off to the Technical College?" he said, with a knowing smile.

I grinned.

"Come on," he said, putting his hand back over the seat and flinging open the rear door with that energetic disregard for other people's plans that the successful often have. "My family are still in Europe and I'm sick of eating at the Rand Club night after night. I'll take you and your young friends out to dinner. Wherever you like. Wherever you kids want to go. It's my party."

I didn't want to go with him, and I was afraid that Dennis and the girls would resent his amusing himself, a spy from another generation, with us and our preoccupations. But at the same time, the other and stronger, expedient half of my nature—the weekend half—was aware that he had said that he had nowhere that he cared to go, that evening; and that, as a young man who was just beginning to make a career for himself in a legal firm in which the elder man was an old client, I had, arising out of my professional obligations, a social obligation not to offend him. Dennis looked a bit put out when the beige and black sedan, with me in it, drew up outside the Technical College again, but the girls—bless them! once they'd said they'd go out with you, they never argued or were willful about where you wanted to take them, the way socially acceptable girls were—climbed meekly and self-consciously into the car without a word. We drove first of all out to McDonald's Drift, because "I wouldn't dream of changing you youngsters' routine," Butters put it. Lily said at once, in an undertone to June, "Now no flowers." And Butters, overhearing, turned with his eyes screwed up in the way that, the first time I had met him, made me think of them as accustomed to looking through field-glasses, and said, "What's this about flowers?" "They all died, last time. Those cosmos she picked," said Dennis. "Ah, what a pity, we should have had a jar with some water, to put them in," said Butters, and June blushed as if she had been reminded of some piece of painful stupidity she had committed.

From the *thé-dansant* at McDonald's Drift, we drove back to town and had dinner at the one really expensive hotel, the one that set the standard for elegance in Johannesburg at the time. We ate a large and elaborate meal, and there was wine—wasted by the girls, who merely made a pretense of drinking it, sniffing their glasses like cats and putting them down carefully again. A trio played the tunes we requested, and Butters told us fascinating stories of his youth in South West Africa; the evening passed very pleasantly. June and Lily had never been in the Carlton Hotel before, and they kept looking round with carefully blank expressions, at the draperies, the chandeliers, and the gleaming spirit-burners on which crêpes suzette were being made before the diners' eyes.

The week after that, my uncle, Oscar, was back at work, and I saw Butters once, at the office, when he was on his way to see Oscar and we met in the corridor, but we merely exchanged greetings; there was no mention of the outing. Dennis and I took our girls, by pillion, to McDonald's Drift again on the following Monday, but our arrangement to go again on the Thursday was canceled because my Indian had developed its old distributor fault once more. When I met Lily for coffee at the Corner Lounge on Friday, after work (there was a trio there, too, I remember, playing musical-comedy selections in the light of fringed silk lampshades), she said huffedly, with the female triumph in finding others out in some slight to herself, "So Dennis and June *did* slip off without us, yesterday afternoon, after all that fuss about they wouldn't dream of going to McDonald's unless we could go together." "But what makes you think that?" "I *know,*" she said, nodding her head tightly. "When I went to June's place to pick her up on the way to the Tech this morning, I saw a great big bucket full of those cosmos standing in the kitchen. She didn't think I saw them, of course, and she didn't say a word. If they wanted to go without us, why didn't they say so?"

"Well, Dennis wasn't anywhere near the Pretoria Road last night, that I can promise you," I said, "because he was at home with me, in my house, playing bridge with my parents."

TWO

I went away to Durban for three weeks, on my yearly holiday, and the first day I was back at the office, Butters was closeted with old Oscar for well over two hours in the afternoon. At some point early in the interview, Oscar gave instructions to the general office that no calls were to be put through to him and no one was to interrupt him on any pretext whatever–I discovered this when I wanted to ask his advice about a contract I was drawing up. I thought nothing of this, since Oscar was far from well at the time, and I supposed he might have decided to save himself the nerve strain of interruption.

I was at my desk, going with what I hoped was a legal hawk's eye over the first draft of my contract, when Butters burst through my door without announcement or knock and strode in. It was as if the calm of the working afternoon had given way under pressure; he stood a moment, brought up short, while I looked up in astonishment. Then, without a word, he returned deliberately to the open door and shut it. He pulled up a chair facing me across the desk and sat down before me, knees apart, both hands resting on them. "I want you to take over the management of my affairs," he said. He spoke with finality, dash, decision, and, the exhilaration of having made it. "I want you to take the whole thing over from today and I want to start dealing with you, right away."

I smiled at him, idiotically.

"I've been arguing with that old man for two hours, and it's either leave this firm or find somebody else. I don't want to leave it after all these years."

The phrase "that old man" caught my ear in alarm. What was wrong with Butters that he could suddenly talk of the confidant of his adult lifetime with that sense of judgment–put himself, in three words, at such a remove from my uncle?

I could only say, "Mr. Butters, you've been with my uncle so long."

"I know, I know. And we've just had the biggest row ever. And that's that. Advice is something one pays for, one mustn't forget that; and one's entitled to take it or leave it, a lawyer must remember, however long and all the rest of it he's known his client. The old man's getting too old, anyway, I'd have had to be handed over to someone else, sooner or later."

Again I was curiously struck by the cruelty of his last sentence. I said, coldly and bewilderedly, "Oscar probably knows the law better than all the rest of the firm put together. But if you and he have quarreled, and you want someone else, wouldn't it be better for you to have one of the other senior men—I mean, I couldn't expect, really—"

He smiled, for the first time. "I don't care a damn for your precedence. You're a qualified lawyer and there's no earthly reason why you can't manage the old legal mumbo-jumbo as well as someone who's become part of the furnishings. And anyway, I like to think of you as a kind of mascot. You're connected with"—he stopped, and his mouth worked, with pride, with some sort of effort at concealment—"what has happened."

I knew at once that he did not mean his argument with Oscar. I said, "I, I? What happened . . .?"

He got up and pushed his chair neatly against my desk and in a no-nonsense voice, authoritative, ignoring in advance all possible reactions, said, "I'm going to marry June Williams. I shall divorce my wife as soon as it can be arranged. I'm going to see the girl's parents and explain to them. I want to be quite frank and fair with everybody. And I don't want to hear another word from anyone on the subject. I just want these things *done*."

"That's why! So that's why you've quarreled with Oscar!"—

and then I stopped. An incredible confusion came over me; he looked at me steadily and I could find no possible thing to say. "June Williams," I said, at last. And he answered, "Yes, June Williams."

I hardly felt I knew whom we were talking about; the surnames of the girls, those girls, were seldom used and did not seem to belong to them. Their identity, their small completeness was always contained in the one or two short syllables of their first, feminine names. June. Lily. (I turned to her, on the motorbicycle under the dark trees and my tongue went deep and thick down her throat.) It was Lily who came to my mind and my senses in a moment so vivid, so sensual, that under Butters' eye, I felt shame for the fantasy he could not guess at.

"I want to make it clear"—he spoke rapidly and without inflection, as a man does when he is repeating something he has decided in advance to say—"that although your"—he gestured, stirring the air for the right word—"connection with the whole thing is closer and more personal than is usual for a lawyer, you'll treat it just as you would any other piece of business."

"Of course," I said. I had never felt less like a lawyer with his client; I was a young man seeing for the first time the force, willfulness, and authority of maturity, used to taking what it wants.

He wanted to begin at once, planning the divorce settlement he would offer his wife— "I'm going to give her half of everything I own," he said crisply—although I told him that I couldn't possibly begin discussing his affairs until I had talked to my uncle.

Yes, of course; he relented—I must fix it up my own way and ring him when I was ready to see him. But it must be soon—at once. Before the end of the week. He obviously was not interested in how I might hope to go about his wishes without offending Oscar, or seeming to presume before my other superiors in the firm. He did not care about me or anybody else. He was in love, and other people did not exist for him; he was ready to buy them off, all of them, impatiently—his old friend Oscar, me, his wife—everybody.

He said, suddenly charming in the old way, at the door, "Well, I don't really blame you for being a bit bowled over. Fix things up. I don't want to go to a new crowd."

But he spoke to me as Dennis might have, or any of my other friends; and I understood why he called Oscar "that old man," now.

When he was gone I was seized by what I suppose was the first experience of melancholy in my life. I felt unaccountably sad and resentful; a strange, becalmed state. What might have been expected to astound me—the spectacle of a middle-aged, solid man ready to throw over his established life for a poor little girl young enough to be his daughter—glanced off my mind. An event finds a different target in each of those whom it concerns; this was a direct hit on the nerve of my adulthood; that state of accepted compromise with moral and social mores that marks the boy from the man. Charles Butters was stretching out his hand and taking what had been agreed (between myself and that order of society in which I wanted my place) must be forgone; that small, sweet, wild apple that was not for daily consumption. He was making the delightfully inconsequent, of consequence; he was plucking the one-day lily. (O my Lily! Who would ever give me the promise that I found in that wet, soft, secret throat?) He was breaking the rules, and it seemed to me, in my sullenness, that it was true—it would be possible, after all, to talk to one of those girls somewhere else than in a teashop or a dance hall or against the wind rushing by on the motorbike; to find some communication with them that would not echo back from the meagerness of their background; to love, instead of to amuse oneself with, one of them. I was a middle-class snob and a coward, myself; but I felt myself a martyr. I was filled with regret; I had already renounced what *he* was about to get.

My uncle Oscar—that old man—looked me over as if he had just learned of some physical characteristic of mine that he had never noticed before. He said, "What can we expect of this girl?"

I felt as though, indeed, I were to blame.

"Since you're the one who knows her, perhaps you can be of some use." He was a man with a fall-away chin and tufted terrier's eyebrows that remained reddish, even though his hair had been brown and what was left of it was white. He had the patient, preoccupied eyes of old doctors and lawyers.

"She's harmless," I said. He lifted his eyebrows and his glasses shifted on his nose.

"Oscar," I said, "it's no good being cross with me. He gave me and my friend a lift, one night, when we had two girls with us, that's all."

He sat thinking; his mild weak-looking face belied all the rules of physiognomy—he was a strong-minded man and for more than forty years his mind had raced like a sheep dog, patient, vigilant, full of tricks for getting strays accepted back into the fold.

He never apologized; he simply forgot that he had ever given occasion for apology; his mind was already somewhere else. "She's under age," he said. "Is there any chance that the parents might stop her? Or are they the sort who'll be dazzled by Butters' bit of cash, never mind his age?"

"I've never seen her parents. I don't know."

He nodded his head to show that he was reminded that these were not the sort of girls to whose homes one went.

"She's a terribly quiet, ordinary little girl," I said. "She's not the sort—" He raised his hand, to show it didn't signify. Talking about the girl, about June Williams, wonder and curiosity began to push up through my preoccupation with my own feelings. Mr. Butters and June Williams! "It's amazing!" I said. "For the life of me, I can't imagine how it could come about! Why, she'd be terrified to say one word to a man like Butters! It's crazy!" He punctuated my sentences with slow confirmatory movements of his head, beating time to an old tune. "They're just girls we take to dance halls, a new one every few weeks, and they're all the same—" How easy it was to talk, and how little was said! Like the clap of a hand, a few plain sentences, and they scuttled, poor little girls, back to their mouseholes.

"It's pointless asking ourselves why," said Oscar, "because we'll only get a half-answer—like putting it down to his age and his glands—that we can't do anything about, and the other half we'll never know will be the one we might have worked on. All I want is to save him from the worst consequences of the reasons why he wants to do this. If she's a quiet girl, as you say, then it's worse. If it were some flighty piece out for a good time, he might be persuaded to string it out, for a while—we could delay the divorce without his knowing—and he might get to the stage where he'd had enough of her. But from what you tell me—a little girl . . . That's much worse. Of course he'll marry her. Unless *she* stops him."

"I can't believe that she'd want to marry him."

"Perhaps she's got no choice," he said. "Now look, the one thing you might be able to do"—the slightest emphasis on the "you" showed a momentary return to the feeling that I was in some way to be blamed—"you could have a talk to the girl and find out, just as a friend, how she really feels about this business."

I experienced one of those moments that come to one quite inexplicably, when surroundings as familiar as one's own skin suddenly appear at once with great immediacy, as they would be seen for the first time, and also with the prescient depth of all those eyes that have taken them in in the past. The huge desk, worn away by touch at the corners, like stone, with its lichen-green smoothness of leather inlay; the brass hand that had withheld from so many staring scrutinies the papers that documented so many lives; the brown plush curtains and the brown carpet that had absorbed so many voices, the glass-fronted bookcases and the reproductions of illustrations to *Sketches by Boz* that had taken on their membrane-thin sheen the shapes of so many heads, transparently superimposed against heavy books and the outline of pictures; the trapped sunlight holding a sediment of dust. So much remained in that room forever, rose, perhaps, when the door opened, and sank again, without getting out; if a wall were knocked down there one day it would all escape in a pouf!—like the past from a broken tomb.

"But I can't," I said, "I can't. That's the one thing Butters has warned me he won't have." At once I realized that what I had just said implied the assumption that already I, and not Oscar, was acting for Butters, whereas, in fact, I had not yet had the courage or found the right moment to broach the subject of the change Butters wished to be made. "Uncle Oscar," I blurted, falling back to the childish form of address, "I don't know what to do about this idea Butters has that he wants *me* to be his lawyer now—did he tell you—it's impossible—"

Oscar made an impatient movement in his big, pendulous throat, like the throb of a bullfrog. "It's of no concern whatever whom he thinks of as his lawyer. What on earth does it matter, if he'd rather talk to you than hear what I think of what he's doing? If he wants it that way, let him have it. I'll have to go on looking after him as I've always done. The point is that he's got to be seen through this mess, whether he likes it or not."

Lily saw what had happened as part and parcel of June Williams' defection as a friend. "All the time you were away, we hardly saw her. Gee, I didn't know what had come over her; I used to go there to fetch her to the tram in the morning, and she'd be waiting at the gate looking as if she'd seen a ghost. We went to McDonald's a few times, but she never came with. At lunch time she'd sit there looking at me over her sandwiches as if she was frightened I'd eat her. And not a word to me. Just like that time with those flowers. *He* must have taken her to get them."

We sat awkwardly, facing each other under the orange light of the Corner Lounge; we had never really talked, only chattered and laughed between dances, but it was the communication that we had had, beneath that, that seemed to have died out.

And it was true that nothing was ever the same, with those girls, after Butters decided to marry June Williams. The easy, happy relationship—not so much irresponsible as without responsibility, for to be irresponsible implies a past and a future to which responsibility is owed, and our relationship with the girls was free of the continuity of our ordinary lives—this lightfooted relationship was hobbled, from then on, and walked with one foot heavily on earth, in the adult world of fate and decision. During the months when Oscar and I were occupied with the drawn-out difficulties of Butters' divorce and remarriage, those girls, McDonald's Drift, and even my Indian, faded slowly into the firmer stuff of my life, the way a painted gauze curtain, on the stage, disappears under strong lights into the scene already set behind it. Lily herself passed her 120-words-a-minute speed test and got a job in the office of a suburban garage. There was a scandal that temporarily closed down McDonald's Drift Hotel. And it was about this time that I sold my Indian and bought a small Austin; about the same time as I began to take out a girl who couldn't be expected to race around on the back of a motor-bicycle. She was a girl who played tennis at the country club and who now extended my weekend interests into the week, until, indeed, such time as they became one and the same.

Opposition to the Butters marriage came from what was to me an unexpected quarter. The wife gave in with no fight at all; it is a common phenomenon, with which I have become familiar in my long years of legal practice, that the "good" wife who has given her husband no trouble in their marriage is usually quite easy to divorce, whereas the troublesome woman, who has herself threatened the safety of the marriage at times, is the one who, when her husband wants to give her the divorce she has seemed to be inviting, does not want to let him get free of her. I don't know what the first Butters marriage was like; I supposed that neither Butters nor his wife had given it any thought for years—it was simply the state in which they lived and expected to live, quite comfortably, for the rest of their lives. His anxiousness to provide for her particularly generously was more than a natural and inevitable guilt at abandoning her in middle life; clearly he felt that she was a person who had done him no harm. I met her only once, on the occasion on which she had to attend a conference between her lawyers (Butters had insisted that she have the services of a sound firm, to take care of her interests and the investments he was handing over to her), Butters, and us. She was a big woman, quite nice-looking, with neatly curled graying hair, young eyes, and a matron's body all weighted to the front; she wore the sort of diamond rings that were obviously her engagement ring and a ring inherited from grandmother or mother, reset by a modern jeweler, rather to her bewilderment, in the cubist-inspired shapes that were beginning to be fashionable at the time. To every request for her opinion, or her preference, she answered, "If it is usual," or, "I don't mind," like a patient undergoing a course of treatment to which he has submitted, but whose progress he does not understand.

It was the parents of June Williams who flatly refused to permit the marriage, and their reason was extraordinary. They did not object to the fact that Charles Butters was more than thirty years older than their daughter, they did not care that he was divorcing his wife and leaving his family for her. Their sole objection to him was that he was the owner of licensed hotels with bars—they would have nothing to do with someone who sold spirits.

That was what they told him when he drove, alone and determined, to see them in the semi-detached house in Brixton where they lived. The beige and black sedan, that had cost more than any house in the mean street, rested outside the broken gate; a cat went to sleep under it, and when Butters drove away again, he killed it. He came straight to our offices and I remember that as he entered my office and looked for somewhere to put down his hat, he said, "I've just run over a cat. The first thing I've ever killed in all my years of driving—you know I had my first car in 1921? It was lying under the car and I didn't know. Just felt the left back wheel go over something." He was still holding the hat, and I took it from him and put it on a chair. He stood in the middle of the room for a moment, as if to sit down would be to indicate to himself a decision. Then he said, "Well—" and sat heavily on the chair before my desk. "Peter"—he smiled as he spoke, but I could see that his mood was serious, even reckless—"The girl's mother and father won't have me so long as I own hotels. Can you believe it? They belong to some Bible-thumping sect or other. There's a 'Jesus Saves' notice in the front window of the house. They won't give their daughter to a man who 'does the work of the devil, selling drink'—the woman said that."

For a moment, I had the faint hope that what he had just experienced of June Williams' background would jolt her out of the focus in which he saw her—romantic and charming, fond of flowers and kisses—a young wife. This latest development must surely make her, along with her dreary family, seem ridiculous in the eyes of a shrewd businessman and investor like Butters. Selling drink, indeed! All Butters dealt in, at his stage of success, was shares and transfers and directorships. Did they imagine him behind the counter with a bottle of gin in one hand and a bottle of *dop*—cheap Cape brandy—in the other?

"Exactly how long is it before she comes of age?" I asked.

He turned on me, almost in fear. "That's out of the question," he said, violently. "Three years, something like that. I'm going to marry her *now*."

"Well, you must get round them. That's all. Nothing else for it."

He thought a minute. He drew the fingers and palm of his hand together over his closed eyes, meeting in pressure at the bridge of his nose. "They—won't—come—round." There was silence, and the feeling of tension that comes to a room where someone's mind is racing, steeplechasing, skimming and bounding.

I waited. Once again I felt, I'm too young for Butters; that's why he wanted me, because he wants to go against himself, and he can't face the reminder of the sight of someone strong enough to stop him.

He made a sudden, swift, vigorous movement toward me, across the desk, the movement of a young man. "I'll sell the hotels"—he spoke as if he had grimly outbidded a tough business opponent in some deal—"I'll sell the lot. To the devil with the devil's work!" But I could see that his sarcasm was directed not so much at the Williamses with their tracts and their hell-fire, as at himself, for having been content so long to spend his life making money and finding nothing in it worth more than money to him.

Butters had begun the ordeal of freeing himself and making his astonishing new marriage in a deliberately calm, controlled manner, determined, apparently, to avoid making a fool of himself, both to himself and others, in the special way in which a man often does when he kicks aside the years and falls in love with some girl whom really he should see in the image of a daughter. What was sad, funny, and distasteful about his situation he seemed sure that, by the exercise of matter-of-factness and good taste, he could escape. But the situation took its revenge on him. Like the man in the fairy story who, once he has put on a certain pair of shoes, is compelled to dance them to pieces, he had to cut the capers of his passion. He, who had conducted his business life by an inflexible rule of patience and negotiation, would have nothing to do with either. He wanted everything hurried up, swept aside, done *now*. He lost his temper too quickly, made it up again exaggeratedly, and, in my office, never looked as if he were there to stay for an hour, but always as if he had just come and were at the same time just about to leave. He sold the hotels at not too bad a price, considering the haste with which he accepted the very first offer for them. He settled, as he had said he would, half of everything he owned on his wife. Oscar was very displeased about this. "I don't like the firm to be party to a bad settlement. The woman is provided for far in excess of her needs. It's bad enough for a man to be making a foolish marriage, he doesn't have to cut his income in half at the same time." But I remembered that Butters had said from the beginning that he wanted to be "frank and fair with everybody," and I came to understand that what he meant by this was that he was ready to stop up the mouths of the gods with the size of his offerings.

He never brought June Williams to the office, while the divorce was proceeding; but the day the decree was made final he said to me, unable to keep out of his voice the pleasure of being able to talk of the girl openly, "I'll bring June in on Monday to sign the ante-nuptial contract."

Again I felt, after many months, a stab of unreality—June Williams; she was a fact lost sight of in the succession of legal processes she had set in motion. And, oddly enough, I saw her, that same day, for the first time since Butters had told me he was going to marry her. I was passing the post office in Rissik Street on my way to a lunch appointment with a client, and there she was coming down the steps. She was putting something into her bag and as she closed it she looked down and saw me, across all that had happened since we had met last. She came down to me as if I had summoned her. I knew that this was the last time I should speak to her in the context of McDonald's Drift, the last time before her marriage and my professional capacity would create a new context to which we both should have to pay a certain due of silence. I forgot about Butters—this one last time it didn't seem to have anything to do with Butters—and I said to her curiously, in the gray embrasure of the steps, where a big pigeon dropped

to rest beside her, and her eyes followed it, "Are you really going to marry him?" And she said, caught in the dreamlike honesty of the off-guard moment between us, "He's so kind. He's so wonderful to me, what can I do?" We saw his generosity, his kindness and consideration—an enormous parcel that had been delivered into her hands, that had been small and empty, destined for the typewriter, and had not expected any sort of abundance to rest in them.

I could not help being surprised to see that she looked just as I had thought she looked; when something extraordinary happens to someone one has always thought of as ordinary, one feels one must have missed some clue that was there all the time. I saw the pendant on her neck, just as it had been the day she bent picking cosmos on the Pretoria Road.

"Do you love him?" I asked. Automatically, she was shocked, she blushed as if I had asked her whether she was in love with the principal of the Technical College, or an employer with whom she had had an interview for a job. And then she realized that the question was not wild, that it actually did have bearing on her own life and possibilities. Again she told the truth. "I don't know," she said, as if we were talking about something neither of us could have experienced, "I don't know what people feel. I—I don't know."

THREE

They were married.

Lawyers usually see most of their clients at times of crisis—misfortune, good fortune, and change make them frequent visitors to lawyers' offices. While their lives are uneventful, they come only occasionally, on routine matters. Charles Butters, with his complex investments, usually had to see us once or twice a month, but even he sometimes had stretches of six weeks or two months when there was no business to be done between us. He bought a house, and we arranged the deed of sale for him. June Williams—or rather June Butters—had two children in just about the minimum time this can be accomplished, and we changed his will in accordance with his elation at these events. Just after the birth of the second boy, he brought her to my office to make a will of her own, and I saw that she had grown up in the sudden and only way in which girls of her kind can—she had changed from a child to a mother. The milk in the now full breasts of her small body was a sap that had pushed the growth of her personality about as far as it would go. She had rounded gently out into concern about what her children ate, how they behaved, and what they wore. She seemed quite unspoiled by the ease and comfort of her life with Butters, and far from wanting to squander his money, was rather distrustful of it, as if she could not believe that it was a factor in his control, rather than in control of him.

He was not as rich as he had been, of course. He was not even as rich as he had been when he had married her, two or three years before. With the money from the sale of his hotels, he had bought two copper concessions in Northern Rhodesia. He was an extremely knowledgeable businessman and there seemed no reason to doubt that he was onto a good thing. But as the twenties turned into the thirties, the demand for copper fell so low that Rhodesian copper mines closed one by one; the miners came back to South Africa to look for work, and the mining towns were left to ghosts and red ants. (During the Second World War, of course, the industry came alive again and the copper boom opened up the whole of Northern Rhodesia—but by then the price of copper was of no concern to Butters.)

Butters was shaken by this reversal; it was as if the qualms that he did not have when he sold his hotels came to him now with double force, when the proceeds of that hasty decision to sell had been lost. He became uneasy about all his investments, and could not seem to let them alone. Perhaps there is a balance of power in a man's dealings with money that must not be disturbed; once he had lost the hotel money in copper, he felt compelled to change the pattern in accordance with the gaping loss. He sold the chrome mine, and put the money into financing light industry, which he did not understand. When the business did not go well, he sold some property in order to provide fresh capital. For a time, he was carried along on the stimulus of the feeling that he was going to make a second fortune for himself, in a new field. Hadn't he made a new life for himself, with a young wife and a family of babies? What was to stop him doing the same thing in finance? And certainly, the success of his marriage must have been a source of confidence in outside chances, to him.

June Williams was content with him, that was clear. The children were beautiful and in a year or so there was another, a girl. She was born just about the time that Butters became impatient with the results of his first venture into light industry, and, selling the firm he had bought, bought another and larger one in its place. To do this, he had to sell another large property. The sale of this property was the last thing Oscar fought against, before he died. "What is that man afraid of?" he said. "Does he think because he's made changes in his life, nothing else will stand?" But I was inclined to be on Butters' side about this sale—in my own life, I was beginning to get the feel of money-making—I thought that Butters, whose needs were expanding rather than static, despite his age, should stake something on the newest phase of the country's development, secondary industry.

Oscar died. The partner next in seniority in the firm moved into his place, and I inherited the illustrations to *Sketches by Boz* and, among other responsibilities, the full control of Butters' affairs. I felt quite equal to all these things, by then. I was married and had a son of my own and was building a house for a family to grow up in. I was at that stage of life when it seems that all of life may be contained in that well-planned house which, after all, has a place for everything, from the cupboard for golf-clubs, under the stairs, to a safe holder for old blades, in the bathroom. There seemed no reason why life should not be this measured cup, poured to a decent level, without mess, by a steady hand.

Secondary industry flourished all right, but Charles Butters' ventures didn't. He lost the scent of money, and somehow he couldn't seem to pick it up again. And the oftener he failed, the more determined he became to go on trying, as if, by repetition, even of mistakes, he must suddenly slip into the old knack of success. At first he took his failures wryly, jauntily, almost, a man skirmishing forth from his fortress of substance. But then he began to seem more and more withdrawn; he was concentrating more and more on this strange phenomenon of his dwindling money; he never, so to speak, took his eyes off it. The sheep farm was sold (he might have made a fortune out of wool, later, during the war, if he had kept it), the greater part of the property was sold and what was left was mortgaged, and the only one of his industrial firms that was making money was being killed by the vast sums that were being taken from it to keep the other two alive. Yet even I, as his lawyer, in possession of all the facts of his finances, found that I had kept some boylike belief that nothing could really go wrong with him, that there would always be some money somewhere in the background that would keep his habits of ease, his rich man's appearance and way of living, intact. It was ridiculous, since I knew his circumstances, but I was startled when he said to me one day, "Do you suppose you know anyone who'd want to buy my car?"

The Cord with the super-chargers had been sold some time before, when he was still prosperous, and had been replaced by something quite as grand—a Bentley, I think it was. But when he said he wanted to sell his car, it was the Cord that I thought of as going. The Cord and everything it symbolized to me, in him. For a moment, I had the wild idea that perhaps I might buy his car myself; a desire not to let it go altogether, to keep it, somehow, in sight . . . But of course that was nonsense; my position did not call for that sort of car.

"June drives me wherever I want to go, now," he said, "and we don't need a driver. We need an ordinary family car, while the kids are small." The mannerism he had always had, of screwing up his eyes, that had suggested to me, when I first met him, a dashing picture of him looking through field-glasses, now revealed itself to have been incipient deafness; he did it habitually, a screwing up of his attention to catch what you were saying. He still dressed well, but whereas before he had always been not exactly fashionable, but inconspicuously up-to-date in what he chose to wear, he now seemed to have chosen a year beyond which he had lost interest, and did not, sartorially, intend to go. As time went by he continued to wear the same cut and kind of clothes he had worn about the time I had met him, and so his dress gradually began to seem a little eccentric.

When he had been married to June Williams for eight or nine years, he went bankrupt. I don't know why, but this disaster shocked me less, seemed less final than the sale of his car had seemed. Like most bankrupts who have been really wealthy, he had some pickings left over, enough to keep him and his wife and their three children going in a flat in the suburb where my wife and I had lived for six months or so when we were first married and could not afford the sort of house we wanted.

I could not imagine Butters in one of those yellow-brick flat buildings, where every balcony had its clotheshorse of washing hung out with the bird-cage. When he told me where they were going to live, I said something personal to him for the first time since he had told me, years before, that I was to treat his divorce and remarriage like any other piece of legal business. "There's one thing," I said, "Your wife—June—she's not the sort of person to mind about"—suddenly I felt I couldn't say "money" because he might think I was referring to the poor background from which she had come to him, so I slipped easily into one of the legal euphemisms that I used all day long—"circumstances. She's got you and her children, and she won't be upset."

He screwed up his eyes again. "What's that? Oh no. No," he said, as if he were naming her for some neglect, "she's never cared at all about money."

I suppose I must have seen Butters now and again, in the next year or so; he must have had to come to us about the slow winding up of his affairs—a process that goes on long after the actual blow of bankruptcy. But I hardly remember him at all, at this time; I have no picture of him in my mind—except one, a brief one that arises not out of the memory of an encounter with him but from one of those moments in a city when you see without being seen, when you have a glimpse of what another person is like outside the inevitable reaction to your presence. I drew up at a robot, once, just behind Butters' car, the "ordinary family car" he had bought in place of the Bentley, and that he had saved from the bankruptcy. June was driving and he sat in the seat beside her; I could see only the backs of their heads. I was about to give a friendly touch to my hooter, just to greet them and attract their attention; but then I didn't. Something in the set of their heads stopped me. I find I can often tell, simply from the set of their heads, whether a couple sitting side by side have quarreled. But the immediate and curiously strong impression that came to me from Butters and his wife was not one of tension; quite the negative opposite. Each of them seemed to be alone; as if the illusion of the presence of the other, in the car, was mine only. And as the light changed and the Butters car turned left before me, I saw at the window his face and a gaze that stopped at the blank wall of glass. It might almost not have been him at all; an old, red, thin-skinned face that did not match any picture of him that I had ever had, at that time.

I saw Butters seldom because I was increasingly busy and he had less and less to be done for him—those hard facts sum it up. I might have wondered, I suppose, what he did with his time—he had no work of any sort; for years his work had been the management of his possessions, and now they were gone—but my own time was so full that I tended to forget other people's. I had been practicing law long enough, and had had clients enough to have learned the doctor's self-preservation trick of allotting my clients' lives only the time appointed to them in the book on my secretary's desk. There was little enough left over for my home, my family, and that busy interlude known as leisure (I played golf to a six handicap, in my young days, and there were dinner parties, like the ones to which we still go, where my wife and I were either host to, or guests of, colleagues from the Side Bar and Bar).

I saw the name "Butters" on my list of appointments for the

day, one morning, and, as I wanted to leave the office for a few minutes just about the time he was due to see me, I told the reception desk that he was to be sent in as soon as he came. When I entered my office again, I was surprised to see June Butters sitting there, tightly, with the look of being watched that people have when they have been shut up alone in a strange room. "Well, a pleasant surprise! I was expecting *Mr.* Butters! Is he meeting you here? How are you?"

She said something about his not coming, but in such a quick, embarrassed mumble that I understood her to mean that she had come on his behalf, or in his place. We exchanged polite questions about the respective ages of our children, for a minute or two, and then came the pause that precedes the turning of attention to business. She fixed her eyes on me with peculiar apprehension; she had always been timid, even of expressing an opinion. I got the impression that the idea of hearing her own voice, saying what she had come to say, alarmed her. Then, too, there was the awkwardness that, ever since she had married Butters, she had never known what to call me—whether to use the formal "Mr." or to admit, between us, the existence of Indian motorcycles and *thés dansants,* and call me "Peter." Her way out of the difficulty was to call me neither. She never addressed me by name at all, and so produced a strange air about our most trivial conversation, as if there were, indeed, some unspeakable intimacy between us.

"He's not coming," she blurted out, "I mean, I made the appointment. I'm the one who's come to see you. He doesn't even know I've come."

"That's all right. It was simply that when I saw the name, I assumed it was your husband, that's all. What did you want to talk to me about?"

The professional quiet of my voice seemed to affect her like sympathy; as I spoke, her eyes became magnified by tears.

"I want him to divorce me," she said, just getting the words out. And she turned her head, glassy-eyed, to the window; by fixing her gaze on some point, she managed to control herself.

Well, it's happened, I thought, with a cold shock. It's come. "I don't know what people feel," she had said to me, long ago, outside the post office. She knows, I thought. It's happened now. She's fallen in love with some young man. She hadn't changed much. She was rounder and softer, and better dressed, but her face was the same. In her trouble, she had the look of one of those slum children who have had life forced on them; she wore responsibility and worry like grime, streaking her soft cheeks.

When she turned back to me, the tears were gone. Staring, staring at me, she put on the desk two thin, trembling hands, on which a vein pulsed distinctly on each. "I'm afraid of him," she begged me. "He's so funny and I'm afraid of him. I can't stand it any longer. He sleeps with a gun in his hand, it's between his pillow and mine, and he walks about at night. Oh, I can't tell you! I'm afraid of what he'll . . . I don't know—I just feel terrified of him. He hardly speaks. He won't let the children play; how can you expect children not to climb? Not laugh, even. They're scared. Please, please, get him to divorce me. I don't want anything. I'll work. Make him let me take the children and go."

I don't know what people feel, she had said; we had stood considering love, two people who could not know what it was like. I looked at her young, trouble-smeared face (she was not thirty yet) and saw that it was true, after all; she still did not know what people feel.

I heard my own voice, cold and angry. "Do you want to marry someone else?"

She said, "There's no one. I don't know anyone. Please, please, all I want is to take the children and go. You must make him let me go."

"He gave up so much to marry you. You realize that? How can you ask him to give you up, now? Have you thought about that?"

"He wanted to marry me," she said. She was the sort of woman who cries easily, but her tears froze into fear.

"He's had some hard knocks to take, lately. Perhaps this mood of his will pass. Perhaps he should go to a doctor. Don't you see—he may be ill?"

"I can't stay with him," she said.

"But you must." I felt strangely alarmed, threatened. "I think it sounds as if he's ill. If you go, and the children, after all he's given up for you—what do you think will happen to him?"

"I don't want anything from him. I'll go just as I am."

"There's nothing left to want," I said in a flash of irritation.

She seemed to be to blame, but was she? Was she to blame for that or anything? If character is fate, it is the fate not only of the individual characterized, but also of those who have to do with the individual.

"All the things about money, I never understood any of it. He was clever. It was all things he did. I don't know what he did. I don't understand anything that's happened to him. It's all happened to him on his own."

"I'll have a talk with him," I said, taking refuge in professionalism. "I'll put it to him that you're worried about the way he's been feeling lately, and that you feel he doesn't confide in you. I'll try to get him to see that this makes life very difficult for you and that he must do something about it. Perhaps I can get him to go to a doctor . . ."

She had on her face the distressed, distrustful look of a not very articulate person who is always afraid her words may be twisted, for his own ends, by someone glibber than herself. "But I'll go," she said, betrayed. "I've told you I can't stay with him. Please, let me go." She was one of those women with flat cheekbones, and the line of her face, three-quarters turned away from me, was defenseless and without pride.

"Look," I said suddenly, "it's not for me to decide. I haven't anything to do with it. It's between you and Butters. Don't make it seem as if I'm not on your side. I'm not on anybody's side. Talk to him, don't be afraid. You need to talk to each other."

She looked terrified. I had seen a cat look like that once, shut out on a narrow window ledge, three stories above the street.

"I can't talk to him," she said at last. "Please, you must do it. You must get him to divorce me."

The idea of "sending for" Butters did not seem right to me; he had always demanded our time, not we his. The beige and black car had waited down in the street; Oscar had set aside an afternoon for him; he had come in, rich, preoccupied with his well-controlled affairs, having about him the air of the powerful man who delegates action to others. But I had to do it; I had to telephone and ask him if he could come and see me.

His voice on the telephone sounded so much the same as it had always been, that I felt some return of confidence in the situation; looking back on my interview with June, I was able to see it rather differently, and it almost came to seem that I was to talk to him about *her* hysterical state.

When he sat down in my office I saw that I had deluded myself.

Butters was one of those slim men who never weigh more than they did at twenty-five. He was over sixty now, but from across the room you would not have put him at past the middle forties. With a desk-width between you, you saw that his rather fine, bright skin was wrinkled all over, like a piece of paper that has been crumpled in the hand and then smoothed out. The lobes of his ears sagged, and his brown eyes, that were still sharp, had a thin milky rim round the iris, like the ring around the moon on a misty night. His old easy way of giving you his attention, while he picked up and put down, as it were, other preoccupations in the privacy of his own mind, had hardened into a self-absorbed withdrawal. It was not the withdrawal of an active mind about its own affairs; it was the stillness of a gaze directed at an empty pool on which no image falls, any more. He could not bear to interrupt this withdrawn gaze and so be reminded of the emptiness it contemplated. Unconsciously, he pretended to be as he was before, a man too busy and too active-minded to give his whole attention to any one thing, but it is more or less impossible to imitate what one has believed to be one's own manner, once that manner has gone.

I understood immediately that June had talked to him, after all. "She's been to see you," he said. And nodded his head and slowly rubbed the angle of his jaw on the left side, as if he were suddenly diverted, as one can be in times of stress, by some slight irritation or pain.

"I'm glad you've discussed it," I said.

"It's not fair," he said, to himself.

"Well, I know, it does seem a bit thick, but you must take into account that she's really very young still, after all, and apparently she's been more upset by this bankruptcy business than we thought. I'm sure that you can reassure her and we can make it all right with her—"

He waved me impatiently off the wrong track. "It's not fair

for her to have had to put up with me. I know, I realize it. Shouldn't expect it."

"Look, all sorts of things are expected of people in a marriage."

"For her, nothing much has happened. She lived my kind of life for a few years, I lived it for forty or more. I suddenly find myself in a little flat, with children under my feet, like a youngster who still has his way to make!" He gave a dry laugh at the absurdity. "I feel I should be looking after her. All I can do is see that the doors are locked. The children are always climbing on the window or getting onto the balcony —what can children do with themselves, shut in . . . God knows what will become of them—but she doesn't worry. She'd be all right, if it weren't for me." He shook his head and his hands opened slowly and rested, lax, on the chair arms.

"You don't want her to stay," I said, afraid to make it a question.

He was not listening to me. "How charming she was, eh, that afternoon."

I remembered it too, suddenly very clearly, the stop by the roadside and the girl picking flowers. I felt embarrassed and on the defensive.

Butters looked up at me suddenly and smiled. "What happened to your girl—the little cheeky one?"

I tried not to answer, to close this digression. But he continued to look at me, inquiringly, reminiscently, amusedly, as if, for a moment, he had taken on the attitude that had been his when he met me—or rather the young man I had been—and the girls.

"Was she cheeky?"

He smiled. "Cheeky smile, she had."

"Oh Lily, you mean. I don't know. Married with a string of children, I suppose."

"No, of course, you wouldn't know."

A pang of regret was touched off in me; instant, ridiculous, meaningless. Why could Butters make me feel jealous—an emotion for which occasion did not arise, in my sort of life? Yet rusty and grating, there it was. Jealous of what? Here was Butters, come to grief, all right.

"You know"—Butters was claimed by the dreamlike present again; remembrance of the past always makes the present seem unreal—"she's never wanted anything. Whatever I gave her, she was pleased with, but she never wanted anything for herself. Funny, isn't it. I would say to her, You want a low chair in your bedroom, so that you can sit down to put your stockings on—and she'd know then that of course that was what she wanted. Now it's her turn and what she wants is to go. The one thing she ever asked of me."

I said, "I think it would be a disaster."

"I know you thought that," he said. "You all thought that."

"I'm talking of now, of this idea of parting."

"Oh now," he said, businesslike. "It's the one thing she's ever *wanted*. D'you see? Poor girl, she's only had what I wanted. It's a sign in her. She was like a toy, to me. D'you understand? When it comes to—this sort of life, the flat, the children breaking things, her cooking and working about the place—I don't know what to do with her. I can't expect her to put up with me. I want to keep *some* clear idea of what I am. I haven't yet got to the stage where I don't see it, thank God. No, I must give her this, this one thing. I can't refuse it. After all, I married her, didn't I? I took her up and married her."

"What do you want to do, exactly?"

He sat back in his chair. "Give her an income, provision for the children, set her free. Yes, I must do that."

"But that means giving her all that's left! If you want to give her enough to keep herself and the children fairly decently, there'll be nothing left for you. Nothing *at all.*"

"Oh I know," he said, as if he were discussing, as he did in the old days, the exchange of one directorship for another, "I shall have to find myself a job." That was exactly the phrase he used to use, in fun, when it seemed certain that he would never have to work as long as he lived.

I looked at him in fascination. Again I could not believe it. Butters, Butters without a large and comforting complex of money and possessions behind him. It loomed there, for me, about his figure, nothing could quite erase it for me. And so, when I thought about his necessity to find a job, I thought in terms of a company directorship or something of that sort; a courtesy sinecure in that world of board meetings and figureheads where his name would carry still the connotations of his vanished possessions.

FOUR

June Butters got her divorce and the custody of her three children and the small monthly income from what remained of Butters' investments. He was left with his personal possessions and about two hundred pounds in his banking account. And then he disappeared. For years he had been drifting to the outer rings of my professional and personal orbit, and now he seemed to have pulled up the anchor of his old life and dropped behind my horizon. Somewhere in my mind was the vague picture of him in, as I say, some modest sinecure, some paper-place of his own world, that would keep him going without complete loss of face. I was busier than ever; further changes in the firm made me senior partner long before I could have expected I might be, and a year later I became president of the Side Bar association, in addition. I had to speed up my way of living if I wanted to fit into my life the things that I had decided were desirable. I bought a luxurious sports car, so that I could make my trips between home and office (we had moved farther out of town, built ourselves rather a nice country place, with a pool and a tennis court for the children) a chance to get some fresh air and sun. I was making a lot of money quite outside my legal practice, with my business interests and on the share market. Often I came home from a theater or dinner party and sat up, working on some case, until three in the morning. My mind was always full of a dozen things at once; a full life, I suppose.

One of these business associates of mine, a man who had a controlling interest in a number of hotels, among other things, said to me one day, "You used to know that chap Butters, didn't you?"

"Yes, I knew him well. Good Lord, it was through me when I was a young man that he met a girl and divorced his first wife. I haven't seen or heard of him for ages. What a fortune went down the drain, there; I'll never understand what went wrong."

"Well, d'you know what he's doing now?" The man looked at me with that fearful yet admiring smile that people flash at the audacity of misfortune. "He's working as a barman in one of my hotels. That's the truth. He came to me and asked me for a job. Of course, he knows the liquor trade, he had some hotels himself, you know."

"Butters as barman?" I said. "But what's happened to him?"

"Down and out," said my acquaintance. "It's a job, I suppose, like any other. I thought I remembered that you knew him. He gets a room, of course, and his meals. I suppose it could be worse. I won't mention anything to him about knowing you, it might embarrass him."

I used quite often to drive past that hotel, and many times I thought: Butters is in there, serving drinks. Past the leather curtain at the bar door, there he is, behind the counter. But I never went in. I always thought, I must go in and speak to him; but I didn't. There is a delicacy toward misfortune; a conspiracy of withdrawal from those it has afflicted, like the conspiracy of withdrawal that sends an elephant down alone to the mythical graveyard waters that those still of the herd never see. Banishment is a state of mind in those who are left in possession; the banished one continues to sleep, to eat, to walk about, and to need, just as he did before.

When at last I did go into the bar, Butters was not there. He had left, they said, a month before. My next news of him came in the form of a letter, written by himself. He wrote to me from Cape Town, asking me to lend him twenty pounds. "Forgive me for bothering you about a trivial sum, you'll no doubt wonder why I don't simply borrow it here, but the fact is, as you know, that I haven't been the sort of man who's been accustomed to touching his friends for a tenner here and there! Well, life brings some surprises to all of us. I happen to need the money quite urgently, and I'd rather ask it of you, since money deals of one kind and another have been the usual thing between us in the past. Of course I shall return it promptly; I hope this whole 'transaction' doesn't embarrass you as much as it does me!"

The tone of the letter was intended to keep the request contained in it on the level of the request of the wealthy friend who comes up to you at the race-course and says, "Lend me twenty quid for the last race, old man; I've run out of cash and I've got a strong hunch I want to follow." And I must say that it did succeed in disguising, for me, the appalling fact that Butters did not have twenty pounds in the world. I sent him the money without thinking much of it, and in the accompanying note I said how glad I was to hear from him again, and to be able to do something for him as a client after so long. I added "What are you busy with in Cape Town—are you living there permanently?" but crossed out the sentence when I read over my letter. It seemed to suggest a polite, mildly patronizing tone I felt I couldn't take, with Butters.

He never replied and he never paid back the money. From time to time there were other letters with requests for money —ten pounds, even five. There was no attempt to keep up the tone of the first; these were curt notes, bluntly asking for a loan. The war was on, by then, and Butters was serving in the pay corps; this I learned from, of all people, his first wife. I was traveling to Durban on a client's behalf, and in the plane I found myself seated next to an elderly woman who kept looking at me, hesitantly, and who, when she caught my eye, smiled uncertainly and said, "You don't remember me—I'm Isabel Butters. We met, long ago, at your offices."

"Of course, Mrs. Butters." She looked much more animated than the woman I remembered—one of those sensibly but attractively dressed, self-possessed ladies with well-kept white hair who are always in the comfortable majority in planes, ships, and motor-coaches. One of those ladies who retire into the world, when family life at home has done with them.

"It's really quite uncanny that you should be sitting next to me," she said, putting a leather jewel box neatly beside her handbag, where it would not be in the way of either of us. "I've been thinking about coming to see you. I just thought I'd put it off until I'd come back from the coast."

"I'm pleased to see you looking so well," I said, and I meant it. All my life in my profession I have never failed to marvel and rejoice in defiance, every time I have met, alive and kicking, someone whom, years or months or even only weeks before, I had seen, crushed, in my office.

"Yes," she said modestly, "I've been all right for a long time. That's really why I wanted to get in touch with you. I wanted to tell you that that whole—idea—my son's idea or whosever it is—is out of the question."

"Mrs. Butters," I said, "I'm sorry, but I know nothing about what you're saying."

She looked at me. "About Charles," she said, "about my husband."

"I know nothing at all about Mr. Butters—I've been out of touch with him for years," I said.

"Is that so? Oh, I thought my son—that's his son, too, of course—I thought he'd been to talk to you. He told me he'd been; he wanted to give some backing to what he had to say, I suppose. I'm surprised to hear that you don't know anything about Charles Butters. But you know that he's lost all his money, of course?"

"Oh yes, I know all about his affairs, up to the time of the divorce—the divorce from his second wife, I mean."

"That poor little girl," she said. And then went on, lowering her voice, "Well, to cut a long story short, Gifford—that's the son who went to Canada—Gifford came back to South Africa a few months ago, and he saw his father in Cape Town. He found him working as a clerk in the Pay Corps"—she stopped shyly; I understood; like me, she had difficulty in contemplating Charles Butters in a mean situation, she felt an old authority of his that made the possibility of pity an impertinence. "Gifford came to me with the idea that I—that we should remarry. I was alone, and his father was alone, and so on, and why shouldn't we put aside what has happened in between. But Mr. Garvus, I'll tell you, I'm not lonely any more. I was, I was terribly lonely for a long time, but I'm not any more. I'm at peace by myself."

I liked this woman, whose presence in our offices that day long ago, when the divorce had been under discussion, I now felt as it really had been beneath its appearance of almost mesmerized quiescence; lost, rent, its consciousness of its identity wiped off as easily as a conversation on a tape recorder. "Well, all I can tell you is nothing's been said to me about all this. I'm sure it doesn't come from Butters himself."

"What I would be willing to do, of course," she went on, "would be to do something for him—some small income, some money." The idea of *her* giving money to *him* seemed unreal to both of us. We surveyed it awkwardly for a moment, between us. "Well, I'll speak to my son about it when I get back to Johannesburg," she said, and that settled it. When the plane landed and she wished me good-by, she added, "I'll probably be coming to see you about arranging that business."

She never came; perhaps she decided that she owed Butters nothing, after all, perhaps he refused to take what amounted to charity, from her. It is possible, of course, that she helped him privately, through her son, instead of formally, through the agency of a lawyer; but I doubt it. I do not think she would have been able to face any sort of personal contact with him.

One autumn morning in 1945, when I had just come back to my legal practice again after two years in the army, my secretary told me that there was "a man" waiting to see me. "He doesn't look like a client," she said. "He was here yesterday, asking to see you, but he wouldn't make an appointment or give his name, and now he's back again."

"Well, tell him I don't see anyone who doesn't give his name."

She said over the office intercommunication a minute later, "He says his name is Butters, and it's urgent."

It would be inaccurate to say that I wouldn't have known him. Of course I should have know that unquenchable wick of identity which burns down slowly within all the distorting, melting change of the shape of a man's outward life. His body was thin and taut—how driven must an aging man's body be, to look like that!—and his face had the bright, tough shine of exposure. The sun had burned hard on him, and the wind blown cold; I had seen such faces on tramps, thumbing a lift on a highway. He was dressed in flannels, shiny and dirty, but sharply creased. He was hatless and tieless.

He stood within the door, I sat at my desk. It was impossible to dissimulate, to get up, hold out a hand, pretend that there was nothing wrong. His look, calling on that old authority over me that perhaps existed for him over no one else in the world, any longer, established the unbridgeable between us. His eyes held me off. All the other lions of the world might have smelled out his defenselessness and leaped at his throat, but for me, there was still a whip in his empty hand.

"I want you to lend me five pounds," he said. His voice was hoarse and distant.

"Butters," I said, "won't you come and sit down?"

He said, "I can't. I'm in a hurry. Well?"

I said, "For Christ's sake, isn't there something I can do?"

He ignored the plea. "I'm going to get married again, if you want to know. I want the money for a special license."

I murmured, "That's good," and I was thinking, Perhaps there's the glimmer of a solution? "Who're you going to marry?"

"Someone I've found," he said. And paused. "She's outside."

"Well, bring her in, bring her in." I was even able to smile. I was prepared for some solid, simple soul, some middle-aged spinster perhaps, who saw Butters' plight as her chance to acquire something discarded by, but nevertheless of a world she could not aspire to. He turned without a glance at me and went out of my office. In a few moments he returned with a street-woman, a creature with a coarse, dull, painted face that had no feeling left in it, lank, unwashed hair, and, in sandals, dirty feet with bare, broken, cracked heels.

When I had gone through the farce of a polite exchange with her, I asked him if I could see him alone again, for a moment. He took her back to the waiting room, and returned.

"Look, Butters," I said brutally, "you can't marry that. I don't care what's happened to you."

But he was glaring at me angrily, with the blind, mean anger that is at the same time puny and meaningless, of a drunk or a child. "Now look here," he said, "are you going to give me that five pounds, or aren't you?"

"Oh that," I said. "That's nothing—"

"Are you?"

Slowly I took my money out of my pocket; four ones, two ten-shilling notes. I separated them from the silver. I gave them to him.

He put the notes into his pocket, hunching himself as if the money would keep him warm. I felt ashamed; I didn't know what of: of him, and myself, and the moment. We were in it together, the shame. At the same time, I was impatient to be rid of him. He wasted no time, and went at once. At the door, he looked round the room where the trappings of my life had accumulated—a sober-looking walnut bureau that contained a portable bar, a cupboard where I kept slippers and a couple of cardigans, the desk-set the staff had given me on my twenty-fifth wedding anniversary. And he looked at me, really looked at me as if he saw me, and smiled, kindly. "You remind me of Oscar, you know, after all."

That was the last time he ever spoke to me.

Less than a month later, the woman came to tell me that Butters was dead. He had had a heart attack, and then had developed pneumonia while he was in hospital. I suppose she came to tell me because she knew no one else who had known him. I myself thought, I shall have to inform—and then came the question, whom? June and her children were living in Rhodesia somewhere. The first Mrs. Butters? I supposed I should be able to find out her address. The sons and daughter of the first marriage? Goodness knew where they had scattered.

What would his death matter to any of them? He had been out of their lives for many years and he left them nothing. In the end, there was only myself. I had come into his way casually, but—unwittingly and without volition on my part—it had not been possible for him to get past me. I had not mattered, and yet there I was, at the last.

I took the afternoon off, from the office—it was very inconvenient, I was in the middle of an important case—to go to the funeral. The woman and I were the only people at the graveside. There were no tears for Butters. She put up no pretense of having, and perhaps had no reason to have, cared for him. I was only his lawyer.

Yet when I left the cemetery, I was in a queer mood. I began thinking about my wife, my children, and my legal practice, and my legal honors; scene after scene, things said, looks exchanged, certain bright mornings, the faces of clients, moments in the street, the sound of a door banging as my eldest daughter came in late at night—they all crowded my mind in a brooding concentration. And a strong and yearning resentment made me turn away, within; turn away and find, on every side, the fastness of these things, confronting me. A mixture of longing and loneliness came to me shockingly, like a cry silencing the babble at a cocktail party. I sat in the back of my open car (I had a driver, by then, to save myself the strain of driving in traffic) and in a trance of regret I watched the veld go by, closed in and brought to the road by the gathering of neat houses in a new suburb. Look at it! Look at it! I told myself. The little life, the little shelter. That's all. If there is longing, it stops at the restriction of the necktie. If there's freedom, it never gets through the expensive felt hat. That was my triumph, that I sorrowed for. It was the last time, ever, perhaps, that I should know it; the other man in me, that had never come into existence, had just been buried under the earth.

And then I saw, as my driver slowed down to take a dip in the road, that the houses had not quite covered all the veld. There was a great open stretch here, and I had been watching, without noticing it, the cream and pink undulation of cosmos, following the rise and fall of the land, all in bloom.